FALLING
WISTERIA

FALLING WISTERIA

A Novel

LAILA IBRAHIM

LAKE UNION
PUBLISHING

Published by Lake Union Publishing, Seattle

www.apub.com

Amazon, the Amazon logo, and Lake Union Publishing are trademarks of Amazon.com, Inc., or its affiliates.

ISBN-13: 9781662514203 (paperback)
ISBN-13: 9781662514197 (digital)

Cover design by Lesley Worrell
Cover image: ©Alexia Feltser / ArcAngel; ©NNehring / Getty; ©Masha Dav, ©olgashashok, ©Oleg Golovnev / Shutterstock

Printed in the United States of America

To all my teachers, from Miss Chance to Mr. Moore and Dr. George. Thank you for your part in helping me to know more about myself and this amazing, complicated world.

If the world were merely seductive, that would be easy. If it were merely challenging, that would be no problem. But I arise in the morning torn between a desire to improve (save) the world and a desire to enjoy (savor) the world. This makes it hard to plan the day.

—E. B. White

Four Freedoms

Freedom of speech and expression
Freedom of worship
Freedom from want
Freedom from fear

—President Franklin D. Roosevelt
State of the Union address
January 6, 1941

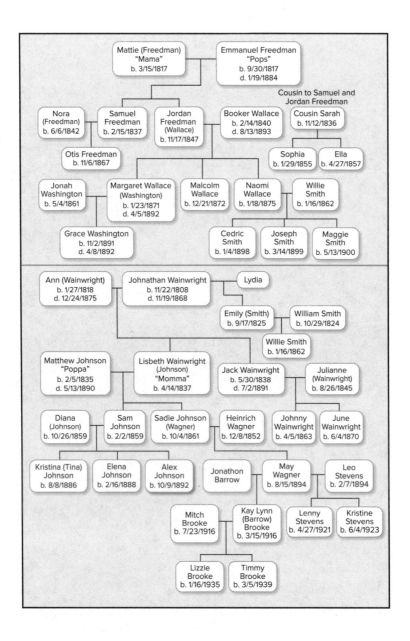

PROLOGUE

Mom prided herself on her ability to talk openly and honestly with me about *anything*, but she didn't reveal her deepest shame until her deathbed.

In a paper-thin voice, she said she was complicit in "evil," no better than those that stood by and allowed the Nazis to take power. That seems extreme. What could she have done?

I don't judge her for the choices she made, though *choice* might be the wrong word—she adapted to the situation she found herself in. Mom was one woman struggling to tend to those she loved in the midst of profound, world-changing forces. As modern people, we like to think we have free will, but in truth we are tossed around by the Fates as much as any character in a Greek myth.

CHAPTER 1

December 7, 1941
Berkeley, California

"Mommy!" Lizzie's bright voice echoed through the house.

Kay Lynn shook her head. She must have scolded her six-year-old daughter a hundred times for shouting from the doorway, but Elizabeth Carolina Brooke had a spirit of her own.

"Mrs. Fujioka needs you!" the girl yelled.

Kay Lynn put on her stern face, attempting to civilize her child once again, but before she could speak, Lizzie continued, "She said, 'Tell her to come straightaway, please,' and she looked like she meant it."

The message delivered, Lizzie ran back to her best friend's house, certain her mother would follow.

Before leaving, Kay Lynn peeked in on Timmy in his crib. Her son's heavy and drawn-out breath meant he wouldn't wake soon, so she left him alone. She couldn't be long, as they had to leave for church in fifteen minutes.

Kay Lynn rushed out the back door into their small, tidy back-yard. Two years ago, she and Kimiko had persuaded their husbands to build a gate in the fence between their yards to allow freer rein between their Edwardian-era homes. Mitch, Kay Lynn's husband, had argued against it since they were renters. But Kay Lynn convinced him it was worth the expense because they would certainly buy their house when it came up for sale. The gate hung wide open, as usual.

To Kay Lynn's surprise, Kimiko's kitchen was empty. A low moan echoed from down the hallway, growing louder. *Kimiko?*

Kay Lynn hurried down the hardwood floor toward the sound, her heartbeat increasing with the intensity of the wail. Lizzie and Kimiko's children, Donna and George, stood in the tight hallway, peering into the bathroom, their eyes wide.

Kay Lynn rushed to them and took in the scene. Kimiko lay on the floor, curled up on her side, facing the tub. Her deep-brown hair was pulled into a bun, and her eyes were shut tight. She clutched at a metal claw-foot, moaning in rhythm. Hazel sat guard at her feet.

The baby wasn't due for three more weeks. Kimiko's moan turned into a scream.

Kay Lynn pushed between the three children to join Kimiko on the cold tile; the small tan mutt moved to guard Kimiko's head.

Kay Lynn leaned over and whispered, "I'm here." Kimiko's eyes stayed closed, but she reached up a shaky hand. Kay Lynn took it and repeated, "I'm here now."

Kimiko's breathing slowed; her moaning stopped. She took a deep inhale, let it out with a sigh, and opened her lids.

Kay Lynn stared into Kimiko's dark eyes and said, "Your baby is coming! This is a great day to be born, December 7, 1941. Shall we get you to the hospital?"

Kimiko shook her head with a tight smile. "It's too late. He'll be here before we can make it to Alta Bates."

Kay Lynn bit her lip. "Are you certain?"

Kimiko nodded, her eyes wide.

Kay Lynn froze inside. She didn't know how to help a baby into the world. Her children's births were like an intense dream. Impactful, but vague.

Should she call for an ambulance? Where was Ken? Mitch was in North Berkeley; he couldn't be back quickly. Maybe her mother hadn't left for church yet; she would know what to do. Lizzie could call her while Kay Lynn stayed with Kimiko.

"Uh-oh, here's an—" Kimiko moaned.

The contractions were close. This baby *was* coming soon. Kay Lynn drew in a deep breath and rubbed Kimiko's leg, an intimate, but hopefully soothing, gesture, until the contraction passed.

Babies are born at home all the time, she reminded herself. *Albeit, with a midwife on hand.*

"Mommy?" Lizzie's voice intruded on her racing thoughts.

"Lizzie, you and Donna take Georgie to our house. You mind him—and Timmy when he wakes." She kept her voice cheerful, wanting to convince the girls there was nothing to be afraid of. "You're big girls. You stay there until I come for you. Mrs. Fujioka is having her baby, and I'm going to stay by her side until he comes. You're going to help her by taking care of the boys. Do you understand?"

Donna and Lizzie nodded.

Kimiko whimpered, "Here comes another."

"Girls, go!" Kay Lynn commanded.

"Oh, oh, oh, oh," Kimiko intoned, higher and higher. Kimiko squeezed Kay Lynn's hand so hard that her wedding ring dug into her fingers; even with diminished sensation on her left side, the pain was so great that Kay Lynn had to fight the impulse to pull her fingers away.

When the contraction passed, Kay Lynn rushed to the linen closet to get towels and to the kitchen to get a glass of water. She washed her hands thoroughly, pulled off her wedding ring, and used her teeth to get the ring off her right finger.

"I feel him," Kimiko whimpered when Kay Lynn returned. "Between my legs."

"Already?"

Kimiko nodded.

"Would you like me to look?"

Dismay distorted Kimiko's face, but she nodded.

Kay Lynn lifted Kimiko's leg just a bit.

"Not yet," she revealed. "I don't see any scalp."

Kimiko's shoulders dropped. "Thank you."

"I'm very glad we hadn't left for church yet."

"Oh, oh, oh," Kimiko chanted again. Kay Lynn let her squeeze her left hand again. Without the ring, she hardly felt it. One small benefit to her palsy.

"He's coming!" Kimiko exclaimed. The laboring woman raised her top leg and wrapped an arm around it. She pulled her leg toward her chest.

A dark scalp bulged out of Kimiko. *He is coming! Right now?!* Kay Lynn hesitated. Should she do anything? Her own births were such a blur. She had no recollection of what the midwife did as her children emerged.

Kimiko stopped chanting. She panted. The infant's smooshed head stayed just at the opening. Kay Lynn grabbed a towel and spread it on the floor; she imagined cupping the baby as it came out. There would be an umbilical cord. She didn't have scissors, but there must be a sharp knife in the kitchen.

Kimiko sucked in a deep breath. "Oh, oh, oh," she started again.

The knife would have to wait.

"Ahhh!" Kimiko screamed. A mushy, dark bulb came out, revealing a mottled forehead. Dark eyebrows emerged, quickly followed by tightly closed eyes and then a tiny, smooshed nose.

"Ahh, ahh."

"I can see him. Keep going," Kay Lynn encouraged. "He's almost here."

Kimiko grunted. The baby was out to his neck. His eyes were closed tight, and he was so still he looked like a doll coated in purple paint. Kay Lynn panicked. Should she pull on him?

Kimiko took in a deep breath, then roared. Suddenly the entire baby flopped out onto the towel, curled in a tight ball like he was still inside Kimiko.

"You did it! He's out!" Kay Lynn declared.

The room became so quiet that Kimiko's panting sounded loud. They should be hearing the baby.

Kay Lynn rubbed her hand in a slow circle around the sticky back, gently rousing him. He didn't move. She patted him, hard and then harder. What would they do if he didn't breathe? She grabbed his arms, ready to shake him, when he jerked and a gurgly wail sputtered through his lungs. His chest moved up and down, and he slowly turned from deep purple to a dark, rosy pink.

Kay Lynn exhaled.

"There you go, little one. You passed your first test, taking a breath. Are you ready for him?" Kay Lynn asked.

"I can't sit up," Kimiko replied, her neck craning to see her baby. Hazel licked Kimiko's cheek, but otherwise didn't move.

"Can you turn onto your back? I'll try to put him on your chest."

Kimiko rolled over. Kay Lynn held the back of the baby's head and cradled the chest with her fisted hand. Her palsy made holding a swaddled newborn challenging. Fearing she would drop the slippery, limp baby onto the bathroom floor, she flipped him over and moved him slowly up Kimiko's torso, getting him to her belly. Kimiko reached with her arms to guide the baby to her chest.

"Oh!" Kay Lynn exclaimed. "It's a girl!"

"Really?"

"Yes, yes, you have another daughter."

"You're here! You're really here," Kimiko cooed to the baby. "You're perfect!"

Kay Lynn remembered telling Timmy those same words. The first time she held him, her heart spread wide as she took in the wonder of the little being that she'd somehow grown.

He must have looked as strange as all newborns do, but she said to him, "You are beautiful and you are perfect. Absolutely perfect."

She didn't remember what she said when Lizzie was born, but her heart broke wide open at their first touch.

Kimiko smiled. Hazel rose to sniff at the infant. Kimiko shook a finger at the dog; Hazel backed away and lay down.

"I think you best stay right where you are until your placenta is delivered," Kay Lynn suggested.

"Yes," Kimiko agreed. "The other children? Are they . . . ohhhh. Here it comes!"

"They're at my house, safe and sound," Kay Lynn explained while Kimiko writhed from a strong contraction. Suddenly, the placenta plopped onto the towel where the baby had just been. Kay Lynn watched the cord pulse between the liver-red organ and the baby.

"I'm going to get a knife . . . to cut it?" Kay Lynn said, but it came out like a question.

Trembling, Kimiko whispered, "Come back quick, please."

The vulnerability in her friend's tone gave her pause. It made sense that Kimiko feared being left alone, even briefly.

"I will," Kay Lynn reassured her as she rose. "Donna and Lizzie will be so happy," she spoke as she walked away, getting louder as she disappeared into the kitchen. "They were certain you were having a daughter."

When she returned, she held a small, sharp knife and a plate. "As I recall, you won't feel this, strange as that seems."

Kay Lynn put the plate on the bloodstained towel. She laid the cord over it and then pressed down hard with the knife. It made a small slice, her hand shaking as she sawed back and forth repeatedly. It was much harder than she expected, more like gristle than meat. After much effort, she separated the mother and daughter.

Kay Lynn thought of all the things she could do next: get a blanket and pillow for Kimiko; call the hospital for advice; contact Mrs. Hori, Kimiko's mother; get Kimiko cleaned up and into bed; wrap up the placenta; bathe the baby; tell the girls the baby was born safe and sound. She'd get to all of those eventually, but for one moment, she would sit on the ground, catch her breath, and slow her heart.

She collapsed onto the floor, feeling the cold tile against her thighs through her thin dress. So much for going to church. Had she really done this? She looked at the back of the baby's head, dark hair plastered against her head. The infant *was* perfect; resting her cheek on the bare skin between Kimiko's breasts. When had she unbuttoned her blouse? Kay Lynn pulled Kimiko's skirt over her hips to give a measure of modesty.

Even at this awkward angle, Kimiko gazed at the baby with devotion. It was beautiful. Kay Lynn had never seen such a look of dedication, though she felt that kind of love when Lizzie and Timmy were born.

Had anyone ever gazed at her like that? Most likely Momma hadn't held or looked at Kay Lynn at all. Her mother intended to give her up for adoption. Why gaze lovingly at a baby you don't want?

Kimiko interrupted her ruminations. "Thank you. I'm glad you were home."

"Me too. Good timing, little one. We were just about to leave."

"She came so fast," Kimiko said. "I couldn't have done this without you."

"Somehow you would have," Kay Lynn replied, "but I'm very glad you didn't have to. I wouldn't want my dear friend to go through childbirth alone."

Kay Lynn squeezed Kimiko's hand. They didn't speak about their friendship directly, so it was unsettling and tender to do so. But Kimiko *was* her best friend as well as her business partner. Their lives had slowly become intertwined since 1934. Painful and fortuitous circumstances had turned them from friendly neighbors into dear companions.

CHAPTER 2

December 1941

"Daddy!" Lizzie ran up to Mitch in the living room before his coat was off. "Donna's baby sister was born, and Mommy was the doctor!"

Mitch, grimy after a day of physical labor assisting his friend Jacob to rebuild the back stairs to his new home, looked at Kay Lynn with his gray-blue eyes.

"Really?" he asked, one of his honey-brown eyebrows raised in a question.

Kay Lynn nodded. "Baby Missy was so ready for her entrance into the world that we didn't have time to get her to Alta Bates or call an ambulance."

"Were you terrified?"

Kay Lynn welled up. "Yes, and I did what I could. Kimiko and the baby did all the work."

"Wow. I'm proud of you." Mitch kissed her cheek and beamed a smile at Kay Lynn.

"Want to meet Missy?" Lizzie asked, pulling his hand toward their front door.

Mitch stood firm. "Mrs. Fujioka doesn't need me to disturb their peace. I'll get to see her soon enough. Do they need anything?" he asked Kay Lynn.

"I already delivered lentil soup. Her mother has moved in with them."

Mitch laughed. "She lives less than two miles away."

Kay Lynn shrugged. "It's a Japanese custom. Kimiko mostly finds it sweet."

"Bad timing," Mitch said.

Kay Lynn nodded. It was nearing the end of the term at the University of California. Kay Lynn and Kimiko had a cottage business typing papers for students.

"We'd hoped the baby would wait two weeks, but I'll manage somehow. Kimiko needs time to celebrate and revel in the new addition to their family, but she'll pressure herself to get back to work soon. Knowing Kimiko, she'll be over here typing up papers by Wednesday."

Anger. Fear. Something flashed on Mitch's face.

"What?" Kay Lynn asked.

He shook his head. He leaned in and whispered into her ear. "The news is terrible. I don't want to speak of it in front of the children."

Kay Lynn's heart skipped a beat, but she kept her voice light as she said, "Lizzie, take Timmy and gather six lemons. We can make Mr. Fujioka's favorite dessert to celebrate Missy's birth."

"Lemon bars, yum!" Lizzie grabbed Timmy's hand and pulled him through the house to the backyard.

As soon as they were out of earshot, Mitch spoke in low tones. "Japan bombed the Pearl Harbor naval base in Hawaii today."

A wave of emotion traveled through Kay Lynn's body. She closed her eyes and inhaled deeply, willing herself not to panic. The advancing anticipation was over; they'd crossed the divide into war.

"What does this mean? For us? For the Fujiokas? For my brother?" She stared at Mitch.

The time for all the theoretical debate was over. She was adamant Mitch should stay out of the war. Of course, she was against the Nazis, but Mitch—her husband and her children's father—shouldn't travel thousands of miles away from home, into harm's way, to fight a European war. She wasn't entirely an isolationist or a pacifist. She wanted to support the right side of history, but she didn't want her husband maimed or killed. Life was enough of a challenge with him here.

Kay Lynn started crying. She grabbed his shirt with her right hand. "You won't go, right?"

"Mommy," Lizzie yelled from the kitchen, "we have the lemons!"

"Lemons," Timmy's sweet toddler voice echoed.

Kay Lynn closed her eyes tight and scrunched up her face, shutting out her children.

"Mommy will be there in a few minutes," Mitch yelled across the house. "Be patient while we talk."

Kay Lynn stared at her husband, waiting for his answer.

"A draft is inevitable. As a father, I may have more time than your brother, but . . ."

"*You* have to prioritize *us* over your duty or your values," Kay Lynn insisted.

"Kay Lynn, I agree. I have no desire to fight on foreign soil," Mitch replied.

"Can you qualify as a conscientious objector?" she asked.

"I'm barely a Unitarian, and it doesn't qualify as a peace religion. You've heard Reverend Reed say the moral course is to go to war against Japan. Even if I did qualify as a conscientious objector, I'd be required to serve in a noncombat role."

Mitch was right. More than a year ago, in September 1940, he complied with the government order directing all men between the ages of twenty-one and thirty-six to register for the draft. That was the day the first drips of alarm landed in Kay Lynn's heart; the drops of dread kept falling as the war spread around the globe. How long would it be before their city would be a target? Would they have blackout curtains and air-raid alarms going off at all hours of the day and night like in London? San Francisco would be the primary target, but they were not far. Would she be forced to run her household without her husband?

Kay Lynn pushed down her fear. "Maybe my handicaps can qualify you for a 4-F exception." She teased, "Or I could pull out half your teeth."

Mitch laughed and took both her hands in his. He kissed each in turn. "I'm sure either of those will work."

"Or maybe the war will be over before your number has to report to the draft board," she suggested.

"I expect fathers will be recused for some time, so I'll keep my teeth until we learn otherwise," he said with a wry smile.

"Okay," she replied, "but I'll think you're handsome even if you take that route. I'll love you, with or without teeth."

Mitch pulled his lips around his teeth. He muttered, "You think I'm cute like this?"

She chuckled and nodded. Then she melted against his body, taking in his warmth and strength. She didn't want to imagine life without him in it.

When she started dating Mitch during their last semester of high school, Kay Lynn hadn't entirely gotten over her first love, but he was a sweet and handsome distraction. They both expected to part ways after graduation.

Family life was thrust upon both of them when her best-laid plans still ended in a pregnancy. Four weeks before finals she told him she missed her monthlies. He blanched, but never said a negative word. Instead of becoming a carefree fraternity brother at UCLA, he became a responsible father in Berkeley. His mother still held it against Kay Lynn, but Kay Lynn believed Mitch was at peace with the turn his life took.

Kay Lynn never made a final plan for after high school. College was out of reach as she was only an average student. Reading came hard and was still slow—most likely for the same reason she was weak on her left side.

If she hadn't had Lizzie, she most likely would have worked at UC Berkeley, like her mother had as a young woman, but she longed to move in with Grandmother Barrow on Nob Hill in San Francisco—working in the financial district and eating out in a different neighborhood each night: North Beach, Russian Hill, the Marina, and Chinatown. She dreamt of being a carefree girl in the big city.

Instead she became a wife and mother almost at the same time. She and Kimiko juggled taking care of their kids and typing papers for students at Cal. Time with the Grands, her parents and her grandmother, was a priority, and there was church most Sundays. Unlike her brother and sister, she'd had to grow up fast after high school. And now this war was going to force her to face the unbearable.

The next morning they stood in front of the Fujiokas' house. Kay Lynn assumed Donna would come out for school at the usual time, but now, she wondered if her parents might be keeping her home today. Either the new baby or the declaration of war could warrant that choice.

"Should I knock?" Lizzie asked.

Kay Lynn stared first at the shiny blue door and then down the street, assessing the urgency by the number of children hurrying down the sidewalk. When she looked back, she saw Mrs. Hori, Kimiko's mother, standing in the doorway. She looked younger than her years, but she was close to fifty. Her short dark hair framed her unlined face. She waved and gave a shallow bow. Kay Lynn bowed back. They didn't share a language, but conveyed a warm appreciation for each other with gestures.

Donna bounced down the stairs and grabbed Lizzie's hand. They skipped down the sidewalk toward Lincoln School. The combination of their love for each other and their innocence about all that had changed was so poignant that Kay Lynn's chest tightened. Would the bombing and the declaration of war be talked about at school? Would any children harass Donna? She wasn't the only Japanese American student at Lincoln Elementary, but there were not very many. Miss Carter would certainly protect her in the classroom, but the playground was another affair.

As they neared the school, Kay Lynn resisted the urge to walk Lizzie and Donna to their teacher. What could she express to Miss Carter that she didn't already know?

The girls stopped at the corner of Ellis and Prince, carefully checking both directions before venturing into the street. Kay Lynn and Kimiko had been standing at this corner for several months now, watching them travel the last stretch into the school unaccompanied. They'd decided that come January, once Lizzie turned seven, the girls would be old enough to walk the whole route on their own. Today they seemed far too young to take these steps alone.

Two days later, as Kay Lynn and Timmy returned from walking the girls to the corner, Kay Lynn heard the particular clink of typewriter keys striking paper. In the office behind the kitchen, she found Kimiko working at the typewriter, a newborn Missy tied tightly to her chest with a strip of Japanese print fabric.

"Back so soon? I can manage without you," Kay Lynn interrupted, and then quickly added, "though I am glad to see you."

Kimiko stopped typing and turned her head. She looked strong and calm. "Baby number three is so very different from the first. I could never have returned to work so quickly after Donna. By yesterday I was restless. I won't stay too long, but she's asleep. I'd rather do this and leave the dishes to my mother." Kimiko laughed.

Kay Lynn walked up to the pair and studied the small, precious face hidden in the folds of fabric. She placed her hand on the warm bundle and whispered, "Hello, little one. It's nice to see you again." Looking into Kimiko's dark-brown eyes, she said, "She's perfect."

"I'm trying to enjoy her, savor this time, since I know how fast it goes."

Kay Lynn nodded. "I truly don't want three children, but I would welcome being the mother of a newborn again."

"Then let's make sure you get your fill of her," Kimiko replied.

Kay Lynn nodded. "Any time—even the witching hour."

"My mom will be back in her own home soon enough, and I'll welcome your assistance."

Missy stirred, her head turned, searching for a nipple.

Kay Lynn's breast tingled. "Oh, my gosh. I swear just seeing her root is making my milk come in!"

The two women laughed.

"I better leave before I leak on myself," Kay Lynn joked.

"And I want to finish this page before she starts screaming for food," Kimiko replied.

Kay Lynn picked up a file folder. "I'm going to use the break in the rain to take these up to the I-House and stop at Alpha Sigma Phi to pick up our final papers of the semester," Kay Lynn replied. "Should I offer to take Georgie with us?"

"Please. He can't make any sense of this. An outing would be very welcome."

Kay Lynn paused, aware of all that was left unsaid between them. Was it her place to bring up Pearl Harbor? The declaration of war? The raids that had already happened on Japanese communities in San Francisco and San Pedro? The cars with drivers that looked Japanese being searched before they crossed the Bay Bridge? She didn't want to bring up the painful, complicated subject if Kimiko would prefer to avoid it.

"I'll stop next door before we go."

She went into the kitchen and brewed a cup of ginger tea for her dear friend, stirring in honey, a spoonful of sweetness in a bitter and beautiful time.

"I expect your milk supply is just fine, but you need to stay hydrated," she said as she brought the cup to Kimiko.

"Thank you," Kimiko said without pausing, her back to Kay Lynn, her fingers flying across the keys.

While Kay Lynn hadn't expected Kimiko to get back to work so quickly after the birth, she was grateful to have some of the typing taken off her shoulders. She did well for someone with only one dexterous hand, but Kimiko was far faster, and they had a lot of papers at the end of the term. Without Kimiko, Kay Lynn would have had many late nights.

She watched her friend from the doorway and thought about the wonderful and strange fortune that brought them together.

In June 1934, the week following their graduation from Berkeley High and wedding, Kay Lynn and Mitch moved next door to Kimiko and Ken Fujioka. Kimiko was also a newlywed from Berkeley High's class of '34, though they'd only known one another in passing. Ken was four years older and a graduate of Oakland Tech.

Kay Lynn grew up in the nearby Elmwood District of Berkeley, where her parents had a small accounting business around the corner from their home on Woolsey Street. Kay Lynn was fortunate to find a rental within walking distance to the house she had taken to calling "the Grands," her childhood home where her parents, grandmother, and siblings, Lenny and Kristine, lived. Kay Lynn thought it was well past time for her twenty-year-old brother and eighteen-year-old sister to make their own households, but her parents said they were welcome to stay as long as they liked.

Initially Kimiko and Kay Lynn were simply cordial to one another. But polite waves turned into front-porch conversations when they discovered they were both pregnant, and lunch visits began soon after their daughters were born weeks apart. Soon they saw each other almost every day.

In 1937 Mitch lost his job. Weeks turned into months without work. They ran through their meager savings and feared they might lose their housing because they couldn't make rent. Her parents had lent them money, but Momma and Poppa's resources were limited.

Kimiko saved them when she invited Kay Lynn to work with her. Kimiko had started the small business after her cousin offered to pay her to type his papers. Word spread quickly that she was affordable, fast, and reliable, and she could not keep up with the demand. She didn't have a typewriter, so she'd used one at the public library.

Kay Lynn wasn't nearly as fast a typist, but she was good with bookkeeping, had a spare room they could use as an office, plus she procured them a used typewriter from her parents.

For four years Kay Lynn and Kimiko had seamlessly shared work and mothering duties. They'd grown the business from a few papers a week to dozens. Each morning one of them walked their girls the two blocks to Lincoln Elementary School, where they were in first grade. Their two-year-old sons entertained each other in the yard or in a house while their mothers typed.

Both Kay Lynn and Kimiko transformed sheets of paper written in longhand into perfectly typed manuscripts without a single mistake. Kay Lynn walked to campus to pick up drafts and deliver final products back to the young men, and some women, who paid them. Kimiko handled the banking.

Mitch started working as a full-time bookkeeper for Kay Lynn's parents in 1938, but she had no desire to stop her business. She liked working, and having a reliable second income that allowed her to be with their children was a safety net that Kay Lynn wouldn't give up easily. They'd made their way out of a huge pile of debt, and Kay Lynn never wanted to be indebted to her parents, or anyone else, ever again.

Since Sunday, everything seemed in peril. Congress already declared war against Japan. Great Britain declared war on Japan as well, which meant the US would soon be at war against Germany and Italy. President Roosevelt was resolved that the United States would win an absolute victory. Young men were enlisting in droves. Bombs were already falling on Manila and Singapore.

Japanese fishermen in San Pedro, as well as leaders of the Japanese community in San Francisco, had been rounded up by the US government. So far, the large Japanese community in Berkeley and Oakland had been left alone, but the threat hung over Kimiko's family.

Kay Lynn's German heritage wasn't apparent, but Kimiko didn't have that advantage. Although she was born in the United States and was a citizen, her name and her appearance identified her as something she wasn't: the enemy. Anti-Japanese animosity had reached unprecedented heights.

Kay Lynn considered what more to say. She and Kimiko didn't speak about their racial differences. It held no significance for Kay Lynn, and it shouldn't matter in the broader world. She didn't want to burden Kimiko with discussing anything she didn't wish to confront.

But the changes were too enormous to simply ignore. She finally settled on saying, "I'm sorry."

Kimiko's fingers stopped their work.

Kay Lynn continued, "We don't have to speak of it, if you don't wish to. But I'm sorry that your nation . . . that our country is at war with the nation of your grandparents. And that people are being so hateful."

Kimiko turned around. She glanced at Kay Lynn and then stared off, her face flashing the same confusing range of emotion that Kay Lynn felt.

Eventually Kimiko replied, "I thought my mother was paranoid to believe she could be forced to return to a country she left thirty years ago. Until Monday, I was certain this country wouldn't abandon her because of the ambitions of the Japanese empire, but now I wonder if it will betray not only them, but also me and my children."

Kimiko shook her head. "The leaders of our community are telling us to prove we are loyal citizens by cooperating." She cleared her throat. "We are loyal citizens. I've never lived anywhere else."

"I know you are," Kay Lynn replied.

Kimiko turned back to her typing. Kay Lynn patted her arm. It was entirely inadequate, but she hoped it was a small comfort.

She glanced through the window. The rain had stopped, but outside it was overcast and chilly. She and Timmy bundled up in their warmest clothes and put the attaché case in the little red wagon.

She knocked next door to get Georgie.

Mrs. Hori answered, her face pulled in with worry until she recognized Kay Lynn.

"Hello!" Mrs. Hori bowed. Kay Lynn bowed back.

Kay Lynn spoke slowly, fighting her mistaken impulse to talk loudly. "We . . . are . . . walking. Can . . . Georgie . . . go . . . with . . . us? Kimiko . . . says . . . yes."

"You . . . want . . . Georgie?" Mrs. Hori asked.

Kay Lynn nodded. "Yes," she enunciated.

"Okay." Mrs. Hori smiled and held up one finger.

She disappeared, presumably to get her grandson, leaving the door open. Timmy pulled at Kay Lynn's hand, ready to walk into the Fujiokas' house. Kay Lynn resisted; instead, she sat on the bench, and Timmy climbed up next to her.

She pointed to the wisteria across the street. "See the pretty red balls?"

It was early yet, but their neighbors had decorated its bare branches with shiny glass spheres. At this time of year, the vine had been cut so far back that it appeared to be dead, just gray ropes climbing around the painted column that supported the roof of the open porch. She appreciated the Thomases' effort to make this dreary time more cheerful.

Hazel darted out the door, leapt between them, and licked at Timmy's face, assaulting Kay Lynn with her fluffy tail. The dog attempted to shower Kay Lynn with the same treatment, but Kay Lynn batted Hazel away. Unlike her children, Kay Lynn did not appreciate the dog's affections.

Mrs. Hori returned with Georgie.

"Thank you," Kay Lynn said with a bow. Mrs. Hori bowed back. They gazed at one another; Kay Lynn teared up, as did her elder.

Would this kind woman be forced to leave her home, her children, and her grandchildren? Was she worried about her parents in Nagasaki? Kay Lynn didn't know any relatives in Germany, but just imagining her parents living there was deeply upsetting.

Kay Lynn took Georgie's hand with her right. Timmy held on to her left. When they got down the stairs, Hazel was in the wagon, her tail thumping in hope against the metal.

"You . . . take Hazel too?" Mrs. Hori asked.

Kay Lynn sighed. How much trouble could a small mutt be? She nodded.

Mrs. Hori smiled and waved goodbye.

The boys climbed into the little red wagon next to the attaché case, and Hazel arranged herself around them. They set out into the bright December afternoon: the slant of the sunlight and the crisp air signaled the holidays were near. Electric lights in some trees and on many houses were already strung up, ready to light up the dark winter nights.

Kay Lynn loved this part of her work: going to the campus. It was her own special world, separate from the cares of domestic life. Usually she came alone, the children staying with Kimiko, and relished the solitary calm as she walked along the creek past stately buildings, wondering what innovations were being conceived behind those walls, propelling future progress. On occasion she would buy a tuna sandwich at the student union and sit out on Sproul Plaza, watching the bustle of students rushing about: mostly young Caucasian men, but there were men of all races from all over the world, and women too. She was still close enough to their age that she could pass for a student.

Best of all was the Campanile, the tall tower in the middle of campus with an elevator to an observation deck. When she really indulged herself, she'd ride to the top. The view from there, like from Indian Rock, made her feel small in a good way. Like looking at the stars on a clear night. It reminded her to put her life within a broader perspective.

Traveling down the streets of Berkeley, toward her peaceful campus, pulling the two boys and a small dog in the wagon, the world seemed the same as last week, but it wasn't. Life as she knew it was over, but what it might become was a mystery. Would San Francisco be bombed? Berkeley? Would they go hungry?

Would Lenny or Mitch be maimed or killed? Her cousins? Mitch's brother?

She wanted a means to view their future, but of course, there wasn't one. Any crystal ball she conjured in her mind only contained the Wicked Witch of the West cackling at her fear. She couldn't know what was to come; she only hoped she had the strength to handle it.

CHAPTER 3

February 1942

Kay Lynn imagined war would lead to sudden, rapid changes, but their world remained mostly the same in the weeks after the bombing of Pearl Harbor. Her brother hadn't rushed to enlist, nor had Mitch, who agreed not to volunteer while fathers were exempt. The new semester started, and there were plenty of students that needed Kay Lynn and Kimiko's typing services. Little Missy was a delight at two months—giving one of her first smiles to Kay Lynn.

Food and goods had been plentiful for the holidays. Lizzie's seventh birthday passed with great enthusiasm. Kay Lynn had lulled herself into believing this war would not be entirely disruptive until she read the headlines.

War Zones for Nation Ordered

Roosevelt Directs Stimson to Set Up Military Zones from Which Aliens or Citizens Can Be Barred or Removed

Oust Japs—Situation Critical Say Farmers

A pit hollowed out her stomach as she read the article. The details were scarce, but it was clear that US citizens could be forced to evacuate without cause as well as residents, perhaps even children and mothers. The article mentioned those of Italian or German heritage might be included, but she hadn't read of any systematic government raids on those communities. She didn't fear for her own freedom in any way.

She scanned the front page. Names from around the globe jumped out at her: Burma. Brazil. Timor Isle. Bataan. Canada. North Atlantic. Port Darwin. British Guiana. London. No wonder President Roosevelt's fireside chat on Monday included an encouragement to have a world map at hand while listening to him.

It was too much to take in, and too important to ignore.

Kay Lynn folded up the paper and went outside to pick some lemons. By the time Mitch was home from work, the lemon bars were nearly finished baking.

She showed him the article. "I made some bars. Let's bring them over to the Fujiokas this evening and offer our assistance."

After dinner the four of them traipsed out the door, bars in hand. Lizzie stopped their family caravan.

"Mommy! I found one!" Lizzie exclaimed.

Kay Lynn looked where her daughter pointed. She smiled. There it was . . . the first crocus of the year, a yellow one. Her heart opened, and she teared up. Life went on, full of beauty, even in these terrible times.

The four of them crouched around the small flower, Mitch balancing the plate of lemon bars with one hand. Timmy's hand darted out to grab the petals.

"No, Timmy." Lizzie stopped him. "We just look; we don't touch."

Kay Lynn smiled. How many times had she said those very words to Lizzie?

"So many signs of spring," Mitch said. He pointed across the street. Pink petals in the cherry tree were in full, glorious bloom.

Kay Lynn remarked, "It happened overnight, because yesterday there were tight buds."

This time of year was like that. The gray ropes of wisteria across the street were bare of leaves and flowers while the cherry tree in the next yard over was in full bloom. The wisteria made spring appear far, far away while the cherry made it seem at hand. In truth, it was both, depending on how you measured spring: light, flowers, rain, warmth, or the position of the sun.

They continued to their neighbors and knocked on the painted wooden door. Hazel barked on the other side, but no one answered their greeting. Kay Lynn shook her head.

"They're likely making plans with their family," she said to Mitch.

"Should I leave these?" He gestured with his head to the table by the door.

Kay Lynn nodded, and they went back home.

The next morning, Kimiko came over to share what they had learned at church about the evacuation order.

"There have been no searches in Oakland or Berkeley, but the JACL, the Japanese American Citizen League, is advising us to remove anything that ties us to Japan or Japanese culture," Kimiko explained.

"Your beautiful painting by Professor Obata?" Kay Lynn asked. "How could that be harmful?"

Kimiko shrugged. "Do you know their store was shot at?"

Kay Lynn bit her lip and closed her eyes tight. She shook her head.

"I'm sorry. I'm outraged for you, but you do not have to justify anything to me."

Kimiko continued. "We *will* be relocated. We don't know when or to where, but all people of Japanese heritage will be removed from the entire West Coast."

Kay Lynn's stomach clenched at this terrible, and truly unbelievable, statement.

"How can we help?" she asked.

Kimiko exhaled hard. "They claim there will be safe storage of our belongings, but I don't trust that offer. Would you have room to store a trunk for us?"

Kay Lynn nodded.

"I'll need time to sort and pack," Kimiko said.

"I understand that you'll need some time off. I can take care of . . ." Then it hit Kay Lynn. It wouldn't be time off. Kimiko would be gone. Their business was now resting entirely on Kay Lynn's shoulders.

She started again, "You need to take care of your family, and I will take care of our customers."

"Thank you," Kimiko said, her voice somber.

"You're welcome. It's hardly enough," she replied. "But . . ." What more was there to say? She felt as helpless as Kimiko looked. Locking away children and mothers wasn't going to make their nation safe, but Kay Lynn couldn't change the hearts or minds of the military men who were making that decision.

A few days later Kimiko was ready to store the trunk in their garage.

Kay Lynn followed her into the living room, noticing a bare spot where the Obata watercolor had hung. It must have been stored in the trunk.

Kay Lynn and Kimiko grabbed the old leather handles. They maneuvered it through the house, down the back stairs into Kimiko's backyard, past the gate, and into Kay Lynn's garage.

Once it was settled, Kay Lynn asked, "May I look inside?"

Kimiko nodded.

The trunk was filled with three neat stacks: papers on one side, beautiful lacquered dishware in the middle, and gorgeous fabric on the left, but no painting.

"May I touch this?" Kay Lynn asked.

Kimiko pulled out the red-and-gold kimono. It was stunning, thick silk rich with bright colors.

"It is so beautiful! I must wrap it more securely, so it doesn't get ruined," Kay Lynn said.

"My mother's wedding kimono," Kimiko explained. "She nearly burned it with their books, documents, and art from Japan. I grabbed it just as she was putting it in the fireplace."

Kay Lynn felt her stomach turn over.

"That's . . . I'm . . ." Kay Lynn struggled for the right words. "I'm sorry." The phrase was so inadequate. "Should I put mothballs in the trunk? To keep it safe?"

"Ruined by moths, or ruined by the smell of mothballs. That's our terrible choice." She laughed. "Yes, to the mothballs. We can get the smell out, but cannot repair the many holes the moths will make. Thank you."

"Where's your painting?" Kay Lynn asked.

"The Obata?"

Kay Lynn nodded.

"We sold it," Kimiko sounded both sad and defiant.

Kay Lynn stopped herself from showing her shock. Kimiko and Ken treasured that wedding present. The practical decision to part with it must have been heart wrenching.

Kimiko folded the kimono in half. Kay Lynn bent over to help. She pushed the fabric into her left hand and took the other corner in her right. Slowly, carefully they bundled it up into a small package and pressed it back into its hiding place.

Feeling unsettled after Kimiko's departure, Kay Lynn sought distraction by taking Timmy on an Indian Rock adventure. He loved climbing on the huge boulder, and she appreciated the view of the bay and the ancient acorn-grinding indentations atop the rock, which offered her a much-needed perspective on time.

On that beautiful March day, she packed up lunch and set out, leaving the cares of the modern world behind to simply be a mother with her son, reveling in the joy of being alive.

"Flowers!" Timmy pointed across the street.

Bright-purple petals dangled from the roof of the porch. The wisteria was starting to bloom—early this year. She looked at her own garden. The crocuses were long gone, but the scarlet carnations and mustard were just blooming, joining the statice and Queen Anne's lace that flowered all winter. She pulled a few clumps of stray grass and tossed them in her small compost pile.

"Let's go!" She reached for Timmy's hand. Joined together, they walked to their stop. On the streetcar Timmy knelt on the bench, facing the back window so he could study the automobiles.

"Hello, Buick. Hello, Oldsmobile. Hello, Ford. Hello, Studebaker." He greeted each one with his sweet voice and waved. She didn't correct him when he got the wrong manufacturer. At nearly three, it was impressive that he recognized any of the makes.

Occasionally a driver or passenger on Shattuck Avenue waved back. Timmy would turn to her with a smile and ensure she was waving too. His joy was infectious and took her mind and heart off the troubles of the world.

At University they got off the streetcar and walked uphill, moving at his pace since she hadn't brought the stroller. He took turns running ahead on the sidewalk, crouching down to look at the plants, or holding her hand while he pointed at cars driving by. A few months ago, he could hardly speak and she would never have trusted him to run ahead on the sidewalk. He was growing up fast, so fast.

It was bittersweet to realize that she was no longer the mother of an infant, and would never be so again. Kay Lynn and Mitch agreed that two children was the right number for them and took every precaution to ensure she wouldn't get pregnant, but she missed the sweetness of her children's infancy and was sad that toddlerhood was coming to an end too.

Timmy climbed ahead of her up the narrow steps that had been carved into the rock that must be three or four hundred feet tall. Kay Lynn held her hands out behind him in case he stumbled, but he was sure-footed all the way to the top.

"Stay where I can see you," Kay Lynn instructed as she sat on the bench carved into the rock at the peak. If he was in sight, he could not be too close to the edge.

The bay sparkled below, with San Francisco in the background. She had a perfect view of both new bridges: the utilitarian Bay Bridge and the artistic Golden Gate Bridge. Even five years after their completion, they still seemed a marvel.

She and Mitch had their first kiss on this rock bench. He'd asked her to walk there with him after school in their senior year. She smiled at the memory. It was such an exciting day, the culmination of their gazing across the room at each other with shy smiles. She had expected it to be a fling, a playful, temporary relationship before she crossed into adulthood. A few months later, they thought a condom was all they needed to enjoy each other and postpone parenthood. Lizzie was proof they'd been wrong.

Kay Lynn loved Mitch and the life they had built together, but she knew they wouldn't be married if he'd gone to UCLA after graduation.

A sudden blare ruined her ruminations. Timmy's screams added to the cacophony. She looked for her son but didn't see him. He'd just been in front of her a moment ago. Her heart raced. She stood. There he was, just over the rise, lying flat against the enormous rock with his hands covering his ears. She rushed to his side and sat down close.

"I'm here," she soothed. Over the sound, she shouted, "It's only a test of the air-raid siren. I'm not worried."

He looked at her, his dark-brown eyes filled with terror. She put her hands around his rib cage in a gentle invitation; he scampered onto her lap and cowered against her, still covering his ears with his hands. She breathed in slowly, trying to calm her own heart.

The horrid sound cut off as abruptly as it had started.

"Stupid siren!" Timmy declared.

Kay Lynn often chastised her children for saying that word, but today she felt the same way. Stupid siren ruining their sanctuary. What had been a joyful day was spoiled by the war.

"I'm sorry, Timmy." She teared up. "I forgot it was the test day, and I didn't know there was a siren so close to Indian Rock."

He shrugged, stood up, and began exploring the rock again, looking no worse for the experience while she was still working to slow her racing heart.

"Ready for your sandwich?" she asked, and gestured for him to follow her to the bench.

He nodded and trotted over to the spot that had changed the course of her life.

CHAPTER 4

March 1942

As they walked from their home to the Grands for Sunday supper, Kay Lynn ruminated about that morning's worship service. She expected Reverend Reed to question the morality of the Japanese relocation order, but he hadn't. For months Reverend Reed had preached taking up arms against fascism, including against the Japanese emperor, but she assumed he would advocate for the rights of individual United States citizens like Kimiko and Ken.

Once they got to the last block, Lizzie ran ahead of them.

"Timmy too?" her almost-three-year-old asked.

She nodded.

He chased after his sister, his arms pumping back and forth as he tried to catch up, but his little legs couldn't. By the time she and Mitch got to the front porch, Timmy was collapsed on the stairs, sobbing. She leaned in and told Mitch it was his turn to deal with their child's emotions.

Inside the house, Lizzie and Kristine sat close on the couch in the living room, already playing one of Lizzie's favorites: Cat's Cradle. She'd also brought her new set of jacks for them to play after dinner.

Timmy would feel left out. Hopefully Lenny would distract him with building blocks.

Kay Lynn's sour mood must have shown at the dinner table, because as soon as Grammy Sadie finished the prayer, Kristine asked, "Why are you out of sorts?"

"I'm bothered that this morning Reverend Reed had nothing to say about the implementation of the evacuation order. Did you read in the paper that they might be held at the Albany Racetrack? It's horrible."

"Who?"

A wave of resentment rolled across Kay Lynn. Kristine was so selfish.

"Kimiko and her family," she snapped. "Your niece's best friend, Donna."

"All of them? *Really?*" Kristine asked. "I find it hard to believe."

"Yes!" Kay Lynn nearly exclaimed. "They expect it will apply to all people of Japanese descent, even those born here."

"Where to?"

Kay Lynn shrugged. "No one knows."

"When?"

"They don't know," Kay Lynn snapped.

Kristine's eyes went wide. "It must be for a good reason. Perhaps they don't have time to sort out who is loyal and who isn't."

Kay Lynn flushed with anger. "I can't possibly imagine why Kimiko, Donna and George, and Baby Missy have to be sent away—even to 'sort things out,' as you say. They have nothing, *absolutely nothing*, to do with the bombing of Pearl Harbor. Kimiko has never even been to Japan." Kay Lynn frowned. "My tie to Germany is nearly the same as her connection to Japan, but no one is rounding me up."

"Maybe if you lived on the East Coast?" her brother suggested.

She snapped at Lenny, "Do not try to justify what our government is doing. It's terrible that children are being sent away for the actions of grown men bent on having power."

Timmy started to cry.

"Mommy is okay, Timmy. No need to be upset," she whispered. Looking at the expressions on her family, Kay Lynn flushed and apologized.

"I feel helpless and confused," she admitted.

Momma spoke up, "The windows at Oshima Cleaners were broken this week," referring to the business three doors down from theirs on College Avenue. "There's absolutely no reason to treat them poorly," Momma said. "It's shameful."

The table went still.

Kay Lynn finally said, "I don't know what I believe anymore. Do I trust our government like President Roosevelt asks of us? When they are behaving like the . . ." She mouthed, *Nazis.*

Poppa said, "You cannot make a moral equivalency. We have not invaded other nations unprovoked. Japan bombed US territory."

"Hawaii isn't a state," Mitch replied.

"But it is a US territory," Poppa replied. "America and Japan have been squabbling over territory since the end of the Spanish-American War."

Kay Lynn asked, "Land in the middle of the Pacific Ocean?"

Kristine said, "The US wants military bases in the Philippines and maybe Guam."

Kay Lynn shook her head. "Baby Missy has to leave the West Coast because of a small island in the Pacific?"

Poppa Leo spoke up. "This is a war between the ideals of fascism and the ideals of democracy. The Japanese emperor wants to build the greatest empire in Asia. Germany wants to rule the whole world, as far as I can tell, starting with Europe. Their aggression makes the strangest of allies—us and the Soviets. They don't want democracy or free markets. I guess the enemy of my enemy is my friend."

"I wish they would just leave us out of it," Momma said. "One world war in my lifetime is enough."

"I have news," Lenny interrupted. He cringed and looked at Momma. "Sorry, Ma."

Momma closed her eyes tight, as tears rolled down her face. She knew what was coming, they all did.

"Go on," she declared, her voice somehow hard and resigned at the same time.

"I've signed with the air force."

A silence descended over the dinner table.

Mitch reached for Kay Lynn's hand.

Poppa asked, "What caused you to settle on the air force?"

"Airplanes!" Excitement shone in his eyes. "They're the future. I don't know if I'll get to be in them or repair them, but I'll be around them. I can't imagine being on a ship for weeks at a time. My apologies to Mr. Kaiser," he mumbled, "but that sounds horrid."

"When do you leave?" Momma asked, her voice so pained it brought tears to Kay Lynn's eyes and raised gooseflesh on her arm.

Kay Lynn looked at Timmy. He was lost in play, zooming two tin airplanes around. Picturing him off to war put a pit in her stomach. She patted his leg; he gave her a quick glance and a brief smile, and then returned his attention to his imagined battle. *Poor Momma.* Kay Lynn loved her brother, and she would worry for him, but her mother's fears must be suffocating.

"I get on the bus at eight a.m. on Thursday."

Momma sighed. "This is our last Sunday supper together. Wednesday, we will have your favorite." She looked at Kay Lynn, letting her know she was expected to join them for Lenny's final meal at home.

"I'll be back soon; I'm certain of it," Lenny declared. "We'll drop a few bombs on Germany, and they'll surrender. They know there's more coming if they don't."

"Son, I respect your choice . . . make no mistake," Poppa declared, his voice so intense that Timmy stopped playing to stare at his grandfather, "but this war will change you, forever. If it doesn't, you're not paying attention. War is not glamorous, nor is it fun. War is not fair. War is not kind."

Poppa never spoke about his time in Europe during the Great War, the one being called World War I since another had begun. Some argued this one was simply a continuation of that previous war. The Wars of the Roses went on for decade after decade. There must have been some breaks that seemed like peace had won out, only to be followed by more conflict. This might be the same: a world war on and off for her lifetime.

Leo was Kay Lynn's poppa, but not her father. She looked nothing like him and was obviously not his biological child. She was two years old when Momma married him so didn't remember life before. But somehow she knew Lenny and Kristine were wanted; she was a mistake.

In 1916 her unwed mother hid her unwanted pregnancy, expecting to give Kay Lynn up for adoption and go on with her life. But on the day of her birth, Kay Lynn had a seizure, prompting the doctor at the Booth Home for Unwed Mothers to proclaim her too defective to be raised in any family. He announced she would be placed in a facility, but Momma couldn't bear that future for the newborn, so she revealed her deep shame to her family and kept Kay Lynn.

Kay Lynn was grateful that Momma had found the strength to take her home. And that they made a family with Poppa Leo. The alternative—being institutionalized—was too horrible to contemplate.

"That is all." Poppa looked around the table, encouraging them to change the topic. He was a man of few words and never liked being the center of attention, not even on his birthday.

"I have a new job . . . ," Kristine declared.

Kay Lynn's heart flipped; everyone's life was changing.

"Building ships in Richmond for Mr. Kaiser to fight the kaiser."

"Building ships?!" Grammy Sadie asked.

"Well, filing papers in the payroll office," Kristine replied. "But I'll be working on the war effort."

"Richmond's far." Kay Lynn asked, "How will you get there?"

"My friend Ginny drives each day and can give me a ride. She's the one who told me they were hiring. They're so desperate for workers that they'll make sure we have the same schedule. And they have doctors we can see for free."

"A young lady with her own car," Grammy Sadie said. "Times sure are changing."

Kay Lynn agreed. She thought her life was complicated by the Great Depression, but that hadn't taken anyone from her. Soon Lenny would be gone, across the sea to Europe, or maybe Asia. Kimiko and her family would be detained in a relocation camp, and Kristine would be driving far to work at all hours of the day. Could she keep her business open without Kimiko?

The decision they faced for Mitch hung over them like the Sword of Damocles: whether to wait to be drafted and deployed anywhere in the world or to enlist with the aim of influencing his assignment to a stateside station. Hopefully, the war would be over so quickly they would never have to make that decision.

Through no fault of her own, Kay Lynn's life was falling apart, and there was nothing she could do to stop it. If she were a woman of prayer like her Grammy Sadie, this would be a time for it. But long ago she'd stopped thinking of God as an entity who cared about her requests. She doubted she'd find solace in prayer. Nevertheless, in the midst of this oncoming storm, she clung to a sliver of hope that somehow, she'd find the strength to weather the tempest of change that was about to engulf her life.

CHAPTER 5

March 1942

They didn't return home after church. Instead, the four Brookes walked to Oakland's Chinatown to celebrate Kay Lynn's twenty-sixth birthday and Timmy's third. Marking special occasions with a meal at Rabbit Moon was a cherished tradition brought from Kay Lynn's childhood. A visit to Chinatown would surely offer them a respite from the world's turmoil. The restaurant's owners, Kai Li and Mei Ling, had once worked for her great-uncle Sam and great-aunt Diana and always welcomed their extended family as honored guests.

As they walked beneath a clear blue sky, Kay Lynn and Mitch moved arm in arm while the children trotted ahead of them.

A large sign in the window of a produce store on the corner of Franklin and Eighth delivered a shock, like a slap across her face.

I AM AN AMERICAN

Kay Lynn felt Mitch contract and exhale hard. She squeezed his arm in agreement. This act of protest might come at a dear cost to the owners.

Lizzie and Timmy stopped in front of the bright-red doors of Rabbit Moon. For the first time, Kay Lynn wondered what the Chinese characters painted over the handles meant. In the past they'd seemed a decoration and nothing more.

Timmy and Lizzie teamed up to pull open the heavy door and held it for their parents. Kay Lynn's heart swelled at their gracious invitation.

The restaurant was nearly empty. Usually they had to wait for a table; today they wouldn't need patience.

"Miss Kay Lynn," Mei Ling greeted her. "Please, sit wherever you like."

"Thank you," she replied, and gestured for the children to make the choice.

Lizzie led the way. "Timmy, this table is the best 'cause we can see the fish!"

They slid into the seats closest to the aquarium. Mei Ling came with a tray bearing tea and menus. When she set it down, Kay Lynn saw she wore a badge on her chest: **I AM CHINESE.**

Her stomach clenched and she closed her eyes. Why did they need to announce to the world that they were not Japanese? It seemed petty and antagonistic. Kay Lynn bit her lip while Mei Ling laid the table. Kai Li came out from the kitchen, also wearing a badge declaring his ancestry.

With a small bow, he said, "Thank you for coming."

Were those tears in his eyes? Kay Lynn looked around the nearly empty room. Had anti-Japanese, anti-Oriental prejudice harmed their business? There was so much she didn't understand about the impact of this war on other people's lives.

Did they have family in China? Sons in the war? She didn't like what the buttons seemed to imply, but who was she to judge them for signaling they were allies and not enemies of the United States? Not that Ken was an enemy. She blinked back more tears.

"Are you okay?" Mitch whispered in her ear.

"I don't know what is right and what is wrong anymore," she whispered back, grateful that the children had turned around to look at the fish. "Those buttons seem hateful, but perhaps they are only self-protection. All I want to do is have a nice lunch with my family for our birthdays, and then I fear I am the one who is selfish and unkind."

"There is nothing we can do to make Japan our ally, but we can be kind to our friends whose business is apparently failing."

She nodded.

"Shall we order chicken chow fun?" she asked her children.

"Noodles!" Lizzie squealed and turned to look at her parents. "And pink pig?"

"Yes, sweet-and-sour pork with rice," Mitch agreed. "It wouldn't be a celebration without it."

"And garlic green beans or broccoli?" Kay Lynn asked.

"Trees?" Timmy suggested.

"Broccoli it is," Kay Lynn agreed.

"I spy . . . something brown." Mitch started their favorite table game.

Lizzie looked around the room, searching for something that fit the bill.

"Bunny!" Timmy pointed at a carved rabbit.

"That was fast!" Mitch replied. "You're right. Who's next?"

"Me," Lizzie shouted, and continued the game.

Kay Lynn took a deep breath. Mitch was correct; there was nothing she could do to repair the terrible treatment of Chinese and Japanese Americans. She'd be kind and hope that was enough to satisfy her own sense of right and wrong.

On a warm day at the end of April, Kay Lynn and the boys were walking the girls to school. The declaration of war had erased any intention of allowing Donna and Lizzie to make this journey alone. They never spoke about it; Kimiko and Kay Lynn simply stayed with them crossing Harper, Ellis, and Prince Streets; through the gate; and all the way to the doors to the building, providing a shield of their mothers' love as far as possible.

Down the block, Kay Lynn could see a large paper notice fluttering against a telephone pole. After they crossed Harper, Lizzie and Donna ran to the sign. From a distance Kay Lynn made out the word *Japanese* in big, bold letters. She knew exactly what it was.

Donna's finger pointed to a word on the paper. The girls were using their budding reading skills to sound it out. Kay Lynn felt ill.

"What's it say, Mommy?"

INSTRUCTIONS
TO ALL PERSONS OF

JAPANESE
ANCESTRY

Kay Lynn skimmed the tightly packed text below the terrible heading. Sentences jumped out at her.

> All persons of Japanese ancestry, alien and non-alien, will be evacuated from the above area by 12 o'clock noon P. W. T., Friday, May 1, 1942.

And further down:

> 2. Evacuees must carry with them on departure for the Assembly Center the following property:

(a) Bedding and linens (no mattress) for each member of the family;

(b) Toilet articles for each member of the family;

(c) Extra clothing for each member of the family;

(d) Sufficient knives, forks, spoons, plates, bowls and cups for each member of the family;

(e) Essential personal effects for each member of the family.

3. No pets of any kind will be permitted.

They had to abandon Hazel. She felt too ill to keep reading. Of all the horrid demands, that one hurt the most.

"We don't want you to be late for school, girls," she replied through a tight throat, working to keep her voice neutral. "This is a long notice. I'll read it on my way home and tell you about it after school."

Oblivious to the menace, the girls skipped forward.

One week. The Fujiokas had to evacuate their home and report to the Congregational Church on Channing by next Friday.

She wanted to rip the sign off the pole, and tear it into little pieces. Did Kimiko and Ken know their time had come? Likely not, because Donna had run out of their house this morning as if this were a normal day, not the start of a doomsday clock.

Now that she knew, should she bring Donna back home? She watched the two girls, skipping down the sidewalk hand in hand, oblivious that they were about to be separated by forces beyond their parents' control. Kay Lynn stopped herself from calling out. She wanted her Lizzie to have one last day of innocence.

"Can we cross?" Lizzie yelled from the corner.

Kay Lynn nodded and followed the girls. When they got to the door of the building, Miss Carter looked stricken. She must have read the signs.

"Donna, can you help me carry these materials into the classroom?" Miss Carter asked.

Thankfully, Miss Carter knew to keep Donna close today. Lizzie and Donna skipped to the front of the line. Lizzie didn't think to stay in the back of the line without her.

Friday. The day had come. Kimiko and her family could bring only what they could carry. Buses would transport them from the Congregational Church in Berkeley to an unclear future. Even with an empty stomach, Kay Lynn felt so nauseated she feared she would vomit. This was wrong, and yet it was happening without any signs of protest. No matter how she thought about it, removing Kimiko and the children from the West Coast was immoral. How could it be necessary for the war effort? Even removing all the men was illogical, but it was happening.

Lizzie rested her chin on the back of their worn couch, staring out the living room window, her look of anticipation rivaling her expression on Christmas morning, but today was a mourning, not a celebration.

"I see them! Can I go now?" her sweet daughter asked. Lizzie wasn't aware of the tragedy that was unfolding. They'd kept the information light and unspecific, telling her Donna was moving away for a while because of the war.

Kay Lynn gave a single nod. Despite the sun, she put a sweater on Timmy, and blinked back tears before joining her friends outside. She didn't need to burden Kimiko with her emotions. Five suitcases, five people, and a dog filled the sidewalk. Lizzie admired the rose stickers she'd given Donna for her suitcase. Kimiko looked at their house, her lips moving, but no sound came out. Kay Lynn watched, uncertain what to say or do, while her friend said goodbye to her home.

When Kimiko turned around, Kay Lynn asked, "There's nothing you need besides forwarding your mail? It's such a small thing."

"Caring for our beloved Hazel is a great gift; I know you aren't fond of dogs."

"I won't mind for a few months. Lizzie and Timmy are very excited to have a pet." The dog would be an annoying burden, but Kay Lynn kept that thought to herself.

Kimiko replied, "We pray it's just a few months. The landlord said he will keep it empty for as long as he can afford to, but I suspect you'll have new neighbors long before we're released."

Kay Lynn wanted to protest, but she also feared they would be detained for the entire war, which looked to be dragging out past the New Year. She didn't fault the landlord; leaving a house empty was an expense few people could afford.

Kay Lynn said, "Donna, you can put your suitcase in the wagon. We'll rearrange if the boys don't want to walk."

"Thank you, Mrs. Brooke."

Ken set out without a word, weighed down by their two largest suitcases. Donna held Lizzie's hand and Hazel's leash, skipping down the sidewalk. Timmy and George toddled behind, and the mothers took up the rear, carrying a five-month-old baby and pulling three bags in the wagon.

The gloomy weather mirrored their mood, as if the sky shed tears on their behalf. Kimiko, Ken, Donna, George, and Missy left their home, perhaps forever, and the world wept.

"Flowers all gone," Timmy said as he pointed to the wisteria vine across the street.

"Next year," Kay Lynn reassured him. "They'll be back next spring." Her heart caught. She looked at Georgie. Would he be here to see them next spring?

Kimiko whispered, "My mother recently told me that she planted that vine."

"She lived on this street?" Kay Lynn asked. "When?"

"She came in 1912—a picture bride. Her parents gave her a pod with four seeds. Can you imagine? Leaving your family to join a husband you had only seen in a picture?"

A wave of emotion raised gooseflesh on Kay Lynn's arms. So much was hidden inside others. In her mind, Mrs. Hori was a doting *bachan*, grandmother, not a brave and bold young woman who dared to cross an ocean. Had she known it would be forever when she left?

"She told you about the wisteria just now?" Kay Lynn asked.

Kimiko nodded. "It seemed her veiled way of saying, 'I've survived worse, so no complaining.'"

No complaining, because it could be worse. Kay Lynn told herself that at least once a day.

Ken called to them from the corner. "We must keep going."

The women caught up, and the group continued their trek. Not too far ahead of them, there was another dark-haired family, weighed down with suitcases, heading in the same direction. They followed them right onto Ashby and then left onto Grove.

"Good riddance!" a voice yelled from a passing car.

Kay Lynn's cheeks burned. "I'm so sorry."

"We are American citizens; why don't they understand we did nothing to deserve this?" Kimiko whispered.

"I promise I'll remind everyone I know."

Kimiko tried to smile, but her lips couldn't finish the job.

They turned right on Dwight and left on Dana to the Congregational Church on Channing. The sidewalk was dotted with families clustered around luggage. Was the church exhibiting a kindness or a cruelty by providing this location for their evacuation?

Kay Lynn wondered if the Berkeley Unitarian church considered providing this send-off, or her own church in Oakland. It was the kind of thing the Unitarians might do to be supportive, but even she hadn't considered it until this moment.

The scene was at once calm and chaotic. Ken ducked into the church building to register them. Kimiko gazed around until she found some family: her cousin Misako and her children. Kay Lynn followed Kimiko with the wagon, lifted out the luggage, and set it by Misako, expanding their own temporary life raft. Lizzie was chatting away with her friend, unaware that she didn't belong.

Kimiko saw her parents a few yards away, standing sentry by two small suitcases, looking aged and confused. She waved them over.

"Should I take Lizzie?" Kay Lynn asked.

Kimiko started to nod but turned to study the girls. They were gesturing with great animation, seeming to be in the midst of a game of pretend. She shook her head and in a somber voice said, "Let them enjoy their last few minutes of innocent play."

Kay Lynn teared up and replied, "Timmy and I will go sit on that wall. Send Lizzie with Hazel when it's time."

Kimiko nodded.

Unwanted tears streamed down Kay Lynn's cheeks; she brushed them away, but Kimiko saw. "I'm sorry. I don't want to burden you with my sorrow."

"Do not mistake my stoicism for indifference."

Kay Lynn's heart burst as she protested, "No! I do not . . . I know you are not indifferent."

"Goodbye," Kimiko said.

A vise clamped Kay Lynn's throat; she nodded and hugged her dear friend. "I'll write," she forced out while they still embraced. "As soon as you send me your address. Lizzie too."

It was a kindness she had to offer. *You will not be forgotten.*

When they released their embrace, Kay Lynn noted the shine in Kimiko's deep-brown eyes. She held Timmy's pudgy hand as they wove through the crowd to sit on a wall and wait.

The mood was somber but polite, and everyone was orderly. Eventually, Ken joined his family. He spoke intently to Kimiko, who nodded. Kay Lynn could only guess what he was saying as he handed Kimiko paper tags.

Kimiko bent over George. When she straightened, Kay Lynn's stomach turned. A numbered tag dangled from George's coat, like he was a piece of luggage. In turn, Kimiko tied one to Donna, herself, and even Baby Missy.

A white woman came through, handing out sandwiches to each family, the pale bread wrapped tight in that new plastic sheeting. It must have been a great expense for that small kindness.

A long, yellow school bus with brown paper covering the windows pulled up, and a wave of families lined up to board. A young man in a khaki-green military uniform, perhaps army, held a clipboard and made notes after speaking to the head of household for each group.

Kay Lynn watched a woman wrestling a bundle of blankets tied with a twine through the bus door when she heard Lizzie's voice at her side, "Mrs. Fujioka sent me to be with you. Their turn is soon."

Kay Lynn looked down; her daughter looked close to tears. Kay Lynn didn't want to encourage an outburst, so she just nodded. Later, she would comfort the girl, but for now they wouldn't draw any attention to themselves. Lizzie settled next to Timmy and sang his favorite song, "The Wheels on the Bus." It would have a different meaning after a school bus took the Fujiokas away.

Too soon, Kay Lynn interrupted her children. The Fujiokas were next to board. Ken carried two large bags, Kimiko had Baby Missy in one arm and a bag in the other. Donna and George wrestled with the remaining bags, pushing them on the ground to get them to the stairs of the bus.

Suddenly Hazel was running through the crowd to Donna. Kay Lynn's breath caught.

"No dogs!" the soldier barked. "How many times do I have to say it to you people?"

Lizzie leapt from the wall and raced to the bus.

"Sorry, sir. It's my fault; don't be mad at Donna."

Lizzie held out her hand to get Hazel's leash from her friend, who'd grabbed it in the chaos.

"We'll take good care of Hazel while you're gone; I promise." The girls hugged tightly.

The soldier looked at the two children, confusion riddled his face. He opened his mouth as if to say something, but nothing came out. He closed it and waited while Lizzie gave Georgie a hug too.

By the time Lizzie and Hazel returned to Kay Lynn's side, their friends were gone, hidden behind the papered windows. Unidentifiable eyes gazed out through the small gaps.

Hazel whimpered and pulled at her leash. "You'll stay with us for a little while. They'll be back soon," Lizzie reassured the dog.

Lizzie asked, "Mommy, Donna will be home by Christmas, won't she?"

"I don't know about Christmas. No one knows. We don't know if they will have to be gone for the whole war, or just while things are sorted out. Last time, America was at war for nineteen months before the armistice, so it may be that long again."

"A year and a half?" Lizzie exclaimed, and then thought for a moment before she declared, "I'll be almost nine! That's way too long! How can I live without Donna for more than a year?"

Kay Lynn didn't have an answer, so she patted Lizzie's leg.

"Shall we head home?" Kay Lynn asked, rising from the wall.

"No, Mommy!" Lizzie responded. "We have to wave!"

Kay Lynn's throat tightened, and she sank back down. Somehow, her daughter was facing this with more strength than she was; perhaps because she was naïve about what the Fujiokas were losing and where they were headed.

Reading her sorrow, Timmy stopped playing and climbed onto her lap.

"Mommy sad?" he asked as he brushed away a tear.

"Yes," Kay Lynn told her son. "Mommy is sad to say goodbye to Mrs. Fujioka."

"Timmy sad too," his sweet voice agreed. "To say goodbye to Georgie."

"And Lizzie is sad to say goodbye to Donna," her daughter chimed in with the high voice reserved for her brother. "And Baby Missy. And Mr. Fujioka."

Kay Lynn smiled at her daughter. "Yes, we are sad to say goodbye to all of them, but we will always love them and hold them in our hearts—no matter where they are."

They watched from the wall as the school bus filled with families. The doors closed, and they anticipated it pulling away. The engine turned on; then a few minutes later, it turned off again.

"Potty!" Timmy exclaimed.

"Oh, dear!" Kay Lynn knew he did not have the training to hold off for long. "I have to take him inside the church. Would you like to come with us?"

"No, Mommy," Lizzie said without looking away from the bus. "I'll stay here in case they leave while you're gone."

Kay Lynn rushed Timmy inside, hoping to be back at Lizzie's side when their friends were driven away, but by the time they walked out of the building, bus number twenty-three had departed and Lizzie was a small figure staring off down the road, her eyes puffy and red.

"She's gone; they're gone. I waved until they turned the corner, but then I couldn't see them anymore, so I stopped."

Kay Lynn squeezed her daughter tight and kissed her on the head. "Donna feels your love."

"Can I write her a letter as *soon* as we get home?"

"Yes, but we can't mail it until we get a letter from them with their address."

Lizzie nodded, wiped her cheeks, and jumped to the sidewalk. She walked toward home, dragging Hazel; the dog resisted every step of the way.

CHAPTER 6

May 1942

Nine days later, Kay Lynn was grateful to have a day filled with distracting activities. Sunday was filled with church followed by family supper. It would be nice to have their familiar routine.

The week had been a brutal adjustment to the Fujiokas being gone. Timmy asked, "Where Georgie?" so many times that she snapped at him—bringing him to tears once, but not deterring him from asking again and again.

Timmy wasn't practiced at entertaining himself while she worked. He constantly came to her with questions or to show her what he was doing. Eventually she let him settle at her feet with his toys while she typed. It was better, but he continued to interrupt her.

She was more productive in the afternoons when Lizzie returned from school. She could be Timmy's companion while he ate, and she could practice her budding literacy skills by reading to him.

On this Sunday, Timmy kept up with Lizzie as she ran the last block to the Grands, her jacks in hand. They were already in the dining room when Kay Lynn and Mitch caught up to them.

"Uncle Lenny," Timmy yelled, "we here! Uncle Lenny!"

Kay Lynn was jarred back into their painful reality.

"He's away, Timmy," Lizzie reminded her brother. His eyes pooled with tears. She soothed him. "Let's find Aunt Kristine. She'll play with both of us."

His little lip quivered, even as he nodded. They went into the kitchen.

Kay Lynn looked at Mitch. She felt terrible. Should she have prepared Timmy for that disappointment? She hadn't even thought to remind him that Uncle Lenny was still gone. Nor had Mitch, apparently. Next week she'd remember to tell him. They followed their kids into the kitchen.

"She's working," Momma told Lizzie and Timmy, presumably speaking about Kristine.

"On a Sunday night?" Mitch asked, his voice tinged with doubt.

"They're welding boats in three shifts, twenty-four hours a day," Momma responded.

Poppa said, "I understand people are renting beds for eight hours in parts of Richmond and North Berkeley. Just time to get sleep, and then they leave it for the next person."

"That sounds horrible," Kay Lynn replied.

Momma nodded. "I don't know how we can possibly fit any more people in Berkeley, though they are coming in droves."

"Kristine isn't welding, is she?" Kay Lynn asked.

Poppa Leo shook his head. "Not yet, but there are a few women welders, and she's put in for the training—to either weld or inspect them."

Kay Lynn imagined Kristine as a Rosie the Riveter, with coveralls and her hair wrapped up in a red handkerchief. Somehow it fit. Her sister would be drawn to the adventure and excitement rather than think about how it might worry their parents. This war suited the young—allowing them an opportunity to abandon their responsibilities and to have new adventures in the name of being patriotic.

She and Mitch continued to bicker about his duty. He wanted to contribute more directly to the war effort. Working as a bookkeeper for her parents didn't qualify in his mind. She understood why he wanted to find a position related to the war, but felt it would be disloyal to Momma and Poppa, who had expanded their business in part to give him a stable job. They'd already lost many of their employees to the military.

Fortunately they were still in agreement that he wouldn't enlist until fathers were being drafted, and there was no indication that was coming anytime soon.

"Happy Mother's Day!" Kay Lynn hugged her mother and then Grammy Sadie.

"You too, dear," Grammy Sadie replied. "Will you three get the carnations for our Mother's Day table? I haven't had time yet."

Lizzie took the garden shears from her great-grandmother. "Come on, Timmy. I'll show you how."

"Get one for Mattie too," Grammy Sadie reminded Kay Lynn, referring to the woman who was like a grandmother to Grammy.

"Of course," Kay Lynn said, but it was likely that she would have forgotten Mattie.

Glad for a distraction from the missing family, Kay Lynn joined her children in the front yard.

"Red carnations for the alive moms, right?" Lizzie confirmed. "You, Nana May, Grammy Sadie, and Grandmother?"

Kay Lynn nodded. She held the stems while Lizzie clipped the flowers and handed them one by one to Timmy.

Lizzie said to her brother in a somber voice, "We honor our grandmothers who died with white carnations." Then she asked Kay Lynn, "How many?"

"Nana Lisbeth, Yaya Athena, and Mattie." Kay Lynn raised a finger for each. "Three."

"Who's Mattie again?"

"Nana Lisbeth wasn't born from her, but she was like a mother to Nana Lisbeth and like a grandmother to Grammy Sadie. They come from the same town in Virginia and moved all the way across the country together in the 1890s."

Kay Lynn didn't tell her daughter that Mattie had been enslaved on the plantation that Nana Lisbeth's family owned. It was a shameful part of their family history that she didn't want to explain to a child. It was long ago, and the racial tensions of the South didn't apply to Berkeley and Oakland. As it should be, Negro people in the Bay Area were treated with equal dignity and respect.

Grammy Sadie kept up with Mattie's granddaughter Cousin Naomi and her great-granddaughter Maggie. Kay Lynn had met them a few times over the years, but they were mostly the stuff of stories. Cousin Naomi, a midwife, had attended both May's and Kay Lynn's birth, but Kay Lynn wouldn't recognize either of them if she saw them on the street. They were their only colored friends, because Oakland and Berkeley had so few Negro families.

Kay Lynn considered the bouquet. If she were being honest, a carnation was missing—for Grandmother Barrow, her grandmother on her biological father's side. She hated to hurt Poppa Leo's feelings by including her, but she *was* important to Kay Lynn. She settled on cutting a mottled carnation for her, a convoluted flower to represent Grandmother Barrow's complex place in her life.

They placed the bouquet in the center of the table, anemic with two fewer plates.

After grace, Momma handed a thin envelope to Kay Lynn. "Lenny's first letter."

Kay Lynn studied the distinct postmarks on the envelope. She pulled out the tissue-thin paper.

Hello Ma and Pops,

I hope you aren't fretting about me, Momma, because I am having the time of my life. I can't reveal my location, but the ocean is warm and welcoming.

Thank heaven basic training is over. It was pure torture-swinging between horridly boring and physically grueling with nothing between, but I came through with flying colors, if you know what I mean. I'm not allowed to tell you my assignment, but I'm mighty pleased, and I've got the finest crew you can imagine. Don't worry about me. We're tough as nails, and we're ready to kick those Japs back to their little island.

Give my love to Kristine, Kay Lynn and her gang, and Grammy Sadie.

Your son,

Lenny

Lenny clearly thought he was clever to tell them he got a flying assignment without saying so outright. His letter got through without any black marks from the censors, so his plan succeeded. He made it seem like a grand tour . . . of the South Pacific? Why else would he tell them about the *ocean*?

The note only added to her suspicion that enlisting was a grand adventure for the young. She truly didn't want any harm to come to him, but it didn't sound like he was making a sacrifice.

Grammy Sadie hadn't said a word since they sat down to Sunday supper.

"Are you feeling poorly?" Kay Lynn asked. Her grandmother seemed to have aged in the passing week.

"This old woman doesn't trust that enthusiastic account," she replied. "I'm aware of the cost of war to the hearts of young men, despite their attempts to hide it from old ladies like me."

"Oh, Grammy," Kay Lynn replied. "I don't know what to say to that."

Grammy Sadie patted her cheek. "There is nothing to say or do about such a situation. It must only be borne with as much grace and kindness as we can offer to one another—and prayers."

Prayers. Kay Lynn didn't understand her grandmother's devotion to the practice. Grammy Sadie was a modern woman who believed in science, a fierce advocate for equality between the sexes and the rights of people of all races. Grammy Sadie was a proud suffragette who'd even shaken Susan B. Anthony's hand in the Starr King Room at their church. They were people of reason, not superstition. Begging for favors from an all-powerful god was at odds with being a forward-thinking woman.

"Enough about this war!" Momma declared. "I want to hear about the birthday party my granddaughter was so excited to attend."

"Nana May, it was the best day *ever*," Lizzie declared. "Mrs. Conyers made a treasure hunt! I want Mommy to make one when it's *my* birthday. Donna is going to love it. She *has* to be back by January."

Should Kay Lynn prepare her for Donna being away next January? None of them knew if the war would still be going. It was premature to make that decision now. But she would have to remember to prepare her daughter for disappointment if the conflict spilled into 1943. That seemed impossible. How could Germany or Japan hold out that long against the combined efforts of England, China, the Soviet Union, and the United States?

After supper, Poppa came into the kitchen with a few more dishes for Kay Lynn to wash. The kids had walked with Mitch and Momma to play at John Muir School.

"Thank you for coming to Sunday supper," Poppa said. "It means so much to your mother and grandmother."

Kay Lynn smiled at her father. Seeing family was just as important to him, though he wouldn't say it.

"We all love being here, even Mitch."

"Your mother attempts to hide it, but she's terrified for Lenny and nearly as concerned about Kristine," he said.

"I understand fearing for Lenny, but Kristine?" Kay Lynn asked. "You see her every day."

Poppa shook his head.

"But she lives here?!" Kay Lynn replied.

"We don't want to ruin her reputation, but she's often out very late. When we press her, she says she's working, or out with friends doing their duty to entertain soldiers. Last night your mother sat up in bed, listening for her to come home. I can't say when Kristine returned, but I know she slept until noon."

Duty to entertain soldiers. Kay Lynn nodded. Just as she had suspected, Kristine's "war effort" was driven more by the allure of freedom and adventure than a sense of sacrifice.

Kristine never thought about how her behavior impacted the others. It was no surprise to Kay Lynn that she was making this difficult situation even worse for their parents.

She and Kristine were so far apart in age that they weren't like true sisters. Kay Lynn tended to Kristine when she was young, but they never played together. By high school Kay Lynn took more of an interest in her friends, leaving the four of them to be a family centered around young children.

Kristine was twelve, still at John Muir School, when Lizzie was born. She was so smitten by the infant that she came over nearly every day for weeks. By the time Timmy was born, Kristine was more intrigued by her friends from Willard Junior High than her young niece and nephew, but she still made time for them: babysitting so Kay Lynn and Mitch could go on a date, taking the kids for adventures around town and occasional overnights.

Kristine showed up at family events and for being with the children, but she didn't really speak about her life or show any interest in Kay Lynn. Kristine was the most private of all of them and had become more so since she graduated from high school last year.

Kay Lynn wanted them to be close, but Kristine didn't share that desire, and she wouldn't force herself on her little sister.

"Can you speak with her?" Poppa asked. "Suggest she consider her mother's feelings?"

Kay Lynn sighed. "She's never liked my input—about anything." Asking her to stop hitting the town would likely cause her to be defensive and angry, not mature. Kristine didn't care that Kay Lynn had two children and a business to maintain on her own. Or that Momma and Poppa didn't need one more thing to worry over.

"Please," Poppa implored.

He asked so little of her, and he looked so confident she could repair this breech.

"I'll talk to Kristine, but I expect it will make the situation worse, which somehow I have a way of doing when it comes to my little sister."

"Thank you," Poppa said. He looked so relieved that she knew he was ignoring her concern.

CHAPTER 7

May 1942

Kay Lynn pushed past her achy fingers and stiff neck to finish the last page. She'd gotten up early to make breakfast and left it on the table for the kids, hoping they would take care of themselves to let her type up this paper before Lizzie left for school.

A knock thwarted her progress. It was early. Who would come by before eight o'clock in the morning? Kay Lynn stretched as she walked through the living room and opened the front door.

Mr. Cuthbert, her new neighbor, stood in front of her with Hazel at his side.

"I'm so sorry! I don't know how she keeps getting out!"

His face stony, he huffed, but didn't reply with language.

"You can put her through the gate in the backyard if that's easier for you," she offered.

"You want me to let this dog in my house?" he challenged. "She'll move back in if I encourage her."

"It's only been twelve days. It's a hard adjustment for all of us," Kay Lynn said. This man had absolutely no sympathy. Nor did his landlord, who had leased the house less than a week after the Fujiokas were forced to leave—so much for saving their home for them. "Maybe if she saw that the Fujiokas aren't there, she would stop scratching at the door."

He scowled as he considered her suggestion. "Come on, then," he growled.

"Now?"

He didn't reply. Kay Lynn followed him down her walkway and over to his porch. Hazel raced beside her and shot past both of them into the house when he opened the door. She yelped in excitement, and her tail swung fast from side to side as she raced in circles, expecting to reunite with her real family. But there was no trace of them, nor any remnants of their belongings. A discolored square where the Obata had hung marked the wall, but it might have only been a shadow in her mind. Kay Lynn ached at the pain Kimiko would feel at the complete transformation of her beloved home.

Hazel ran through the dining room and out of sight, her nails clicking frantically on the exposed hardwood floors as she rushed from room to room. A loud, canine howl resounded from the back of the house, reminiscent of Kimiko's wail during her labor just six months ago.

"I think she's learned her lesson," Mr. Cuthbert said.

"Hazel." Kay Lynn's voice broke. She cleared her throat. "Hazel," she called out. "Let's go home."

The dog emerged, her ears low and her tail down. She slunk low and close to Kay Lynn's side all the way out the front door.

"You're okay, girl," Kay Lynn soothed. "They'll return for you soon." Kay Lynn boldly declared a future she wanted, but couldn't create.

Back in her house, Kay Lynn found Lizzie standing over the kitchen table, the *Oakland Tribune* open before her, her breakfast untouched. She pointed to a picture of evacuees at the Tanforan Racetrack. Several teenage girls were perched on a railing, grinning from ear to ear. "They look happy, don't they, Mommy?" Lizzie declared. Kay Lynn's stomach sank. Those girls *did* look happy, and she wanted to assure Lizzie that her friend was safe, but she hated to mislead her daughter into thinking it was right or kind for them to be relocated. What was enough information to give an innocent and curious seven-year-old?

They'd written letters to the Fujiokas but had yet to post them, nor had they received any mail from them. As far as Kay Lynn knew, they were at the Tanforan Racetrack, but Kay Lynn didn't know how to address the letters so they would arrive into their hands. The rumor was that Northern Californian citizens and residents would eventually be sent to Topaz, Utah.

"They do look happy," she replied.

"Read it to me, please," Lizzie requested.

> California's Japanese youth find sports in a favorite American game these days at Tanforan, the horse-racing track converted into an assembly center for evacuees. It's baseball season, but the racing strip is ideal for football. While brothers and boy friends play a "tight" game, the girls look on as "railbirds," perched on a fence, rimming the track.

"What does this one say?" Lizzie pointed to the picture below of the boys playing football.

Kay Lynn read,

> And here's the game itself. The halfback leaps high to pass the pigskin (circled), while his teammates neatly block out opponents. Some of the barracks erected at the track can be seen in the background. Jap youth, at least, are Americanized.

"The newspaper wouldn't lie to us, right, Mommy?" Lizzie asked. "They *are* having fun at camp."

Amazed at Lizzie's direct question, Kay Lynn paused to consider her words before replying. She feared that the newspaper *was* lying to them every day. She wanted to trust the news, but it seemed to be propaganda, advocating for patriotism.

She replied, "I believe those teens were having fun right then. But the newspaper isn't showing us the pictures of them missing their home, and their friends, wishing they didn't have to stay at camp. It isn't *all* bad, but it's wrong that they have to be there. Do you understand?"

"I think so."

"That's enough newspaper for you. Go wake up your brother and bring him down to breakfast."

Kay Lynn read the rest of the page. There was a long article about the situation in Tanforan, including a strangely upbeat paragraph about a nurse mixing up formula for a two-week-old baby. She shuddered at the thought of a baby being born at the racetrack, and wondered why the mother wasn't able to breastfeed. A pit hollowed out in Kay Lynn's stomach.

The article right below was headlined

Rivet Passer Falls 65 Feet to Death

Kay Lynn read the tragic news that ended with a short sentence about the riveter's wife, Mrs. Nellie Lane. That woman's life was changed forever because a strong gust of wind came at the wrong time. *This is a job my sister wants?* Kay Lynn couldn't help but wonder what Kristine was thinking.

Every time she read the paper, Kay Lynn felt ill for hours afterward. She wanted to be someone who kept up with the news, but reading the *Tribune* consistently crushed her spirits. Kay Lynn scanned the rest of the headlines, ignoring anything that didn't concern her or someone she loved directly, searching for a glimmer of hope amid the disheartening reports, but there wasn't one to be found.

For the rest of the morning, Kay Lynn felt behind. She managed to finish typing a paper while Timmy occupied himself in the backyard. They rushed to campus to get it delivered on time and swung by the store to get food for supper on the way home. The highlight of the day was finding an envelope addressed to her in Kimiko's handwriting in the mail. She set it aside to let Lizzie open it. Timmy resisted his nap, but finally fell asleep, giving her the opportunity to listen to her radio show in peace while she folded laundry.

Lizzie looked close to tears when she got home from school.

Kay Lynn asked, "What happened?"

Her daughter pulled a card out of her knapsack.

"I made this card for Donna for her birthday and invited everyone to sign it." She unfolded it. There were only seven names: Lizzie, Connie, Ronda, Ben, Janie, Millie, and Miss Carter.

"No one cared!" Lizzie declared. "Willy and Johnny said very mean things about the Japs. Donna isn't a Jap. She's my friend."

"It's hard when you really care about something and other people disagree or don't think it matters," Kay Lynn explained to her daughter. "And I think it is very sweet that you gave those six people a chance to show Donna that they miss her too. You can focus on the hurt, or you can focus on the kindness."

Lizzie sighed and sat quietly for a moment. "I think this might be one of Grammy Sadie's 'easier said than done' situations."

Kay Lynn nodded and smiled at her daughter—so mature, so sure of herself. She wished she could protect her from the cruelty of the world.

"We got a letter from Mrs. Fujioka today. I waited to open it until you got home."

Lizzie jumped as she exclaimed, "Hooray!"

They used a knife to pry into the space behind the glue, careful not to tear any of the notepaper inside.

One folded-up pack was addressed to Lizzie written in Donna's young hand; the other was Kimiko's neat writing. Lizzie read out loud:

I mis you very much. We are on the bus, and I waved and waved and waved. I saw you waving to me. I didn't cry, but I wanted to.

Now we are at the racetrac. It still smells like horse you know what. Mama says Berkeley usto smell like that too, when she was reely little and there were only horses—befour cars. Our bed mattriss is fill with hay they left behind. It's poky, but not as bad as you mite think.

I hear the family next to us because the wall is only part way. Mama says I shouldn't listen, but they are too loud not to hear. The mom doesn't like the teenagers to go out. She is sad that they don't eat together. At night she tells them they are bad kids, but they go again the next day.

The food here is not as good as my mama's, but I like the hot dogs. We have them every day, but I am not tired of them yet.

(Sorry. I got intrupted.)

There is always something fun to do here. We play tag after dinner. There is no school, but Papa believes there will be when we get to camp in youta. No one knows when we will go, but we think we might have our own huose there.

Give Hazel kisses and pets from me. I miss cuddling with her.

Write back!!!!!!

Your friend forever and always,
Donna

"Do you think she'll make a new best friend, Mommy?" Lizzie asked.

Kay Lynn understood her daughter's fear. She'd been lonely since Kimiko left. She still expected them to return, and it was sad to know that when they were released, they were unlikely to be neighbors ever again.

She missed Kimiko, not just for getting work done or childcare, but also sharing the small joys and triumphs of her own life. She'd taken for granted expressing her fears and hopes to Kimiko.

Telling Momma wasn't the same, because she fretted over Kay Lynn, and while she had girlfriends from high school and church whose company she enjoyed, they didn't share as openly and honestly with one another the way she and Kimiko did.

"Honey, Donna loves you very much. And I hope you each find good friends while you are apart."

"But she has been my best friend for my whole life. No one else can ever take her place!"

Kay Lynn responded, "There's room for more than one kind of friend in our lives. You are right that no one else will be all the things Donna has been to you: neighbor, friend, classmate. She will have a special place in your heart forever. Making new friends won't betray her or replace her."

Kay Lynn was telling her daughter what she herself needed to hear as well. Kay Lynn unfolded Kimiko's letter. Her neat handwriting was blacked out in a few spots.

Dear Kay Lynn,

I write from our temporary home, a former horse stable at Tanforan Racetrack. It is not as unpleasant as it could be. We are together and healthy, for which I am deeply grateful. My parents are in the next block over, so I can check on them easily ███████████████████████

███████████████████████████████

█. We do not have the same assignment for our meals, but we visit nearly every day. My auntie and cousin are not so fortunate as to see each other most days.

The time I save because I'm not allowed to cook, I spend on laundry. With only one washroom, I send Donna to wait in line before breakfast. I eat quickly and then take her place. Most mornings I can get the diapers washed out and drying before 8:00. They get dusty as they hang; there is no stopping the racetrack from leaving its mark. A good shake before I use them is in order.

I have tried to keep up with Donna's lessons, but it has not been easy. Some of the high school and college students are going to be forming a school for the younger children. They do not have any materials, but it will be a productive use of her time. As of now, the children are either cooped up in our small stall, or they run freely without purpose. Donna is a good girl and does everything I ask of her.

Kenji has joined the maintenance team, and I am on dish duty. While it is tiresome to wash hundreds of dishes, I can do it while tending to Missy. My mother has offered to watch Timmy and Missy if I prefer to do office work. I will stick to the dishes while we are in Tanforan but may switch once we are settled in ▮▮▮▮▮▮▮▮▮. We do not have a date for our transfer.

How is Berkeley? I miss it, and you, dearly. Please send me as many details as possible. I long to hear about my lost home.

Lizzie interrupted Kay Lynn's reading.

"Tanforan is in San Francisco, right?"

"It's south of the city, in San Bruno," Kay Lynn explained.

"So we can visit Donna there?"

Lizzie looked so hopeful it made Kay Lynn's heart hurt.

"Please, Mommy. When school is out, before they move to Utah, which is really, really, really, really, really far away? We can bring Hazel. Uncle Sam will let us use his truck to drive there, don't you think? When we explain why we need it."

Kay Lynn nodded.

"Hooray! I'll write to Donna right now to tell her we're coming! That will brighten her spirits."

Kay Lynn hadn't intended to agree that they could go, just that Uncle Sam would let them borrow his truck, but now Lizzie thought she'd consented to a visit. Were visitors even allowed? Borrowing the truck was easier than finding a driver.

Mitch would drive if they went when he wasn't working. He got his license a few years back, though they didn't have a car. Perhaps the war would end before she was faced with disappointing Lizzie or finding a way to drive to San Bruno. This gave her yet one more reason to wish for a swift end to the war.

"Mommy," Lizzie yelled from the yard. "I can't find Hazel."

Kay Lynn got up with a groan. *That stupid dog.* Hazel continued slipping away despite their efforts to keep her contained. Kay Lynn regretted showing her the Fujiokas were not next door. Now when she escaped, Hazel searched further and further away, hoping to find her beloved family. Kay Lynn understood. She also ached for the warmth and laughter of the Fujiokas' home, and for the friend she so dearly missed.

CHAPTER 8

June 1942

"What's on your heart and in your mind?" Momma asked Kay Lynn as they stood at the kitchen sink.

They'd just finished a Sunday supper with the extended family. A crowd had shown up to honor Uncle Sam's belated eighty-third birthday, which they'd combined with a celebration of Kristine's nineteenth. Grammy Sadie's older brother had been too ill for a party on his actual birthday in February, but he'd made a full recovery, so they were celebrating him now.

Kay Lynn gently washed one of Momma's fine plates. "I don't want to burden you with my worries. We're fine. Mitch is home, the children are healthy, and compared to how little we had during the Depression, we have plenty."

"And yet . . ." Momma encouraged.

"I don't seem to know how to be a good mother to Lizzie," Kay Lynn confessed.

"That can't be true!" Momma insisted.

"How do I protect her from the pain of the war and Donna's absence? I want to assure her they're fine . . . that Lenny is safe. I've taken to *hiding* the newspaper from her." Kay Lynn continued, "I'm no better. Mitch threatens to keep the paper from me. I have to steel myself before I listen to the radio. Often I take the children out during President Roosevelt's fireside address. Mitch wants to hear it, and I find that I don't. We're six months into this war. What if it goes on for another year? How do I manage honesty and harmony?"

Momma replied, "If it's any consolation, I also found it easier when you children were too young to be concerned with much outside of our home."

Kay Lynn shook her head. "Lizzie draws a picture for her uncle Lenny *every night* and declares, 'So Uncle Lenny *knows* I love him, Mommy.'" Kay Lynn teared up. "She thinks I mail him every picture. How long do I let her believe that?"

"Do you want to know what I suggest?"

Kay Lynn nodded.

"Teach my granddaughter to pray . . . for Lenny, for Donna, for everyone she is scared for."

Kay Lynn's stomach knotted. "You know I don't really know where I stand about prayer and God."

"I know." Her mother smiled at her. "I don't know where my prayers go, but I know that I feel more connected to Lenny every time I pray for him. Who else cares enough about him to want him to return safe? You? Me? Lizzie? The list isn't very long. I told him I'm praying for him. He knows he's in my heart and in my mind every single day. There isn't much else I can do for my son, far off in East Asia."

"Oh, Momma! How do you bear it? How do any of us bear this?" Kay Lynn asked.

"If our young men can confront the prospect of taking lives and losing their own," Momma responded, "then we can endure the fear for their well-being."

Kay Lynn didn't bother to wipe the tears from her cheeks. "What was it like for you when Poppa was in the war? Mitch still wonders if he should enlist before he's called up. I want him to wait until we are certain they will draft men with children."

She didn't tell Momma that he wanted to contribute more directly to the war effort than he was now. Kay Lynn didn't see the point in causing her mother concern about losing her best employee. For the moment, Mitch agreed to give it more time.

"Poppa wasn't my husband then, remember? We were friendly—my cousin Elena's cousin by marriage—but he wasn't at the center of my heart."

"Right," she said. Kay Lynn was so young when Momma and Poppa married, she didn't remember her parents as anything but the two of them.

"But Nana Lisbeth said the time when her husband, Grampa Matthew, was fighting in the Civil War was the worst time of her life. And she lived through some hard, hard times."

Kay Lynn shook her head. "It seems like the Civil War should be further ago than Nana Lisbeth."

"It wasn't ancient history," Momma replied. "Grammy Sadie was close to Timmy's age when it ended. She says she doesn't remember her father being away, but it must have had an impact. Her father missed her early years; her mother was left to care for two young children in Oberlin, not knowing if her husband would return."

Kay Lynn suddenly saw her great-grandfather's Union service in a new light. She had previously viewed it as simply noble, fighting on the right side of history. She hadn't considered that while it was happening, no one knew how long it would last, who would be killed or maimed, or how the men would return.

Momma dried a plate. "So much changes in a lifetime, especially now—with these new technologies. You might ride in an airplane sometime in your life."

Kay Lynn scoffed, "Do you think I'm going to enlist in the WAACs?"

Momma laughed, and then her expression darkened.

A horrid thought rushed into Kay Lynn's mind. "Kristine wouldn't join the Women's Army Auxiliary Corps?! Would she?!"

Momma released a deep breath. "I pray she won't. She seems enchanted by the prospect of welding. Let's hope her pursuit of that goal will give her enough of a challenge."

Kay Lynn rinsed a dish in silence.

"Thanks, Momma," Kay Lynn said.

"For what?"

Kay Lynn shrugged. "For asking. For sharing your thoughts. I feel so alone most of the time. Mitch knows how I feel, but he says there's nothing to be done but face each day as it comes."

"You miss Kimiko," Momma stated.

Kay Lynn nodded. "I do. I counted on her for the small details of my life—a cup of sugar, keeping Timmy while I ran to the store, complaining about my husband. And she did the same. I took it for granted at the time. And I miss feeling safe. I'm scared all of the time, for something that might never happen."

"It takes a lot of bravery to wait." Momma stared at Kay Lynn, studying her face like she was searching for something. "And it takes courage to be honest with your children about your own fears and limitations."

Momma had brought the conversation back to Lizzie.

"I know you want to protect her, but you cannot protect her from something as great as a war, but you can sit with her as she bears the pain of it."

"She's so young, too young."

"I agree. Too young to be troubled by war, and yet she is. As are the children in Germany and England and Japan and the Philippines . . . the list goes on and on."

"Every day in the paper, Momma. It's too much to bear."

"It doesn't end, you know."

"What doesn't end?"

"The desire to protect your children, even when they're all grown and have children of their own."

"Oh, Momma."

Tears glistened in both of their eyes. Kay Lynn hugged her mother. "I love you."

"Mommy!" Lizzie ran into the kitchen. "Uncle Sam says we can use his truck to visit Donna! Isn't that wonderful?"

Kay Lynn pasted on a smile. She'd hoped Lizzie had forgotten about that desire. Kay Lynn didn't relish the idea of a long drive to an unknown, and likely uncomfortable, situation. It might be sweet to see Kimiko, but it was just as likely to be unsettling.

"You asked him?"

"Yes! He said"—Lizzie deepened her voice to sound like the older man—"'For my favorite great-great-niece? Of course! Anytime.'"

Lizzie looked at her grandmother. "Nana May, I'm sorry that we can't drive to see Uncle Lenny in East Asia."

Momma opened her arms, and Lizzie leaned into her Nana May's wide embrace. "Me too, Lizzie, me too."

Kay Lynn's heart filled with sorrow and love. *Please, God, end this war soon and bring them all home safe to us.*

She wasn't certain who or what she was praying to, but Momma was right . . . asking made her feel better.

Back in the dining room, Kay Lynn gathered up her courage and looked for Kristine to fulfill her promise to Poppa. She found her standing with a group of second cousins. Kay Lynn slid into the circle of relatives she hadn't spent time with in far too long. It was sweet to see them. Over the years they got together less and less as they grew too busy to visit. Now they only seemed to get together for occasional events that brought together Uncle Sam and Grammy Sadie's descendants.

When the group dispersed, Kay Lynn saw her opportunity to ask Kristine to be more considerate of her parents and less selfish.

"Kristine, will you help me in the kitchen?"

Her sister let out an audible sound and practically rolled her eyes, but she nodded and walked to the other room.

Kristine gestured at the clean space. "What do you need me to do?"

"Momma is worried about you. She hasn't said anything, but Poppa asked me to speak with you."

"You and Poppa were talking about *me*!?" Kristine glared at Kay Lynn.

"Nothing bad. We love you. He's just worried about you."

"I can take care of myself! I'm fine."

Kay Lynn felt her anger rise. "Momma isn't *fine*. Can't you see how worried she is about Lenny? You're only adding to her burdens— gallivanting out late at night. Lying about where you are and who you're with? They know you're not 'working.' They aren't stupid."

Kristine hissed, and then growled, "If Momma and Poppa don't want me to live with them, I'll move out."

Kristine was being overly dramatic. "I didn't say that, nor did Poppa. I'm simply asking you to be a comfort to them and not a worry."

Arrows of hate shot from Kristine's eyes.

"I'm an adult," she replied. "How I live my life is not yours to think about or talk about with Momma and Poppa."

"We truly mean no harm, we're only thinking about your well-being." Kay Lynn looked down. "You must take precautions, you know . . . against pregnancy."

"You don't care about me. You're only concerned with pleasing Momma and Poppa, Miss Perfect," Kristine retorted. "Unlike you,

I want to do *my* part to win this war. Stay out of my life." Kristine stormed out the back door.

Kay Lynn stared at it. Kristine's contempt and words hit hard. *Miss Perfect?* Did Kristine really feel that way about her? What did that even mean? Kay Lynn was so far from perfect: Was she taunting her about her imperfections?

Kay Lynn wanted to have a respectful conversation, while Kristine was being cruel. Kay Lynn wasn't too old to remember being young and excited about love. She hadn't asked Kristine to stop her behavior altogether, only keep it more private to protect their parents and to be responsible.

But, as she feared, speaking to Kristine had made the situation worse. Instead of agreeing to take reasonable precautions and be considerate of their parents, she was threatening to move out. Kristine was too self-centered and immature to make these terrible times easier for their parents. Kay Lynn was left to do that on her own.

CHAPTER 9

Summer 1942

"We aren't taking Hazel," Kay Lynn declared. "If you ask me again, none of us are going." She stared at her daughter with her sternest look.

"Yes, Mommy." Lizzie looked adequately chastised.

The girl was excited beyond reasonable measure. She'd been preparing all week for this visit as if she were going to see Princess Elizabeth of England. Kay Lynn wasn't confident this was a good idea. So many things could go wrong between here and there, and then the camp itself might be a grave disappointment. They weren't going to a picnic, but Lizzie wouldn't listen to reason.

Kay Lynn packed up a duffel bag with the supplies they'd purchased for the Fujiokas. Kimiko requested toilet paper, Coca-Cola, and the handmade ointment for diaper rash from Star Grocery.

"Here, Momma." Lizzie held out a book. It was her favorite: *Little House on the Prairie*. Kay Lynn felt a chill pass through her.

"Are you certain you want to part with it? I thought you wanted to read it again and again."

Lizzie nodded. "Donna will love it as much as I do. I can borrow it from the library when I want to read it again, but she can't."

Kay Lynn took it and added it to her duffel with the other books they'd collected.

After church they walked to Uncle Sam and Aunt Diana's shop. Momma's cousin Alex ran the business now, but she would always think of it as her great-aunt and great-uncle's. A 1930s truck stenciled with JOHNSON PRODUCE MARKET in white was ready for them. They loaded into the cab with the metal pan of lemon bars resting on Lizzie's lap and Timmy sitting on Kay Lynn's. After a few jerky blocks, Mitch got the hang of the old clutch. It was a beautiful day to cross the Bay Bridge. Visiting hours were between 1:00 p.m. and 4:00 p.m. They should get there with time to spare.

"Thank you, Mitch," she said over Lizzie's head.

"For what?" he asked.

"Making the time. Caring about this too. Not every father would indulge his wife and daughter."

He smiled, took his hand off the stick, and reached out to her. She took it and squeezed it tight.

Lizzie grabbed their clasped hands and kissed them three times.

"Thank you both!" she exclaimed.

Kay Lynn couldn't do anything to end this war and make life return to normal, but she had managed to make her daughter's dream to visit Donna come true. And they were showing their friends a measure of support proportionate to their devotion.

Suddenly, the car jerked and Mitch took his hand back. Kay Lynn clutched Timmy close and held out her left arm to stop Lizzie from flying forward.

Kay Lynn's heart raced as Mitch slowed the car. A loud thump accompanied each jerk of the car; he turned down a quiet side street. She waited until he stopped the car to ask, "Flat tire?"

"You can fix it, right?" Lizzie said. "We can still go?"

Mitch looked at Lizzie. "I'll do my best, but I won't make you a promise that I don't know I can keep."

They piled out of the truck and confirmed: the black tire on the back passenger side lay flat against the street.

Kay Lynn pointed to a worn spare resting in the bed of the truck. "Doesn't look bridge-worthy to me."

Mitch looked and nodded. "I agree."

"Can we buy a new one?" Lizzie asked.

"It's Sunday," Kay Lynn said, not mentioning that they didn't have the means to simply pay for a tire.

Mitch pulled out the jack and assembled the parts. Timmy stood close, holding Kay Lynn's hand and watching his father's every move. Lizzie sat on the curb, crying quietly.

An hour later, they left the truck in front of the produce market and walked the two blocks to her cousin's apartment.

"Back so soon?" Cousin Alex asked.

"Flat tire."

"I should have warned you," Alex replied. "I knew that tire was unreliable, but we can only get new tires when they are beyond hope. Rationing, you know. The other three are in good shape, so once we get this one replaced, I hope the war will be long over by the time we have to worry about tires again. I'm awful sorry."

"You're kind to lend us the truck," Kay Lynn reassured Cousin Alex. "And we're grateful we weren't on the bridge when the tire went flat."

"When we get a new one, you're welcome to borrow it again."

"Thank you." Kay Lynn smiled.

Lizzie's mood was somber as they returned home on the streetcar. Kay Lynn worried about her daughter, who took so much to heart. She was too sensitive for these tumultuous times.

"Daddy, will you help me write to Donna?" Lizzie asked, her eyes red and puffy from tears.

Mitch agreed. Kay Lynn listened as they sounded out the words to explain why they had broken their promise to visit.

A few weeks later, Kay Lynn made preparations for the journey to Tanforan with unease looming over her. She explained to Lizzie that they might not succeed in getting there, but they would try, and sometimes the trying is what mattered. But Kay Lynn didn't want to be disappointed again, nor face her daughter's sorrow if they weren't able to see the Fujiokas.

They set out with the packed duffel and a fresh batch of lemon bars, skipping church to give them more time to make the drive to San Bruno.

As they drove away from Johnson's Produce, Lizzie said, "Timmy, cross your fingers, like this."

She showed him her hands, her index and middle fingers wrapped around each other.

"Yes!" she declared when he'd done it. "Will you too, Mommy? To help us get to Donna?"

Kay Lynn nodded. She used her right hand to twist the fingers on her left and then crossed her pointer and middle fingers.

"God, please get us to Tanforan," Lizzie prayed with her eyes closed and her crossed fingers pressed to the edges of her lips. Timmy mimicked his sister. They held that stance as they traveled across the bridge.

Kay Lynn relaxed her fingers once they were in San Francisco, but the children held tight while they traveled southward.

"Almost there," Lizzie chanted under her breath.

Kay Lynn navigated, using the map on her lap. Lizzie looked near to bursting as they pulled into the packed parking lot. Mitch drove up and down the dirt aisles until he found a spot in the back.

"We made it!" Lizzie declared, clapping her hands, with a huge grin from ear to ear. The sheer joy on Lizzie's face made it worth all the effort. Kay Lynn smiled at Mitch and mouthed, *Thank you.*

Climbing out of the truck, Lizzie looked toward the camp, and her face fell. Kay Lynn looked too. Barbed wire capped the chain fence surrounding the racetrack.

"Is Donna in prison?" she asked, her voice quivering. "Mommy, the newspaper made it seem fun, like a picnic party."

In an instant Kay Lynn regretted bringing her children here. What had they been thinking? She'd imagined it would be unpleasant: simple, crowded barracks, but not a prison with barbed wire. How was this different from the Nazi camps?

Mitch walked ahead, the duffel on his back and Timmy in his arms. They caught up to them and joined the long line of people waiting to pass through the gate. Kay Lynn was surprised that people of all races were queued up. They waited in silence.

Close to the front, Kay Lynn read the wooden sign attached to the fence:

TANFORAN ASSEMBLY CENTER—SAN BRUNO, CA

NOTICE

VISITING HOURS: 10:00 A.M. TO 12:00 NOON AND 1:00 P.M. TO 4:00 P.M.

VISITORS AND OTHER CONTACTS DURING THE ABOVE HOURS. ONLY VISITORS SHOULD NOTIFY THE CENTER IN ADVANCE BY MAIL. ADDRESS TO WILLIAM R. LAWSON, CENTER MANAGER, TANFORAN ASSEMBLY CENTER, SAN BRUNO, CA, GIVING DATE PERSON TO BE CONTACTED AND PURPOSE OF VISIT.

VISITORS' PRIVATE CARS WILL NOT BE ALLOWED WITHIN THE GROUNDS.

ALL PACKAGES AND PARCELS MUST BE LEFT AT THE INTERNAL
POLICE HEADQUARTERS ADJACENT TO THE MAIN GATE.

VISITORS ARE REQUESTED NOT TO BRING FOODSTUFFS OR OTHER
PERISHABLES TO THE CENTER.

PACKAGES AND OTHER PARCELS WILL BE ACCEPTED ONLY DURING
THE ESTABLISHED VISITING HOURS.

ALL VISITING MUST BE DONE AT THE RECEPTION ROOM IN THE
MAIN BUILDING.

VISITORS MUST LEAVE THE GROUNDS PROMPTLY BEFORE THE END
OF ESTABLISHED VISITING HOURS.

WILLIAM R. LAWSON,

CENTER MANAGER

Her heart raced. They hadn't written to William R. Lawson. She looked at Mitch and leaned in to whisper. "This was a mistake. She's going to be so disappointed."

He squeezed her hand. "There's nothing to do but ask as kindly and forcefully as we can."

"Names?" the young, blond soldier asked when they got to the front.

"Mitch Brooke," her husband replied.

The boy looked at the paper in front of him. "You aren't on the list."

"We weren't aware of that requirement," Mitch replied.

"It's new. Send your letter and come back in a few weeks."

Kay Lynn squeezed Mitch's hand hard.

"We've come a long way," Kay Lynn replied, working to keep her voice calm. "As you can see, my daughter is very excited to see her friend. We had to go to the trouble of borrowing a truck to get here."

"The tire went flat last time we tried," Lizzie added, her voice quivering as she teetered on the brink of tears. She bit her trembling lip.

The boy sighed. "I . . . it's not my . . ."

Lizzie buried her face in Kay Lynn's waist. The boy stared at the side of Lizzie's head, then at Kay Lynn. He looked flustered and confused.

He sighed again. "Write down your names and the reason for your visit. I'll ask my CO to put you on the list for the afternoon. I *can't* add you. He has to do that; do you understand? I would if I was allowed."

"Thank you," Kay Lynn replied. "It gives us something to hope for."

He tried to smile back.

"Can we leave the things we brought even if we can't go in?"

He nodded and pointed. "Leave them there. Put the name for who they go to. You can't leave any homemade goods or take them in with you if you get on the list; only packaged food allowed now."

Kay Lynn bit back her desire to yell, *How can lemon bars be harmful to the war effort?*

They trudged back to the parking lot and climbed into the bed of the truck. They watched the line shrink as people made their way past the checkpoint. New people joined the end of the queue, so it never was gone altogether. A few people pulled up, unloaded supplies from their vehicles, and left without going through the gates.

It was heartbreaking, but also touching to know that the Japanese community wasn't entirely abandoned.

"I have a memory," Mitch declared. "Want to guess what it is?"

Kay Lynn smiled. Leave it to Mitch to find a fun way to pass this miserable time.

"Yes," Lizzie responded, and then she asked, "Were we . . . inside?"

"Yes," Mitch replied.

"Were we at home?" Kay Lynn asked.

"Yes."

"Just the four of us?"

"No."

"Was Grammy Sadie, Nana May, and Poppa Leo there?"

"No!" Mitch smiled.

"Hmmmm," Kay Lynn said. "How about the Fujiokas?"

"No!"

"Ummmm." Lizzie drew out her thinking. "Grandma and Grandpa?"

"Yes!"

Lizzie clapped. Timmy stood up and danced. They all laughed.

"Santa?" Timmy asked.

Mitch smiled and nodded, his face beaming encouragement.

Lizzie burst out, "When Timmy saw the Christmas tree and started crying because he was afraid Santa was there, but then he got so happy that he cried because Santa wasn't there, and the tree was so pretty and we had presents!"

"You got it!" Mitch declared.

Lizzie smiled and let out a big breath. "That was a good memory."

"It was," Kay Lynn agreed.

"Grandma and Grandpa made it special." Lizzie asked, "Are they coming next Christmas?"

"I hope so," Mitch said.

"You miss seeing them more often, don't you?" Lizzie asked.

He shrugged and nodded. He never said so out loud, but she believed he missed them, despite the complication their obvious dislike for Kay Lynn added to their lives.

Carolina and Harry expected their entire family to relocate to Southern California after Mitch graduated from high school. He was going to follow in his brother's footsteps by attending UCLA. Kay Lynn's pregnancy put a wrench in that dream. Soon after Mitch graduated from Berkeley High, his parents sold their house and moved to Santa Monica without him.

Kay Lynn appreciated that they made the effort to visit once or twice a year. While she didn't exactly enjoy their time together, she wanted her children to know Mitch's parents, so she hid her hurt and did her best to be gracious and welcoming.

Mitch changed the topic. "The line is growing. Should we get in it even though it isn't time to go in yet? It will give us more time once they open again."

"*If* we're on the list," Kay Lynn said.

Lizzie resumed the prayerful stance she had made on the trip over, closing her eyes and holding her crossed fingers by her lips. "Please, please, please . . . Put our names on the list."

Timmy mimicked his sister's actions and said, "Please, Santa, please."

Kay Lynn considered correcting him, but in truth they'd taught their kids that Santa could make their wishes come true. She grabbed the basket with their lunch.

They ate tinned tuna sandwiches, fruit, and cookies and played a few more rounds of the memory game before the soldier came back. It was the same boy.

Kay Lynn tried to make eye contact with him, hoping he'd signal success or failure before they got to him, but he never looked down the line. His gaze was limited to the person in front of him and the paper on the table.

"Name?" he asked when it was their turn to get his attention.

"Mitch Brooke."

The boy's pale pointer finger slid down the list of names, stopping at Mitch's.

"Go through the gate, first building on the right," he explained without looking up. He continued without emotion, "You aren't allowed anywhere else and will be escorted out if you are found outside of that building."

Mitch walked away.

"Thank you very, very, very much!" Lizzie exclaimed.

The boy looked up. A question on his face.

Kay Lynn reminded him. "We were here this morning, but we weren't on the list. You asked your CO to put us on it. Thank you," she said sincerely.

He blinked up at her and then recognition dawned. A small smile rose from his dry lips. "Yes, ma'am. You're welcome. Glad I could be helpful to you. Have a good day."

Lizzie started to skip through the gates, but the spirit of the place quashed her excitement. She took Kay Lynn's hand, and they crossed into the compound.

The reception building had unfinished plywood walls, with rows of tables on a dirt floor. Groups of Japanese people sat around them, some watched the entrance while others already sat with their visitors. Kay Lynn searched the space, but none of the faces were familiar.

"Let's sit here." She pointed, and her family followed.

Hundreds of people could fit in the room. Had the Fujiokas sat here for hours a few weeks ago, waiting for friends that never came? Would they wait for the Fujiokas for hours? Had they been notified the Brookes were here?

"Georgie?" Timmy asked.

"I don't see him," Mitch replied.

"They'll be here soon," Lizzie declared, her fingers crossed tight. Kay Lynn held up entwined fingers, joining her daughter's ritual of hope.

She didn't placate her children with reassurances they would see them soon, nor did she share her doubts. Instead, she sat quietly, pretending she wasn't listening to the conversations around her.

Kay Lynn chastised herself for not bringing a deck of cards. Go Fish or Old Maid would have passed the time well. And they would have been a nice gift.

"You're here!" Donna's high voice drew her attention.

Joy shot through her chest. The five Fujiokas were right in front of them. Donna and Lizzie hugged, rocking from side to side so far over that their long hair swept across the dirt floor. Mitch and Ken shook hands. Kimiko smiled at Kay Lynn, and they shared a brief, sweet hug.

"We got your duffel. The books will make our librarian very, very happy," Donna said.

The girls sat close on a bench. Georgie and Timmy took a moment to warm to one another, but then joined the girls.

Kimiko sat down and said, "Thank you for coming. We weren't certain you would be let in because of the change in rules. My last letter explained the new procedure, but I imagine it won't arrive at your house until next week."

"A soldier took pity on us and asked his CO to add us for the afternoon."

"You've been here since morning?"

Kay Lynn nodded.

Kimiko's lips pulled in. "Thank you for your kindness."

"You shouldn't even be here," Kay Lynn replied. "The newspaper makes it look like you're on a vacation."

"I assure you, we aren't," Kimiko replied. "Dorothea Lange took many pictures last week. Perhaps they'll be printed in the *Tribune*."

"May I?" Kay Lynn reached out her arms toward Missy.

Kimiko passed the girl, who had grown in two months. Her cheeks had filled in, and she could sit up. Kay Lynn dangled her necklace, inviting Missy to play with it. She'd missed out on so much, not getting her fill of the precious girl as they'd hoped.

The two women chatted about their lives. Kimiko assured Kay Lynn that she was genuinely interested in hearing about Momma, Poppa, and the rest of the family back at home. She appreciated remembering the life waiting for them in Berkeley.

Too quickly a soldier arrived to say visiting hours were over. Kay Lynn felt physically ill as they said their goodbyes. No one said they would see one another soon, because the future was unknown.

Kimiko expressed deep gratitude for their visit, but as much work as it was for her to go for the visit, Kay Lynn couldn't possibly feel like it was enough. It didn't change the fact that Kimiko was being unjustly treated like an enemy of the United States. Perhaps their visit had been a kindness, but it felt like a taunt as they walked away, going back to their lives, while the Fujiokas had to stay in that horrible place.

After the kids were in bed, Mitch asked, "Are you all right?"

It had been hard for Kay Lynn to hide her sour mood. "After that visit I'm more confused. Was it a mistake to show that to Lizzie? How can President Roosevelt say we're fighting this war to spread the four freedoms, *and* sign the order to force the Fujiokas to evacuate from their home?"

"It wasn't a mistake to bring Lizzie. She'll remember forever that we're loyal to our friends," Mitch stated. "And neither you nor I can change the politics of the world. President Roosevelt doesn't care what you think about him."

Kay Lynn nodded. "Then why do I need to know what he's doing?"

"Maybe you don't," Mitch said. "I appreciate that we want to understand the state of the world, and yet if it means that you are unduly disturbed by circumstances that you can't change, then maybe it isn't helpful."

Kay Lynn hugged him tight. How would she get through each day if he was drafted? She wanted to appreciate that he was here now, but her gratitude was sullied by the knowledge that he could be taken away from her too, and she would be plagued by even more worry and rage.

CHAPTER 10

October 1942

Kay Lynn pushed Timmy in the stroller to Nana Lisbeth's gravestone. In previous years he stayed with Kimiko when she made this visit on the anniversary of her death. Once again, she was reminded that her friend was gone. *I miss you, Kimiko.* She telegraphed a silent greeting across the miles—now all the way to Topaz, Utah, in the middle of the desert, according to their map.

Momma rested a bouquet of white carnations and purple statice gathered from their garden on the headstone. Grammy Sadie placed her hand on the marker, and her lips moved in a silent prayer or conversation. Kay Lynn read the engraved words.

LISBETH JOHNSON

4-14-1837 TO 10-31-1918

BELOVED WIFE, MOTHER, GRANDMOTHER, AND FRIEND

Just next to it the gravestone read,

MATTHEW JOHNSON

2-5-1835 TO 5-13-1890

WE MISS HIM SO

Kay Lynn did the math in her head.

"I never noticed how many years she lived past him. Twenty-eight years is a long time."

"Nearly as long as they were married," Grammy Sadie replied. "None of us knows how many days we're given."

Momma spread out a blanket. Kay Lynn unbuckled Timmy and pointed to it. She placed a picnic basket on the fabric and pulled out their lunch.

"Anything you want to say about your mother before we eat her favorite foods?" Kay Lynn asked.

"Twenty-four years later and I still miss her." Grammy Sadie's voice caught. "I love you, Momma."

Kay Lynn recounted what she knew of the story. "She died of the flu, *and* it was the war, *and* I was little, less than two years old. It must have been awful."

"Those were hard times," Momma said.

"Harder than now?" Kay Lynn asked.

"Comparisons are difficult," Momma said. She thought for a moment before replying. "I suppose it depends on how Lenny comes back." Her voice caught. She cleared it. "If he doesn't return at all, well, nothing could be worse."

"Oh, Momma, I don't know how we can bear this waiting, not knowing."

"We have no choice," Momma whispered in a hoarse voice. "He's a soldier, and I am the mother of a soldier."

They fell into a silence, each in their own thoughts. Momma laughed.

"What?" Kay Lynn asked.

"I just pictured hordes of mothers traipsing through the jungle in Asia, shouting their sons' names, and telling them to come home now." She shook her head. "I could laugh, or cry, at the thought. Today I go with laughter."

Kay Lynn pictured it and laughed as well.

"Thanksgiving will be sad without him," Kay Lynn said.

"Naturally," Grammy Sadie agreed. "And Christmas."

"And Lizzie's birthday," Kay Lynn added. "The family I don't want will be there and the family I do want will be missing."

"Carolina isn't any kinder to you?" Momma asked about Mitch's mother.

Kay Lynn shook her head. "She still acts as if I conceived Lizzie by myself and her precious son had nothing to do with it. He was there, I promise you."

The two older women laughed.

Momma took a slice of apple. "When you have expectations for your children, it's difficult to accept when they go awry."

"I didn't intend to marry right after high school either. Both of us had to change our plans. It's been *eight* years—I wish she would accept me as part of her family by now. Mitch assures me he doesn't need college."

"And he's being honest?"

"Mostly," Kay Lynn admitted. "How can we regret Lizzie and Timmy?"

Momma patted her leg.

"May I be excused?" Timmy asked.

Kay Lynn replied, "Yes. You may walk around, but stay where you can see me." She turned back to her mother. "Thankfully she's warm to the children. Lizzie has no idea how Carolina feels about me."

"There's a small blessing," Grammy Sadie reminded in her typical fashion. "We must take our blessings, no matter how small, wherever we find them. Today I'm counting this as my blessing. Thank you for making this outing with a sentimental old woman."

Kay Lynn took Grammy Sadie's hand. "As sad as it is, I like to remember Nana Lisbeth. Somehow she is in me, even though I never met her."

They packed up their leftovers and walked to another gravestone before heading home.

Jordan Freedman Wallace

Born November 17, 1847, in Charles City, Virginia

Died July 15, 1923, in Oakland, California

Passionate Educator and Reformer

Grammy Sadie set a single purple salvia against the granite. She touched the top of the headstone, her lips moving in a silent, private message.

Kay Lynn was raised on stories about Miss Jordan, the bold suffragette; her wise mother, Mattie; and her courageous daughter, Cousin Naomi. Their families had ties going back to Oberlin, Ohio. Miss Jordan had been Grammy Sadie's first teacher in Oberlin, an especially impressive accomplishment given she'd been enslaved when she was born. Jordan's mother, Mattie, had been the midwife for Great-Uncle Sam and Grammy Sadie.

Both families settled in Oakland in the 1890s. Miss Jordan's daughter, Cousin Naomi, was also a midwife, and a genuine hero. She saved both Grammy Sadie and Momma when Momma was born weeks and weeks early, on a moving train. And she'd been the midwife when Kay Lynn was born in Oakland. After being at Missy's birth, Kay Lynn had more awe and respect for all midwives.

Timmy zoomed past, his tin airplane soaring around the head-stones. Kay Lynn teared up. Momma put her arm through Kay Lynn's.

Kay Lynn explained, "He'll have one of these someday. He's so *alive* right now. It seems wrong that he'll ever end. I know we all die, but it's as if I will myself to forget. And then it hits me, hard. Grammy, you, Mitch, me . . . Timmy. All of us will be gone someday. Will it matter that we lived?"

"It matters to me that you lived. You are my dearest Kay Lynn."

Kay Lynn looked at her mother. "It matters to me that you're alive." Her voice choked up. "I can't imagine living without you."

Kay Lynn looked at Grammy Sadie. Her breath caught.

"What?" Momma asked.

"This sounds so ridiculous. You loved your Nana Lisbeth like I love Grammy Sadie."

Momma nodded.

"How do we miss these things when we're young?" Kay Lynn asked. "It's so obvious right now, but I never let myself notice or feel it before."

"Those glimpses make life sweeter, but if we lived every moment in that awareness, I don't think we could let our loved ones out of our sight. And that's no way to live."

Kay Lynn said, "This is the moment I wish I believed in an after-life: the Universalist heaven or Hindu reincarnation."

"I understand," Momma said. "I've settled on mystery: we come from mystery and we return to mystery."

"But will *I* know I'm there?"

"That's part of the mystery. I trust if creation, or evolution, wanted us to know that, we would."

"Ready?" Grammy Sadie asked, interrupting their theological conversation.

The two women nodded.

"Let's go home, Timmy." Kay Lynn held out her hand. Her son ran to her, connecting their bodies. She reveled in his warm touch, not taking it for granted as she so often did. Her heart opened. *Thank you.* Who or what she was thanking, she didn't know, but it felt good to say it in her mind.

CHAPTER 11

March 1943

The holidays and Lizzie's birthday came and went, but this year they felt the impact of the war. Food rations and redirected manufacturing led to modest meals and simple gifts. Inflation forced them to make do.

Timmy no longer expected to see Uncle Lenny when he went to the Grands. He'd stopped calling for him some time ago, though he could name him when he was pointed out in a picture.

The war was showing no sign of winding down. If anything, it was escalating around the world, with the draft continuing at the same rate as in 1942.

Lizzie stopped asking when Donna would be home. But she was proficient at writing letters to her friend. Kay Lynn struggled to keep up with her drafts. She had a difficult time knowing what to say. Details of their own lives seemed a taunt, news of the world was only disheartening, and expressing her own concerns was insensitive. She wanted Kimiko to know she was loved and missed, but after writing every letter, she was unsettled and uncertain, questioning every sentence.

She reminded herself that she loved getting Kimiko's letters, regardless of the news they held. There was an enormous gulf between them, but she was grateful that on occasion it was bridged. She was determined to respond to each letter, even if she could only include a newspaper clipping or small anecdotes. She unfolded Kimiko's latest letter.

Dear Kay Lynn,

I imagine you have read about the loyalty questionnaire in the newspapers. We had no doubt that we were loyal to the United States and that Ken would be willing to fight. However, the questions were stated so oddly that we feared we were declaring the opposite of our intention. There were many debates in the camp. We must have filled it out satisfactorily. Some of our neighbors have been moved to Tule Lake, but Ken has been given his orders, and we are staying here.

The 442 regiment will be entirely US citizens of Japanese descent, Nisei. He left yesterday, proud and heartbroken. The camp is strange without our young men. We suspect they will be serving in Europe rather than the East. Time will tell.

We are keeping our spirits up as best as we can. Missy is a delight; she chatters on in gibberish, though she is quite convinced that she is speaking English. I prefer her toddling about rather than crawling in the dust and muck.

Last week we witnessed the most unexpected and entertaining scene. All of the aunties insisted on making a large batch of mochi for the children. They are trying so very hard to instill Japanese American culture to the younger generation. The children were delighted for the mochi, but the aunties didn't realize they wanted it for a food fight, not as a tasty delicacy. I didn't have the heart to tell my mother why the children kept returning for more. It was quite a sight, watching the small balls sail across the desert sky.

It's becoming increasingly difficult to keep the children close. They enjoy one another's company so much that it's painful to require them to eat with us at every meal or return home after school, because our cramped home isn't a pleasant place to spend time. Donna and George spend hours in the library, reading books and magazines, and playing games with their friends. When the bell rings for dinner, they run straight to the line, and often I don't catch up with them until they are finished with their food. They are here when it is time to sleep. I can hardly say they are home for sleep because this is not a home in any true sense of the word. Only a way station.

Here I am pouring out my troubles to you. I know life in Berkeley has become topsy turvy as well. I pray for Lenny every night. I hope you will add Kenji to your prayer list.

Your friend,
Kimiko

Kay Lynn closed her eyes and took a deep breath. She pictured Ken in a uniform, his family waving goodbye. Tears pushed at her lids. To ask for prayers meant Kimiko was terrified for him. Would Kay Lynn and her children be doing the same too soon?

"Mommy?" Lizzie's voice broke into her thoughts.

Kay Lynn opened her eyes and looked at her daughter. She cleared her throat but her "Yes" still came out raspy.

"Did Uncle Lenny die?" Lizzie looked near to tears.

Kay Lynn's heart twisted, "No, honey. I'm scared for Mr. Fujioka. Did Donna tell you he's enlisted?"

Lizzie nodded.

"There's no reason to think he isn't safe, except—" Kay Lynn stopped. She had to consider her words. "You know I'm sad for all the people that have to be away, right?"

Lizzie didn't look reassured. "Will Daddy have to go soon too?"

A shot of adrenaline made Kay Lynn's heart race. "Why do you ask?"

Lizzie shrugged.

"We don't need to borrow trouble. Daddy and I are thinking about the best way for him to serve the country and stay safe. You know we believe the effort to stop Hitler is right, even though it's sad to have soldiers away for the war."

Lizzie didn't look convinced.

"Is that your letter from Donna?" Kay Lynn changed the subject. "Will you read it to me?"

Lizzie read without hesitation, her skills having grown so much that her sweet voice came out loud and clear.

Dear Lizzie,

My daddy looked so handsum in his unform. When he lined up with the other soldiers, I could hardly tell which one was him. It was strange to feel sad and proud at the same time.

He left yesterday, and Momma says we don't know when we get to see him next. We don't know where he is going like when we left Berkeley. Maybe he will return to Utah after boot camp.

It is still very, very, very, very, very, very, very (times a hundred) cold here. We shiver between all the buildings and hudle close to the stoves at night. I don't like playing outside when it is this cold, so I go to the libary after school. George is big enough to go with me. You would be surprised at how big he is now—or maybe not since you have Timmy. Missy walks all over the place. Momma says she's glad that she doesn't spend so much time on the dusty floors or ground.

Thank you for the books you sent. I read them and then added them to the libary to share. We are very lucky to have good friends who keep our libary filled with good books.

Love, love, love, love, love (times a thousand),

Donna

"Sad and proud. Donna has a very good summary of this time, don't you think?" Kay Lynn asked.

"Yes." Lizzie smiled. "And she loves me a thousand times, so I don't think she has a new best friend."

Kay Lynn replied, "I agree. Ready to go on a sugar hunt? Some store must have enough so we can make a cake for Timmy's birthday."

Star Grocery was out of sugar this late in the day. If she had more time, or a car, she could go further afield. But she didn't.

"Let's try the Grands. Grammy Sadie and Nana May might have a cup of sugar to spare."

When they got there, Lizzie shrieked, pointing to a black Chevrolet parked in front of the house. "Is that Poppa Leo?"

"I don't think so," Kay Lynn replied, but then peered through the open window to the driver side and saw her father.

He grinned at them. "Surprise!"

"Up!" Timmy said as he popped out of the stroller.

She lifted him to see. Timmy leaned into the car, climbed through the window and across the bench seat to Poppa Leo's lap. He placed a hand on each side of the steering wheel and pretended to drive.

"*You* bought a car?" Kay Lynn asked.

"I can see where things are heading," her father replied. "It's getting harder and harder to get by without one. So . . ." He shrugged.

Kay Lynn sighed. She wanted to know how to drive, but wasn't certain that she would be capable of working a clutch safely. Would it be embarrassing or even dangerous to try? So far, she'd put it off.

"What's wrong with your arm, Poppa Leo?" Lizzie asked, pointing to a bandage around his elbow.

"This arm just saved a life," he declared, and then explained. "I donated plasma to the Red Cross."

Kay Lynn smiled. Her father had been a faithful donor at the blood bank since it opened. He said it was the least he could do for the soldiers. He didn't know where his plasma actually went, but he hoped it was sent overseas to the young servicemen. Kay Lynn felt proud but also guilty that he'd found a way to contribute to the war effort but she couldn't bear the idea of someone sticking a needle into her arm.

"Let's get you inside so you can rest," Kay Lynn suggested.

"Don't you want a ride in our new car?" Poppa Leo asked.

"Yes!" Lizzie clapped with joy.

"Okay," Kay Lynn agreed. "You two get in the back."

Timmy climbed over the seat to the back, and Lizzie joined him there.

"How about a ride to the market on Broadway? I believe they have sugar."

"Sure," Poppa replied.

"Let me just put the stroller on the porch and see if Momma needs anything."

As he drove, Kay Lynn studied her father's movements. He switched between two pedals with his right foot and one with his left. When he did the one on the left, he also moved the shifter on the steering wheel. *Could I manage that?* Her left hand would have to hold the wheel steady while her right was shifting.

"The right pedal is the gas, and the middle is the brake, correct?" she asked.

"Yes. And the one on the left is the clutch, to change the gears as you go faster."

"Is it hard to hold the wheel steady with one hand?" she asked.

"Not at all . . . oh." His face pulled in. He gave it some thought and eventually said, "You can steer a bike with your left hand; I don't believe this is harder than that. You have to have your foot off the gas, so maybe your right leg can help steady the wheel."

"Are you going to learn to drive, Mommy?" Timmy asked from the back seat.

She watched her father control the car. It was complicated, but not impossible. She had to at least try.

"I am, Timmy. I'm going to learn how to drive," Kay Lynn told him.

"Hooray!" the two children cheered.

The store had sugar plus some tinned goods that Kay Lynn was always short on. The car made what would have been more than an hour-long journey by streetcar a twenty-minute errand. Soon they were back home, and the cake was nearly finished baking.

"Can you get nasturtium from the front yard for the top?" Kay Lynn asked. Frosting was out of the question.

Lizzie returned to the kitchen with the orange flowers. "Mommy, there were lots of crocus leaves, but no flowers. Did I forget to see them this year?"

Kay Lynn thought for a moment.

"I guess they bloomed, and we missed it. They come and go very fast. Next year we'll have to keep a closer watch."

Lizzie nodded and added the bright flowers to the top of Timmy's cake.

"I wish I could send Donna a flower-topped cake for her birthday," Lizzie remarked.

She said it so matter-of-factly that it hurt in a new way. Lizzie had become resigned. The war, these separations, were normal.

"We can press some flowers and include them in your next letter," Kay Lynn suggested.

Lizzie consented with a smile and a shrug. It would do.

"I'll put in some carnation petals for Kimiko for Mother's Day, so she'll know we're holding them in our hearts."

"Okay," Lizzie replied. "I'll go pick some right now."

She trod off—making do, but not happy. Kay Lynn was glad for a kind action in the face of an abhorrent situation; like her daughter, she was making do, but not happy. Sending petals was better than doing nothing, but hardly seemed enough.

CHAPTER 12

June 1943

After the children left the dinner table, Kay Lynn slid the *Oakland Tribune* to Mitch. She pointed to the front-page article. She needed to have this conversation when the children were out of earshot.

"We're out of time. It's now or never for you to take matters into your own hands." She tried to keep her voice light, but there was no hiding her dismay. She reread from the article while Mitch read it for the first time.

78 Percent of Fathers Face Draft in 1943

Washington

June 1

AP

Dependency alone will be virtually eliminated by the end of this year as a reason for keeping fathers out of uniform, Manpower Chief Paul V. McNutt indicated today.

The Armed Forces will need so many men, he said, that only 22 of every 100 able-bodied fathers still will be deferred at the end of 1943 because their families need their support.

General Induction of Family heads is due to start August 1. Navy announcement yesterday lowering physical standards for draft may slow up induction of fathers slightly, McNutt said, but he emphasized that even if the army follows suit adopting new standards the general effect on father induction will be "only a delay."

Inductions have been proceeding at about 300,000 a month. If this rate is continued in 1944, McNutt said it would be necessary to lower physical requirements still further.

"Urgh," Mitch groaned, and sat back. "I'll speak with recruiters tomorrow. Navy and army are near the office. Your dad is losing everyone. He said they're going to start hiring women."

"Maybe I'll go work for them," Kay Lynn responded. "It would be ironic, wouldn't it?"

Simply the thought of it made her blue. In high school she swore she would never become a bookkeeper or work for her parents. Suddenly overwhelmed, she covered her face and pressed her fingers into her eyelids. She must have looked like a pouty child, but she didn't care.

"It will be okay," Mitch assured her. "We'll be okay."

Kay Lynn looked at him; tears burned her eyes. Through a tight throat, she could barely squeeze out, "You might be sent far away to be maimed or killed."

"Let's not borrow trouble," he replied. "There are many stateside positions."

She scoffed. "I said those very words to Lizzie today."

"You're so wise."

She glared at him, and then leaned against his chest. He kissed the top of her head. Mitch was her rock. How could she possibly get through the war without him by her side? She was a ball of nerves without adding him to her list of worries. Many women were managing so much more. Kimiko was in a camp and somehow bore the indignity and physical hardship as well as the fear.

"Our lives are about to be divided into before and after . . . ," she said.

"I'll have to make a fast decision. This article will make many men in my position turn up. What they offer me tomorrow may not be an option the next day. Do you trust me?"

Kay Lynn felt a tear slide down her cheek. "I trust you, but not . . ." She let her voice trail. "The army and navy have one job: to win this war. To them you aren't a husband, a father, or a son . . . my Mitch; to them you are only a tool."

Kay Lynn started to sound like a war protester.

"I'll do everything I can to stay stateside," Mitch said. "I promise. And I'll delay my report date if I can."

She pulled her lips inward.

"What?" her husband asked.

"It's not in your hands."

He nodded, fear in his eyes.

"We'll be okay," she reassured him. "It's just . . . well, I love you."

Tears sparkled in his eyes. "I love you too."

The next morning, Kay Lynn walked Lizzie to school but didn't want to return home right away; the nerves in her body urged her up Woolsey, past her childhood home at Claremont until she got to the redwoods in the median. She walked to the largest, put her hands on the enormous trunk, and rested her forehead against it.

"Are you hugging the tree, Mommy?" Timmy asked from his stroller.

"Give me strength," she whispered into the rough bark. "To bear what will come."

She looked at her son, her heart twisted as she pictured him as a grown man with a uniform on. He stared at her, expecting a reply.

"Yes, I hugged the tree, to thank it for all that it gives us."

"Are you sad, Mommy?" he asked.

It was hard to hide her emotions from a four-year-old.

She nodded. "I miss Mrs. Fujioka and Uncle Lenny."

She wasn't ready to tell him that his father would be gone soon as well. She wanted to protect him, let him keep his innocence, at least for this day. Later she would consider how to prepare him for living without his father.

She turned the stroller toward home. She considered making a big loop, walking through the serene campus, maybe taking the elevator to the top of the Campanile, but instead she turned down Claremont. She had the time to head home on Alcatraz and give her son the small delight of seeing the distant island prison on this clear day.

CHAPTER 13

August 1943

Kay Lynn let the tears fall freely while she washed up the dishes, her own reflection in the kitchen window the only witness. The giggles from the kids' bedroom sharpened the pain in her heart. This was their last certain night as a family under one roof; tomorrow Mitch would leave them for basic training. He'd postponed his departure as long as possible. Eight weeks in San Diego were guaranteed. After that, his future, and Kay Lynn's, was cloudy.

She listened hard as Mitch read bedtime stories, using the voices for characters that the kids loved so much. They'd started *The Wonderful Wizard of Oz* a few weeks back. Kay Lynn would finish reading the story about a girl who just wanted to get home. *Is there a book about Auntie Em longing to know what happened to Dorothy?* Kay Lynn had never thought about the story from the vantage of those left in Kansas. Too soon, she'd know what it was like to be alone with her worry.

Kay Lynn was joining the ranks of all those wives, waiting and wondering, chasing out imagined fears with prayers. For more than a year, she'd been walking by many of those wives and parents as they went about their lives, pretending they were okay, when inside they were tamping down their panic at what might be.

Grammy Sadie reminded her that often the only thing she could control was her own breath. At any time, she could soothe her heart by sending it a lungful of oxygen. She wanted to be calm for Lizzie and Timmy, but somehow it seemed a betrayal of Mitch and their marriage to act as if she was fine with his departure.

He returned to the kitchen and said, "They're ready for your good-night kisses."

When she turned around, her tears made her distress obvious.

"Oh." He breathed out audibly.

He opened his arms, ready to embrace her, but she shook her head.

"Not now," she whispered. "Let me hug them good night before I fall to pieces."

She wiped her face dry with her flowered apron, but was grateful the lights were already out in the children's room. The dark night was a welcome cover while she gave each of them a wordless hug.

"Pancakes for breakfast, right, Mommy?" Lizzie asked.

"Of course, we have to send Daddy off with a treat."

"Wiff sugar?" Timmy asked.

"We have jam," Kay Lynn told him.

"'Kay. Night. Love you," he replied.

"I love you . . ." Kay Lynn cleared her throat. The enormity of this change was lost on a four-year-old but hit her all at once. He trusted them so much, and they couldn't protect him from this. "I love you too, Timmy. Up to the sky."

Both children chanted back, "And down to the ground."

They went to bed early. Mitch's small bag was packed with a few items. He'd been told he didn't need to bring anything, as they would be supplying him everything from clothes to razors. A picture of their family and one of his parents and brother, *Walden* by Henry David

Thoreau, a small paper notebook, and the pen he got when he graduated from Berkeley High were easy enough to carry.

"I'm late," Kay Lynn told him, pulling the covers around her. Hazel licked her hand and curled at her side. She stroked her warm, soft fur.

His eyes went wide, knowing exactly what she meant. "How many days?"

"Only two," she replied. "I expected my monthlies yesterday. It might be nerves, but I didn't want to tell you in a letter if it's otherwise."

Mitch turned to face her. "How could you? I . . . I don't know what to say," he stammered.

"We were as careful as I know how to be," she replied. "I just . . . I don't know how to bear any of this. Everyone around me seems capable of bearing so much. I don't want you to leave. I don't want a third child. I don't want a war. I don't want the Fujiokas to be in a camp. But I don't get to decide any of it, do I?"

Kay Lynn sounded angrier than she wanted. She rested her head against his chest.

"We will love this child if it comes to that," he reassured her.

"If you ever get a chance to meet him." Kay Lynn caught herself. None of this was her husband's fault. "Sorry," she whispered. "Thank you. Yes, we will."

"I'll kiss you every night . . . all three of you. And if a baby is born while I'm gone, I'll draw him in and kiss him too."

Kay Lynn laughed. "Stick-figure baby . . . Adorable."

She brought her head up to look at him. "I'm going to miss you so much . . . and we will be okay. And"—her voice broke—"I'm grateful you are my husband. Thank you for being my Mitch."

There was nothing else to say. Kay Lynn had no more words. So she kissed him, and he kissed her back, their lovemaking poignant and bittersweet.

———— ❧ ————

"Mommy, we're singing in front of the *whole* school. Principal Bartley will be there. I have to look my best!"

"Lizzie, there is nothing I can do to have your poplin dress clean, dry, and pressed before you need to leave."

"But, Mommy!" Lizzie argued back.

Just then Timmy did it again: knocked over his *entire* cup of milk. White liquid spread across the brown table like a foreign invader.

"Oops," he declared, smiling as if he were playing a game.

He looked at Kay Lynn, searching for assurance that she wasn't mad, but her face gave away her frustration. Timmy burst into tears.

Adrenaline shot through Kay Lynn; she stood up and declared, "I'm going to the bathroom."

"But, Mommy! There's a big mess!"

"Clean it up, Lizzie," Kay Lynn barked as she stormed away.

In the bathroom, she allowed her tears to flow. Every single morning had been hard since Mitch had left for basic training a week ago, but today was the worst. Timmy woke up crying and was at the edge of tears ever since, and Lizzie's back talk was exhausting and infuriating. Kay Lynn stood at the sink in front of the mirror when she felt a telltale cramp. She rushed to sit on the toilet, hoping not to soil herself. Her body flushed with heat and sweat, and then she shook with a chill. A huge cramp forced her to bend over and bear down; she felt the flow leave her womb. Relief, sorrow, and pain poured out with the end of the pregnancy. She *was* relieved, but surprised to feel a measure of sadness too. Somehow, in just a week, she'd opened her heart to another child.

She wiped away the smear of red, then dug out her menstrual supplies and pinned a pad to her underwear.

She rose and searched in the toilet bowl. This early it was small. Would it even be the size of a grain of rice? However large it was, she could not make out anything different from a typical period on a high-flow day.

Kay Lynn washed her hands, splashed water on her face, and wiped her eyes. She gazed in the mirror. It was obvious she'd been crying, but she looked put back together. She went into the closet in the kids' room to find a dress for her daughter.

In the kitchen, Lizzie sat by Timmy at the now-cleaned table.

"Thank you, Lizzie, for mopping up your brother's mess. Someday someone will invent a cup with a lid."

"Sorry, Mommy." Lizzie teared up. "Hazel helped too."

Kay Lynn pulled her lips in. "I'm sorry as well. We're all extra sad and mad without Daddy here."

"Is he coming back soon?" Timmy asked.

Kay Lynn exhaled. "He'll be away for at least eight weeks. He asked to be assigned near us, but Uncle Sam decides where he goes— not him, or me, or you."

"Uncle Sam the government, not Uncle Sam Grammy Sadie's brother, right?" Timmy managed to make the sentence a statement and a question at the same time.

"Correct," Kay Lynn replied.

Lizzie nodded. She'd already known the answer to that question.

Kay Lynn continued, "We have to give each other extra love while Daddy is gone. And extra grace when it's hard to be kind. Do you know what grace is?"

"Patience from God? Maybe with love?" Lizzie thought for a moment. "There is also *graceful*, which means pretty. Or something like that."

Kay Lynn agreed. "It is one of those words that means a lot of things. The kind of grace I'm talking about is a gift that we didn't earn, but we give to each other. Really the gift of forgiveness."

"Okay."

"I think this will do just fine for today, don't you?" Kay Lynn held up the hanger with the flowered dress.

"Yes, Mommy."

Lizzie grabbed the hanger and skipped off to her room. Kids moved on from spats so quickly. Perhaps it was only on the outside, but Lizzie looked perfectly fine.

Kay Lynn took a deep breath. She searched for the right words. *Calm my heart. I miss you, Mitch. Send me patience.* Those weren't right. She wished she had a simple prayer; then she remembered what she asked of the redwood tree up Woolsey Street. *Give me strength.* She imagined her hand on the tree and her feet on the earth. *Give me strength,* she repeated in her mind as she took deep breaths until she felt something give way in her shoulders.

"Go get your shoes on," she told Timmy. "We're going to walk Sissy to school."

"When do I get to go to school?"

Soon enough. "After you turn five years old you will go to school with Sissy."

He trotted off to find his shoes.

Kay Lynn cleared the table and glanced at the front page of the newspaper. A picture of a navy officer was surrounded by headlines: Big Income Tax Increase Asked and Cut Use of Milk, Plea to the left; Navy's Needs May Swell Father Draft on the right; and Dead Officer's Letter to Kin below it.

She read the caption under his face: *His widow lives at 2703 Woolsey.* Her heart raced. Happy to Die for Great Cause, Says Posthumous Message. Disgusted with the blatant propaganda, she stopped reading.

"Mama, is *Negro* a bad word?" Lizzie asked as they walked home from Lincoln School that afternoon.

Oh, dear, Kay Lynn thought. She didn't feel ready to discuss race relations with Lizzie. Her daughter stared at her, waiting for an answer.

"No, it isn't a cruel word, though it sounds close to the word we don't use in our family," Kay Lynn replied. "Why do you ask?"

"Jimmy says his dad says the Negroes are ruining Berkeley. He doesn't like how many there are in our classroom. He said it like I agreed, but I was too embarrassed to say I didn't."

A confused expression on her face, Lizzie looked to Kay Lynn for an answer. Kay Lynn hated that her daughter was being exposed to hateful assertions about race. Berkeley should be better than that.

"Next time Jimmy says something like that to you, you can say to him, 'In my family we measure people by how they behave, not by how they look.'"

Lizzie nodded. "What's the new-fashion word?"

"For Negro?"

Lizzie nodded again.

"Colored."

"What makes someone colored? And why are so many colored people moving here?"

"We look like the people we are born from, our mothers and fathers."

"That's why you don't look like Aunt Kristine and Uncle Lenny, because Poppa Leo isn't really your father."

Kay Lynn took a breath. "Poppa Leo *is* my real father. I never lived with Jonathon Barrow. He gave the seed for me to grow, but he was never my father. Your real parents are the ones who love you in life, not the people whose egg and seed made you grow to begin with."

"I'm glad my real parents are my egg and seed parents too. It makes it less complicated in my heart."

Kay Lynn snorted. She felt insulted and understood at the same time. Lizzie skipped ahead, satisfied with the conversation without hearing the answer to her question: "Why are so many colored people moving here?"

Kay Lynn had more time to ponder the answer to a very complex history. Lizzie knew something about slavery and the Jim Crow laws in the South, but they'd protected her from the grim realities of racial segregation, lynching, and sharecropping.

Kay Lynn thought it right that the war was an opportunity for colored people to improve their lives. Their family were devoted advocates for racial equality. Henry J. Kaiser was sending recruiters specifically to colored communities in the South, offering staggering wages. However, those recruiters didn't volunteer that housing and food prices were just as staggering.

Colored workers were given a great opportunity, but they were also struggling to be accepted and to make ends meet—and often facing shameful racial hostility that shouldn't be in California.

CHAPTER 14

Four weeks later, Kay Lynn lay alone in their large bed. She had yet to change the sheets, wanting to keep that minuscule bit of Mitch. Her hand rested on his pillow as she drifted into a dream. In it, she heard an officious knock that filled her with dread for the news that lay on the other side of the door. She woke with a start, her heart racing. Kay Lynn sat up and took deep breaths. *Don't borrow trouble. Do not borrow trouble.* Adrenaline coursed through her body.

Too agitated to fall back asleep, she rose and checked on the kids. Lizzie and Timmy were in a deep slumber, with Hazel curled up by Lizzie's side. Feeling trapped, Kay Lynn made the decision to walk in the dark night to calm her nerves. Hazel trailed her to the door, looking hopeful, but Lizzie closed the door in the dog's face. A low whine came through the wooden barrier, followed by a sharp bark and frantic scratching. Kay Lynn sighed; she didn't want Hazel to wake the children.

Lizzie opened the door. "Come on, then."

They walked up Prince Street, the cool air shocking the emotion out of her. By the time she reached Telegraph Avenue, she felt calm enough to turn back. She made a right turn, passing Woolsey. As she approached the next block, the sight of the lively crowd overflowing from the White Horse Inn onto the sidewalk gave her pause. It wasn't a seedy bar, but one that welcomed a wide range of people from students to soldiers and rumored to welcome homosexuals.

She felt self-conscious walking by so many young men. She continued at a steady pace, not looking at the soldiers, but Hazel didn't keep up with her. Kay Lynn turned back to call the dog to her side, but stopped when she saw that Hazel was enjoying the attention of two men in uniform who had crouched down to pet her. Kay Lynn took a few steps back.

One of the soldiers looked at Kay Lynn. "I miss my dog so much!" he said with a sweet Southern drawl. "He's adorable. Aren't you?" He kept petting Hazel, who had sat down in front of him. Others crouched down, hoping for a chance to pet a dog. Hazel traveled from person to person, relishing the attention.

"What's his name?" someone asked.

"Hazel."

"Oops!" a heavily made-up woman said. She shrugged and declared, "Sometimes, you can't tell who's a boy and who's a girl." She looked at the dog. "No offense intended, Hazel."

Kay Lynn laughed. "None taken, I'm sure."

She waited while each person got their turn. She'd been afraid of them just a few minutes ago, and now she wanted to lift their spirits. It was the least she could do for these young men, most of them soldiers far from home. Hazel was good for boosting morale. Kay Lynn had found a very small way to contribute to the war effort.

"Come on, girl," Kay Lynn said when the petting party was over. "Let's go home."

Hazel trotted beside her up Alcatraz Avenue, a few lights from Alcatraz Island and Angel Island flickered in the distance ahead.

The next day Kay Lynn was tired from lack of sleep, but her spirits were still oddly lifted by the interaction with the young soldiers. While Timmy was napping, she focused on meeting her deadline for a thesis paper. The handwriting was tricky, and she had to stop often to decipher certain words, but she wanted to finish so they could go to campus right after getting Lizzie from school.

She heard the front door open and close.

"Hello," she called out.

When there was no response, she walked into the living room. Her parents were sitting on the couch. Her eyes darted to the telegram Poppa Leo was holding. Fear shot through her, making her hands go cold. Momma's face told her everything . . . Lenny.

Kay Lynn sank down by her mother; her father handed her the paper.

> The secretary of war desires me to express his regret that your son Leonard Stevens has been reported missing in action since 17 September in the Southwest Pacific area. If further details or other information are received, you will be promptly notified.
>
> Ulio the Adjutant General

Kay Lynn exhaled. He wasn't dead. But he wasn't alive either. He was . . . missing.

"Oh, Momma!" Kay Lynn cried.

Her mother grabbed her hand. They sat in silence, tears streaming down Kay Lynn's face. Kay Lynn pictured Lenny: captured, dead, in a prison, wounded, crowded, alone. He was all of them and none until they learned more.

Hazel came close and licked her arm.

Kay Lynn took a deep breath. Her eyes traveled around the edge of the carpet, following the flowered pattern. She had to act strong for her parents.

"We'll get in touch with the Red Cross. They may have access to information that the US military doesn't have."

"And we will pray," Momma said.

"Every day," Kay Lynn agreed.

"Every moment," Momma replied.

Kay Lynn nodded. A new wave of emotion hit her as she imagined telling Lizzie the news. *Give me strength.*

Kay Lynn looked at her father. His face was hard. She could mistake him for calm if she didn't know he cared so much about Lenny.

She reached for him with her fisted left hand. He took it, connecting them all.

Kay Lynn said, "This is terrible, terrible news. And I am going to hold out hope for his well-being and strength to get through whatever he is facing."

They nodded.

"Does Kristine know?"

Her father nodded. "She was home when the officers delivered the news. And then she left for work with hardly a word."

"She assured me that he'll be fine," Momma said.

"As if saying it would make it so," Kay Lynn replied.

Momma said, "We are each going to have our own way of coping. Please don't judge her way, and I will do my best not to judge yours."

Kay Lynn, feeling the sting of her mother's reprimand, replied, "I just told Lizzie that we need to extend each other more grace. I will try to offer Kristine grace, but I don't like that she's causing you both concern. She should be a support, not a burden."

Momma's face hardened. "It's getting to the point that I don't want to see you two together. That is a burden, too. Kristine is young. I know you believe we've always spoiled her, but it isn't fair to judge her by your stage of life, or your choices." Momma shook her head and rolled her eyes, obviously frustrated.

Kay Lynn wanted to defend herself, to explain that Kristine was the one being immature, but that would only add to Momma's agitation.

"I'm sorry, Momma. For *you*, I'll be more patient with *her*," Kay Lynn replied. "How is Grammy Sadie taking the news?"

Momma's chin quivered, and her eyes filled with tears.

"As you would expect, Grammy Sadie said, 'And now we wait, holding both hope and devastation for as long as it takes to learn his status.'"

Kay Lynn looked through her pantry. She wanted to bake something to soften the blow when she told Lizzie that her uncle Lenny was missing. Just the thought of the conversation put a pit in her stomach.

She had enough flour, baking powder, and cinnamon to make cookies, but their sugar ration was down to just one cup, and they wouldn't receive another coupon until next month. The natural sweetness from the apples on the tree in the yard would have to suffice.

Her concoction was cooling by the time Lizzie walked through the door.

"Yum!" her daughter called out. "Did you make cake?! Whose birthday is it?"

"They're apple biscuits." Kay Lynn wanted to lower Lizzie's expectations. "Have a seat. I have something sad to tell you while you eat your snack."

"Donna isn't moving back to Berkeley, is she?" Lizzie's lip quivered.

A different arrow pierced Kay Lynn's heart. "Oh, Lizzie, I don't have any news about Donna. I didn't know you were worried about that."

"Mr. Cuthbert is nice enough to me now, but it isn't the same as having Donna as my neighbor."

"I agree," Kay Lynn replied. "When . . ." Kay Lynn stopped herself. She didn't want to tell Lizzie a falsehood. "I believe the Fujiokas will move back to Berkeley, but I think it's unlikely they'll be our neighbors again."

Lizzie nodded and squeezed her eyes, trying to keep the tears in. "When I was little, I thought after the war, everything would go back to how it was before the war started, but now I know it won't. Sometimes, I wish I was a little kid like Timmy. He doesn't remember before."

Lizzie was more aware of the awfulness of the world than Kay Lynn had realized. Kay Lynn thought she'd shielded her daughter from thinking about the war, but now she saw that wasn't true. It was probably natural for an eight-year-old to be aware of the troubles of the world, but it was also sad.

"What's the news you have to tell me?" Lizzie asked. "Is Daddy being sent to Europe? Or East Asia?"

"We still don't know where Daddy will be assigned. The sad news is about Uncle Lenny," Kay Lynn said.

"He was killed!" Lizzie shrieked.

"No, but he's missing." Kay Lynn kept her voice calm.

"Missing? How do we find him?" Lizzie's face expressed all the agony that Kay Lynn felt.

Kay Lynn started to say that they don't. But the look on her daughter's face stopped her. They had to do something . . . take some action, on Lenny's behalf.

"First, we will ask for more information from the army. Where was he last seen, and where do they want him to be? We will write to the Red Cross and ask them to look for him."

"Do Nana May and Poppa Leo know?"

"They came over this morning to tell me."

"Did the soldiers come to their house with the letter?"

Kay Lynn nodded.

Lizzie looked near to tears. "I don't want that to happen with Daddy. I know I should be sad about Uncle Lenny, but I'm also scared for Daddy. And then I think about Donna. Mommy, it's a lot to think about. My heart doesn't know who to be saddest about."

Kay Lynn leaned into her daughter's chest and said in a firm voice, "Lizzie's heart, you don't have to rank your sadness; it can be all jumbled up. And you can be happy too, right along with the sadness and fear."

Kay Lynn laughed at herself. It was much easier to say that to Lizzie's heart than to know it inside her own.

"I bet Grammy Sadie and Nana May are saying prayers for Uncle Lenny."

"I'm quite certain you're right."

"Can we pray for him too?"

"Have I given you the idea that you cannot pray?"

Lizzie shrugged. "You say you don't believe in prayer. I don't want to do something you think is bad."

Another arrow pierced Kay Lynn's heart. "Oh, sweetie," Kay Lynn replied. "Prayer is *not* bad, even if I don't believe in doing it. If prayers make you feel better, then I believe in it, for you. Maybe it's like ice cream flavors: if you like strawberry, eat it; if you don't like strawberry, don't have any."

"Mommy, do you or don't you believe in God?"

Kay Lynn's heart dropped into her stomach. How had she gotten here with her daughter? She took in a deep breath and composed her thoughts. She felt Lizzie's eyes on her.

"Do you know what free will is?"

Lizzie shook her head.

"It's hard for me to believe in a loving and powerful God when there is so much that is unfair and unkind. Free will is the idea that everybody gets to decide how to be for themselves. In contrast, predestination is the idea that God decided before you were born what your life would be like. These are very big ideas. Many people say that humans have free will, so God isn't responsible for these bad things that we do to each other."

Lizzie nodded. She looked like she was composing a thought.

"Could God be loving, but not powerful enough to make things fair and kind?"

Kay Lynn smiled. "That is exactly what your Grammy Sadie would say when I talked to her about God. She says we are the hands and hearts of God, making the world more fair and kind. She prays to remind herself how she wants to be, not to get God's favors."

"So I shouldn't pray for Uncle Lenny to be found, Daddy to come home, and Donna to be my neighbor?"

"Lizzie, you may pray for whatever you like. I just suggest you take action as well."

"Such as writing to President Roosevelt, asking him for those things too?"

"Yes, that's a splendid idea."

Lizzie ran to the secretary and returned with two pieces of paper.

"I'll write to President Roosevelt *and* Donna. I'll tell her about the Halloween carnival we're having at Lincoln School. I wonder if they dress in costumes in Topaz? We have stamps, right?" Lizzie asked.

Kay Lynn nodded.

"Will you please, please, please write to Mrs. Fujioka today? I don't want Donna's letter to wait and wait like last time."

Kay Lynn nodded again. In truth, they'd never been out of stamps. Writer's block—not a shortage of postage stamps—was to blame for the delay. Each time she put pen to paper to write to Kimiko, Kay Lynn struggled. Should she be entirely honest, but perhaps insensitive? Or chatty and superficial, but then also insensitive? She had yet to come to peace with what to say about her life while Kimiko was forced to be in Topaz.

"I'll do it right now," she told her daughter.

Dear Kimiko,

Lizzie is back at school. Timmy is frustrated that he has to stay home with me. Our home is very quiet.

The emptiness is disconcerting in a way I hadn't expected. It gives me too much free time to think about war. I learned today that my brother is missing, so I imagine that is all I will think about when I should be typing papers. We are in sore need of my income. Mitch's military pay doesn't cover our expenses. I hope I can keep our business afloat, but as you know, I don't type nearly as quickly as you do. And Timmy is constantly interrupting my work.

I keep picturing my brother—bleeding to death alone in a jungle. Or worse, alive, but without companionship or food or water or shelter. I'm consoled to imagine him as a prisoner of war even though I've read of the atrocities in the camps.

I never seem to sleep through the night anymore. Mitch has been gone for six weeks. I keep expecting to get used to it, but that hasn't happened yet. The bed is SO empty. I reach for him, and when I find only a mattress, my heart races. The only way to console myself is to walk.

I leave the children alone in the house, even after finding Timmy crying in his bed one night when I returned. I don't know how long he was calling out for me. I tell myself I should stay home, or only walk around the block, but somehow I'm only soothed by a walk to Telegraph and back on Alcatraz. I'm strangely uplifted by taking Hazel by the White Horse Inn on Telegraph. He was awake only that one time, and he wasn't crying long enough to wake Lizzie. And she's here if he is upset enough to wake her.

My sister is no help to any of us. She's only concerned with herself, and when I point that out to my parents, they blame me for creating conflict.

I want my life back. How are you?

Love,

Kay Lynn

Kay Lynn read through her letter. *I want my life back.* "I want my life back," she whispered to herself.

She couldn't possibly send this letter to Kimiko, who had lost so much more than she had.

Kay Lynn held up the note in her left hand; with her right, tore it down the middle. She took those two halves and tore them into little pieces. She swept the bits of paper into her trash can and then wrote another letter.

Dear Kimiko,

Lizzie is back at school. Timmy wishes he was old enough to be at Lincoln School as well, but must make do with me. He doesn't enjoy a quiet house with only my company. I am distracted with our business for much of the day.

Our sad news is that Lenny is missing, his status unclear. As you can imagine, it is painful for all of us. We hope to hear soon that he is in a prisoner-of-war camp.

Lizzie and Timmy are very excited for Halloween. Each day they decide on a different costume. They are going through my parents' closets as well as our clothes. I have offered to tailor anything they wish.

Hazel has proved to be a lovely addition to our family. She often sleeps with me, which is especially soothing with Mitch being at basic training. Many nights, she and I walk together. She enjoys the attention of the soldiers hanging around the White Horse Inn, and they vie for the opportunity to pet her. The children love taking her on outings, and she stays close to them. I can

*say that she and Mr. Cuthbert are finally good
friends.*
   Much love, your friend,
   Kay Lynn

This one was still honest, but not self-indulgent. She could send
it to Topaz. As soon as it was addressed, she sent the kids to post
their letters.

CHAPTER 15

Fall 1943

That fall, on the many nights Kay Lynn woke with a start or couldn't settle her mind well enough to fall asleep, she walked with Hazel. She'd come to appreciate taking her time by the bar on Telegraph. Inevitably one or more of the soldiers standing on the sidewalk delighted in petting the dog. It was bittersweet to bring a touch of home to those young men; bolstering their spirits was her tiny contribution to the war effort.

As much as Kay Lynn yearned for their life to return to normal, there was nothing in the newspaper to indicate it was happening anytime soon. Every morning, for one moment before she opened her eyes, Kay Lynn believed Mitch was asleep next to her, but then she would lift her lids and face the reality of an empty pillow.

Everything in Berkeley and Oakland had changed: traffic, housing, people. With each visit, the market seemed less and less stocked and more and more expensive. Whenever she went out, she saw men in uniform, reminding her of her missing brother, her absent husband, and of the battles raging far away. At home she felt Mitch's absence every morning and every night, and often in the middle of the day too.

Kay Lynn felt sorry for herself, and then felt shame at her own immaturity. Her brother was missing: dead or in a prisoner-of-war camp. Kimiko was in an internment camp. In small towns all over the world, homes were being bombed, men were being killed, and children were starving. She shouldn't be upset that she lacked enough sugar to make lemon bars and her husband was in San Diego.

The morning of the Lincoln School Halloween carnival, Lizzie ran into the kitchen while Kay Lynn cleaned up breakfast.

"Mommy, do I look like a real angel?" Lizzie asked.

Kay Lynn beamed at her daughter, who wore a long white gown sewn from an old sheet. Lizzie had reshaped wire hangers and wrapped them in tinfoil to make wings and a halo.

"Your wings are perfect. The halo too. You look just like an angel in the movies."

"Arghhh!" Timmy roared. He had a patch over one eye and a papier-mâché sword in his hand.

"Oh!" Kay Lynn pretended to scream. "Pirate, I don't have any gold!"

Timmy pulled the eye patch up. "It's just me, Mommy; you don't have to be scared."

"Thank goodness," Kay Lynn replied with a laugh. "You two will look wonderful at the carnival this afternoon. Lizzie, leave your costumes here when you go to school. Your teacher was very clear that she doesn't want any costumes in class—only for the party on the playground. I'll bring it to you after school."

It was going to be tight, rushing to the cemetery to visit Nana Lisbeth and then returning home for the costumes. But bringing them on the streetcar would have added even more stress than going home before going to Lincoln School.

"Hold tight to the picnic basket," Kay Lynn instructed Timmy later that morning. She ran down the sidewalk, pushing the stroller while he gripped their lunch balanced on his lap. Truly he was too big for a stroller, but she didn't have time to move at a four-year-old's pace. She needed them to get to the Grands, then on to the cemetery, and back home in time for the school carnival. She regretted the obligation at Lincoln School, but she didn't have a true choice. Mrs. Grant hadn't asked *if* she would volunteer, but rather *where* she would. The ring toss seemed innocuous enough.

"No Kristine," Kay Lynn observed when she got to the Grands.

"She's working," Momma replied.

"So she says," Kay Lynn retorted.

Momma's face flashed with hurt and anger.

"I didn't ask her to come, because she has work. And to be honest, I don't want to be around the two of you."

Kay Lynn immediately wished she had kept her comment to herself.

"I'm sorry, Momma," Kay Lynn replied.

"Ready?" Momma asked without accepting her apology.

They walked toward their Key Route stop. As they turned onto College, Kay Lynn saw the back of the streetcar traveling away from their stop. Her heart clenched in frustration. If she already had her license, she could have driven Poppa's car and they would be at Mountain View Cemetery in ten minutes. Now they would have to wait at least that long for the next trolley. With all the stops, they'd be fortunate to be there in forty-five minutes. She had to find the time to learn to drive.

The carnival started with a costume parade. Lizzie scolded her for being late with the costume, but both kids were dressed by the time

the music started. There were no prizes because some of the mothers didn't want to cause rivalries. Kay Lynn didn't mind. These kids were too young to be anything but tearful when they lost.

For a moment, while watching the kids march, Kay Lynn forgot about all the stresses in her life and simply took joy in the delight of the children. Timmy, at his sister's side, waved at her from multiple points on the trek around the playground. Lizzie was too busy talking to her friends to look at her mother.

When the parade ended, Kay Lynn took up her station at the ring toss. A line of children formed, supervised by another volunteer that Kay Lynn didn't know, Mrs. Fortich. The older students loomed over the young ones, but they didn't look to be harassing them.

"Next," Kay Lynn called, summoning a young witch forward. "You won't cast an evil spell on me, will you?" she asked.

Laura giggled. "I'm only pretend, Mrs. Brooke. Here's my ticket!"

Laura took the three rings Kay Lynn offered to her and immediately tossed one toward the nine milk bottles; it landed short.

"Witch Laura, you can take a step forward, to the next line," Kay Lynn told her.

The little girl moved forward, tried again, and overshot the bottles.

Kay Lynn crossed her fingers for Laura's third and final toss; she hated it when the children didn't win. Laura's last ring sailed through the air and landed right around the top of a milk bottle.

"Hooray!" Kay Lynn cried out. "Go see Mrs. Washington. She has a prize for you."

The little girl skipped over to get her popcorn ball while Kay Lynn collected the rings.

"Next." She called a clown forward.

"Daddy!?" a child yelled from across the yard. Jealousy squeezed Kay Lynn's heart. She wanted her children to know the joy of having

Mitch at this Halloween carnival. She shook off her self-pity and turned her attention back to the game. Two rings were already on milk bottles.

"Mr. Clown, you may get a popcorn ball from Mrs. Washington." She heard the tightness in her own voice. She cleared her throat.

"Next," she called out to the column of contestants.

Past the ring toss line, on the other side of the playground, a ball of costumed children swarmed around a soldier in a military uniform. One child was picked from the crowd and pulled up into a hug that included a full spin around. The boy was small, Timmy's size. Kay Lynn's heart jumped. A chill ran through her.

Was that? Timmy! In Mitch's arms? She raced across the schoolyard.

"Mommy, it's Daddy!" Lizzie pointed. "He's home. He's really home!"

Mitch stopped spinning. He stared at her; his eyes moist. A huge grin lit up his face. "Surprise!"

She fell against his chest, clutching him and Timmy at the same time. Lizzie's arms, waist high, wrapped around them too. Kay Lynn closed her eyes tight to hold in her tears. She breathed in her husband. Mitch was here, in Berkeley!

"What?" she broke away to ask.

"I got my orders: naval weapons depot in Port Chicago. If we can manage to get a car, I can live at home."

Gooseflesh raised on Kay Lynn's arms. "Truly?"

He bit his lip and nodded.

"Oh, Mitch." She let her tears fall. She didn't care who saw her. She was so happy, she thought she might burst. Mitch would be safe in Contra Costa County.

CHAPTER 16

Winter 1943

"This came yesterday," Momma said as she handed a paper telegram to Kay Lynn. They were in the kitchen, preparing Sunday supper.

Adrenaline poured through Kay Lynn. Was the telegram good or bad news? She couldn't tell by Momma's face.

> The name of Leonard Stevens has been
> mentioned in an enemy broadcast as a Jap-
> anese prisoner. These enemy broadcasts'
> aim is at getting listeners for their pro-
> paganda; however, the army is checking for
> accuracy and will advise you as soon as
> possible.
>
>
> Foreign Broadcast Intelligence Service
> Federal Communications Commission

Relief and sorrow swirled in Kay Lynn. *Alive.* Lenny was most likely alive. She hugged Momma.

"Are you relieved?" she asked.

"Yes. And . . . it's unbearable to imagine him in one of those camps." Momma teared up. "Your brother is a sensitive man. Like his father, he wasn't made for the cruelties of war."

Kay Lynn didn't know what to say. Every encouraging phrase seemed an empty platitude. *He's strong. He'll be okay. I'm sure he's fine.* None of them were right.

Kay Lynn finally said, "I miss him too. And I'm scared for him."

Momma smiled a tight, sad smile; handed Kay Lynn a dish of scalloped potatoes to carry to the dining room; and yelled, "Supper!"

Momma placed the broiled chicken at the table, and they all sat around it once Kay Lynn positioned the potatoes. They joined hands for grace, a practice in this home, but not the Brookes'.

"Timmy, hold my hand," Lizzie reminded her brother. He did, and the circle of hands around the table became complete. Timmy gazed at the circle of family. Most of them had closed their eyes and bowed their heads. Mitch winked at their son; Kay Lynn's heart filled with love. It was a moment of grace. Not the forgiveness grace, but the blessed grace.

Grammy Sadie prayed, "God of connection and creation, we thank you for this day and for our time together. Watch over those we love, especially our Lenny, and place love and compassion into the hearts of all men and women so that we may end this terrible war soon. Amen."

Amens echoed around the table, including from her children. Kay Lynn had to admit that it was soothing. She pulled an envelope from her pocket and slid it to her father across the table.

"Your payment for the loan for the car we bought. Thank you very much."

"I'm grateful we had the money to lend you," he replied.

"How's the drive to the weapons depot?" Grammy Sadie asked.

"Quite lovely. This time of year, the hills are bright green, and there are rarely backups in either direction in the tunnel."

Poppa Leo replied, "Those highways have changed everything. Mark my words, people will start living out there and working in San Francisco."

"And your work, Mitch?" Momma asked. "What do you do at the naval weapons depot?"

Mitch paused. A shadow crossed his face. "We're loading tons of weaponry onto ships. We're working at full speed, but there are few safety precautions in play. I expressed my concerns to my commanding officer, but he brushed them aside, saying the artillery isn't yet armed. Most aren't, but I did see some artillery pieces already fitted with caps."

"You load the weapons?!" Momma asked.

"No, only the colored men are loading the weapons onto the ships. The white enlisted bring the weapons to the loading dock. I know it isn't right, but it isn't my place to do anything about it."

"If only the federal government enforced Executive Order 8802 instead of Executive Order 9066," Kay Lynn barked.

Lizzie leaned over and asked in a whisper, "What does that mean?"

Kay Lynn explained to her daughter, "President Roosevelt said there will be no discrimination against minorities for government work with Executive Order 8802, which the military ignores all the time. And he said people who are of Japanese ancestry, even if they are United States citizens, had to relocate away from the West Coast in Executive Order 9066. We think one is fair and one is unfair; do you understand?"

Lizzie nodded. "The second one is what made Donna have to live in Utah, right?"

Kay Lynn nodded.

"I agree. President Roosevelt isn't being fair," Lizzie said with a scowl.

Lizzie truly was growing up. A few months ago this conversation would have sailed past her. Kay Lynn was glad to share their family's values with her daughter. Even the prayer from Grammy Sadie was a lesson that she hoped Lizzie took in: love and compassion for all people. That was the key to ending the war and returning life to normal. If only Hitler could agree.

Twice a year Kay Lynn visited Grandmother Barrow in San Francisco: on her elder's birthday and near Christmas. Up until ten years ago, her grandmother shared the burden of travel. She reliably visited with Kay Lynn in either San Francisco or Berkeley, first with Momma and eventually just the two of them. They went to extravagant restaurants like Alioto's on Fisherman's Wharf, the Cliff House on the Pacific Ocean, or the Claremont in Berkeley. These were the only times she went into the stately white hotel.

When Grandmother Barrow's health had started failing, she stopped traveling to Berkeley. They didn't see each other as often, but Kay Lynn came to San Francisco for a meal out near her grandmother's house. The last two visits, her grandmother suggested they simply have tea in her home.

This year she would bring Lizzie. Now that she had her license, it would be easy to bring her daughter. The girl was finally mature enough to be a welcome companion and to learn more about Kay Lynn's complicated start in life. Grandmother Barrow asked for Lizzie and Timmy at each visit, but Kay Lynn hadn't brought them since they were babes in arms. Controlling young children in a fancy restaurant or grand house was too difficult. As kind as her grandmother was to her, Kay Lynn never fit in on Nob Hill.

"Lizzie, this is my first time driving to San Francisco, so I will need to concentrate. I may ask you to look for signs. Can you be my navigator?"

"Yes, Mommy. I'm glad we don't need a gunner," Lizzie quipped.

Kay Lynn cheerfully agreed, but inside she was pained by her daughter's matter-of-fact talk about warplane crews.

The route was well marked, and even at highway speeds, Kay Lynn navigated from Route 24 to the Bay Bridge without a problem. A Saturday meant less traffic than she might face on a workday. Thankfully, she'd been practicing and perfecting parallel parking, which was essential on Nob Hill.

"The buildings are so tall," Lizzie remarked.

"You've been here before, but you were very little."

Grandmother Barrow invited Kay Lynn's father, Jonathon Barrow, to every visit. For years she would get her hopes up and then have them dashed when he didn't come as planned. He never said no directly, but offered an excuse and apology for his absence at the last minute.

Grandmother Barrow had said he would be there today, but Kay Lynn was doubtful. She considered preparing Lizzie for his possible presence, but didn't want to face the girl's questions and curiosity, and disappointment if he wasn't there. If he was there, they could discuss it afterward.

A servant Kay Lynn didn't know showed them to Grandmother Barrow in the parlor. Lizzie clutched Kay Lynn's right hand with both of hers. This home *was* intimidating.

"It's so fancy," Lizzie whispered as they walked across the thick Persian carpet.

"Good thing you're wearing your fanciest dress," Kay Lynn replied.

"Come in. Come in," the white-haired woman declared. She'd aged in the six months since Kay Lynn's last visit, but she looked as elegant as ever with her pearl necklace and custom dress in her favorite shade of blue.

"You must be Lizzie, so grown up!" She beamed. "Come, give me a kiss and take a See's chocolate. Only the best for my great-granddaughter."

Kay Lynn led the way, kissing her grandmother's hollowed cheek and grabbing her favorite—dark-chocolate-covered almonds.

Lizzie followed suit with the kiss, but then stared at the variety of chocolates laid out before her. Kay Lynn brought a pound of See's home with her from each of these visits, so Lizzie was familiar with them, but she seemed hard-pressed to choose one.

She eventually settled on the light molasses chips and said, "Thank you," followed by a small curtsy.

"She is charming!" the old woman said with a tear in her eye. "Thank you for bringing her for this visit. It means very much to me to know my great-granddaughter."

The woman raised the bell next to her and gave it a clear shake. The ring echoed through the house.

"Hannah will bring tea and sandwiches. I'm afraid Jonathon will not be joining us. He telephoned to say he'd been unavoidably detained."

Just as Kay Lynn expected, he had failed to keep his promise to see her. She glanced at Lizzie to see if she took in the information, but the girl was looking at a vase of flowers.

"Tell me about your school, young lady," Grandmother Barrow went on.

The visit continued with pleasantries. Grandmother spoke about her garden and the theater. She asked about Timmy, Mitch, and Momma. They avoided speaking of the war or her health, but it seemed to be fading.

As always, she finished the visit with gifts. She handed Kay Lynn a wrapped present for Timmy and a two-pound box of See's candy, and a beautifully wrapped box directly to Lizzie. Kay Lynn smiled. Grandmother Barrow used to present her with a custom-made dress once or twice a year. Likely a gorgeous dress was inside that box.

"Thank you very much," Lizzie said. "Should I open it now?"

"Young lady, we do not open gifts in front of others. You may have your own reaction in private," Grandmother Barrow replied.

Lizzie nodded with wide eyes, taking in this old-fashioned etiquette.

When she was young, Kay Lynn proudly handed presents to Grandmother Barrow at every visit: trinkets bought with money she saved over time, pictures she drew herself, and bouquets made from flowers she collected in their garden.

Soon after her tenth birthday, she'd flushed with embarrassment as she handed over her gift. The contrast with the beautiful objects from around the world, framed oil paintings, and hot-house-grown flowers in gorgeous vases was humiliating. Her grandmother had only ever expressed delight at her tokens of love, but Kay Lynn saw them for what they were: meager. She never brought a present again, though she carefully chose a card from the stationery store for every birthday.

When they were walking away from the house, Lizzie asked, "Are you sad that your daddy didn't come to see you?"

Lizzie had been aware of that exchange.

"Long ago I stopped thinking of Mr. Barrow as my father. Poppa Leo is my real father," she said. "The people that pay attention to you and take care of you are your family."

"So Grandmother Barrow is really your grandmother because she cares about you so much, but Mr. Barrow isn't really your father."

"As strange as that sounds, that's exactly how it feels to me," Kay Lynn replied. "People make family in all sorts of ways: by marriage, by birth, by adoption, or . . . I guess, love."

"What about in here?" Lizzie asked, pointing to a pawnshop.

Confused at her daughter's question, Kay Lynn asked, "For what?"

"Timmy's Christmas present?"

They seemed to be finished talking about Jonathon Barrow. Kay Lynn peered through the window. She saw a variety of tools and several radios, but the only toy was an old rocking horse.

"I don't believe they have many toys," Kay Lynn said.

"I think Timmy would be *very* happy if Santa left him a radio under the tree," Lizzie declared. "So he can take it apart and see the insides."

"Santa?"

"Mommy, you know I'm too old to believe that Santa is really real. I know he's really you and Daddy."

Kay Lynn didn't know Lizzie was too old to believe in Santa. They'd never had that talk. Somehow she'd figured it out by herself.

Kay Lynn smiled. "You really are growing up."

"Is that a yes?" Lizzie asked.

"Yes, Timmy would love a radio as much as a toy. Let's see what it costs."

Thankfully Lizzie wasn't too old to hold her hand as they walked into the shop.

CHAPTER 17

Spring 1944

A few months later, Kay Lynn and Timmy headed to the Grands house. Momma had invited her to join in their visit with Cousin Naomi and her daughter, Maggie. Kay Lynn couldn't remember when she'd last seen them. Seeing these distant relatives wasn't a priority, but today she had the time to please her grandmother by joining in the visit.

The four women were seated in the living room when they walked into the house. Timmy clung to her arm, shy once he realized there were guests. The two colored women rose with huge grins on their faces.

Naomi had a halo of white hair contrasting with her smooth, dark-brown skin. Her daughter, though she was in her forties, didn't have a single fleck of white.

"Kay Lynn, it is a joy to see you so grown and looking so well," Naomi exclaimed.

She patted Kay Lynn's cheek after they hugged. It was sweet and intimate. Kay Lynn felt like a long-lost, treasured child.

Naomi turned her attention to the five-year-old. "And you must be Timmy. I'm your great-aunt Naomi. It is delightful to meet you, young man. This is your auntie Maggie."

He stared wide eyed at the two women.

"He's so grown," Maggie said. "It has been too long since we've seen one another. He was a babe in arms last time we saw you."

"Has it been that long?" Kay Lynn asked.

"Time does fly," Maggie said. "Especially those years with young children. You blink and your babies are ready for school."

"He starts kindergarten in the fall," Kay Lynn replied. "Each week seemed never-ending when he was an infant, and now that it's over, I already miss having babies."

When they sat again, Timmy leaned in close to her ear and whispered, "Momma, I have a question."

Kay Lynn replied, "Your question can be spoken out loud, or it can wait."

He stared at her, and then looked around at the other faces.

"I'll wait."

She nodded at her son. "Go play in the backyard while we visit. I'll come for you when it's time to leave."

He ran off while the women returned to their conversation.

"Best wishes on your birthday, Kay Lynn," Naomi said. "I hope you will feel it as more of a blessing because of these hard times. No day is promised to any of us. Each one is a gift from God."

"Thank you," Kay Lynn replied. "I can't believe you remember it."

"I've attended hundreds of births," Naomi said, "and yours was one of the more memorable ones."

Then she looked at Momma and said, "Yours too, May! I wasn't in the slightest prepared for it, but I was too young and self-certain to be terrified. A preemie on a moving train!" She shook her head. "It's a wonder you survived!"

The women laughed.

"Our family owes you a debt we can never, ever repay," Grammy Sadie said.

Kay Lynn thought of the midwife at Lizzie and Timmy's births. She had so much appreciation for the kind and competent woman. After being at Kimiko's birth, her respect and devotion had grown. She looked at Naomi's face and then at her hands. *Those were the first hands that touched me.* She felt a chill go down her spine. Did this woman help Momma choose to keep her?

Naomi raised her chin. "Most of those babies I caught I never got to see again. It's such a blessing when the Lord allows me to use my midwifing gifts for those I care about. You two are some of the ones I got to see grow up. What a joy!"

She turned and patted Kay Lynn's cheek again, as if she were a child. It was intimate.

"Do you miss it?" Momma asked.

"Every day . . . and every night I'm grateful to be finished with it," Naomi replied. "Now I'm content just holding the babies after they've arrived. I'm too old to stay up at all hours waiting for an infant to come."

"And I don't miss fretting over her being out late," Maggie added, and then she changed the topic. "We visited with Lisbeth after we paid our respects to Gramma Jordan last Sunday."

"Oh, that is lovely," Grammy Sadie replied. "What a blessing that they share a final resting place."

"Indeed," Naomi replied.

"Sadie, I thought on the day you and I hid at that cemetery," Naomi said.

Kay Lynn's interest was piqued.

Grammy Sadie retorted, "*I* was hiding. You were keeping me company as a kindness."

Shocked, Kay Lynn asked, "Who were you hiding from?"

The women looked at one another. An uncomfortable silence filled the room.

"My father," Momma finally spoke. "You know he wasn't a kind man."

Grammy Sadie said, "Somehow, I picked a mean one. We have so many kind ones in our family." She shook her head. "But I got myself rid of him when he left for Hawaii, and I refused to go with him. I had to hide so he couldn't force me on that boat, away from my family."

"It was a triumphant day!" Naomi said.

Grammy Sadie took her hand. "It was—only because of you and Jordan. I'm grateful with every breath."

"The Lord works in mysterious ways!" Maggie said.

Lord. The word bristled at Kay Lynn. The thought of God as a master was repulsive. She thought it especially strange that these colored women would be comfortable with such a term, given the history of slavery in their family.

Grammy Sadie changed the topic. "Tell us your news? How are your grandchildren faring in these trying times?"

Kay Lynn wanted to hear more about her grandfather. She'd heard he was a terrible man, but never any details. Grammy Sadie had to *hide* from him? She'd have to press Momma or Grammy Sadie for more details. There were more secrets in their family than she realized. She stared at the women in front of her. She'd been told that Naomi was Grammy Sadie's cousin, but now that didn't make sense. How could a Negro be Grammy's cousin?

Maggie replied, "They're scattered—like so many families. Our happiest news is that Billy is posted at the Port Chicago depot. When he has a spare day, he can come to see us, and we hope to get there to visit sometime soon."

Same as Mitch, Kay Lynn thought. *But he can commute each day because we have a car.*

"That is wonderful," Momma said without mentioning that Mitch was stationed there as well. "And the others? Are they in Europe? Or Asia?"

It wasn't even a question if they were serving. It was just presumed that all young men were enlisted.

Maggie replied, "Asia as far as we know. All of the boys. So far none have been taken from us or taken prisoner. Any word about Lenny?"

Momma said, "None. We sent a Christmas package through the Red Cross, but we don't know if he got it. They know they're delivered but not if they're distributed."

"What's a mother to do, except pray," Naomi said.

Kay Lynn felt a chill go down her back and arms. Prayer seemed so inadequate in the face of fighter planes, submarines, and machine guns, and yet, Naomi spoke the truth. What else was a mother to do? Or a sister? Or a father? Or a friend? How did all of them bear this every single day?

The conversation continued. Kay Lynn saw for the first time how well these women knew one another. *Dawn, Cedric, Joseph.* The names and their children were a jumble to Kay Lynn, but Momma and Grammy Sadie knew them all. She didn't interrupt with her questions, but just watched the visit until it was time for her to go.

"I must get home before Lizzie gets worried. I told her I'd be there when she got back from school."

The four women rose and hugged her goodbye.

"I have an odd question before Kay Lynn leaves. None of our crocuses flowered this year," Momma said. "Did yours?"

Momma and her crocuses. For years she'd been devoted to keeping them flourishing. Hunting for them was a February tradition.

Maggie shook her head. "Not one bloomed. Plenty of green, though."

"Us too," Momma said.

"Some years are like that; not enough rain or cold or something they need," Naomi explained.

"Is there anything we can do?" Kay Lynn asked.

Maggie said, "We'll separate them in the fall to give them some space, put some bones in the ground to give them extra food, and pray for the right weather. So far, they've always flowered again eventually."

"Thank you," Kay Lynn replied. She'd put their advice to use. She hadn't once separated the crocuses Momma planted seven years ago on Prince Street.

"I wonder how many generations it is for the crocuses?" Grammy Sadie asked. "It's just a few for us humans. My mother, your great-grandmother, ordered the first bulbs before I was born. She said they seemed an extravagance at the time but ended up being a bargain since they flowered year after year."

"What year was that, Grammy Sadie?" Kay Lynn asked.

"I was born in 1861," the elder replied.

"Eighty years." Kay Lynn sucked in her breath. "That's amazing!"

Naomi said, "As the good Lord reminds us, we reap what we sow."

Maggie added, "We just don't know how long we'll reap from what we sow. Or how the seeds will keep spreading, long past our sight or lives."

"Like the stained-glass window in your church," Naomi said. "I've always loved that best about your building. The Parable of the Sower, right up front, reminding me to spread seeds of love and justice."

"You've been in our sanctuary?" Kay Lynn asked.

"Many times from when Mama was working on women's suffrage. This hand"—she held up her right hand—"shook the hand of the great Susan B. Anthony, in your church."

"Like you," Kay Lynn said to Grammy Sadie.

"It was that same day. She only came the once that I know of," Grammy Sadie replied, and then added, "with the brave and true Ida B. Wells."

"God bless their souls," Naomi said.

Kay Lynn teared up. These women were so lovely. How had she missed what a treasure they were? They'd been invisible to her, but they were true heroes, helping babies be born and working for women's right to vote.

"It was lovely to see you. I promise I won't let it be so long before I see you again," Kay Lynn said.

She got Timmy, hugged them goodbye, and rushed up the sidewalk toward home.

"Momma, why do those ladies have dark skin?" Timmy asked. He stopped walking.

Kay Lynn was taken aback by his question, but then remembered that Lizzie had asked similar questions at the same age.

She looked at him as she replied, "They look like that because their parents had dark skin. Their ancestors come from Africa, where everyone has dark skin to protect them from the sun."

"One was dark dark, but the other one was only a little dark," he said.

There was so much more to say about what having dark skin meant, the ugly history of slavery.

She thought for a moment and then replied, "Mrs. Hays is Mrs. Smith's daughter. Mrs. Hays's father isn't so dark. We look like our ancestors. Though some families are more mixed up than others, so people look different from each other."

And somehow they were related to Grammy Sadie, unless they weren't actually related and just called each other cousins. Kay Lynn would have to get to the bottom of that question.

"Where do my ancestors come from?" Timmy asked.

"Germany, mostly, we think," Kay Lynn replied.

His eyes welled up, on the verge of tears. "Are we bad?"

Kay Lynn sucked in her breath. "No, Timmy, no! We've been in America for a very long time. My grandfather was born in Germany. But Nana May and I were born here."

"Poppa Leo is German?" He looked alarmed. "Is he our enemy?"

Kay Lynn's mind swirled. Had she never told Timmy about their family tree?

"Poppa Leo is your grandfather, not mine. Grammy Sadie's husband was my grandfather, Nana May's father, but he died a long time ago, so you never met him."

His eyes moved up and down, and his head nodded, as he worked out the relationships in his mind. Kay Lynn considered whether to say more, and decided this was as good a time as any.

"Timmy, it takes a seed and an egg to grow a baby. The seed comes from a man and the egg is inside a woman."

He nodded, though this was new information for him.

"Grampa Leo isn't my seed father, but he is my father in all the ways that matter."

"Who's your seed father?"

"A man named Jonathon Barrow. You never met him."

"Has Lizzie?"

"Once, when she was a baby."

"Is Daddy my seed father?" Timmy asked.

"Yes," Kay Lynn replied.

Timmy nodded. Looking satisfied, with no more questions, he resumed walking down the sidewalk. She was glad he'd finished asking hard questions. She ran it through her mind, wondering if she'd answered well. Satisfied that she had, they finished their journey home in a comfortable silence.

When Mitch climbed into bed that night, Kay Lynn said, "I had 'the talk' with Timmy today. Sort of two talks, really. Maybe three."

He sighed and then laughed. "Go on."

"He asked why Grammy Sadie's Negro friends, Maggie and Naomi, have dark skin. I explained that their ancestors are from

Africa, which led right into conception, which led right into Jonathon Barrow being my seed father."

He pulled his lips and eyebrows into a challenge.

She shrugged. "Our children are curious; I *like* to answer their questions."

"Don't you think he is a little young to be thinking about such things?" Mitch asked, sounding annoyed.

A flash of anger heated her chest. She'd been proud of her honest answer, and Mitch was criticizing her.

"If he's old enough to ask the question, he's old enough to get a respectful and thoughtful response. I don't want them to be ashamed of their curiosity about the world."

"He's five years old, learning about sex?"

"I didn't mention penises go into vaginas," she snapped back.

"Your family is more complicated than mine," he replied.

"My family *is* his family. I'm sorry if you didn't realize that your children would be in a *complicated* family." She felt tears push at her eyes. "Good night."

She lay down, and turned her back to him.

"I'm sorry," Mitch said. "I didn't intend to insult your family. You know I love them, all of them."

"Shh!" she snapped at him. "I'm tired, and I don't want to talk about it anymore. I'm going to sleep."

She couldn't possibly sleep after that flash of anger, but wanted Mitch to know she was upset. She lay still, radiating hurt. Kay Lynn sensed Mitch looking over at her from his side of the bed. She knew he was still sitting up. He touched her arm, a peace offering, but she shook it off. She wasn't ready to move on.

He finally turned off his bedside light and lay down. His soft snores filled her ears before she was asleep. She took in a few breaths. Should she get up and walk around the block to cool down? She felt for her watch, turned her light on, saw it was nearly midnight, and quickly turned it off. She'd been stewing for more than an hour.

Hazel jumped on the bed. She licked Kay Lynn's hand and then curled against the back of her knees. The comfort of the dog transformed her anger into sorrow. A few tears streamed down her cheek to her pillow. Shame gummed up her heart.

Was Mitch ashamed of her?

She was barely hanging on and didn't need his judgment.

But maybe she was the one who was ashamed . . . of her family. They *were* complicated.

She could never think of any time Poppa Leo treated her as if she were different from Kristine and Lenny, but that wasn't the case for his mother, Yaya.

The flash of a Christmas tree popped into Kay Lynn's mind. Her heart raced, and she pushed the memory away. It came back, insistent.

Poppa and Yaya were arguing. He had tears on his cheeks. Her present was in his hand, and he was shaking it at his mother.

She let the memory come from the beginning.

She was nine years old, and it was Christmas Day. Their family was at Yaya's house with their aunts, uncles, and cousins for Christmas dinner. After dinner they opened presents, going from youngest, two-year-old Kristine, to oldest, twelve-year-old Micaela.

Kristine tore her package open. Inside was a deep-red velvet dress with black satin bows. It was beautiful. Jealousy shot through Kay Lynn.

Three-year-old Joseph opened a mechanical train set with a track you could put together.

They continued with four-year-olds James and Lenny getting train sets and four-year-old Kim and six-year-old Sonia getting dresses that matched Kristine's.

Yaya handed Kay Lynn her present with a smile. It was a box just like the other girls'. Her heart raced with excitement. She tore the paper and lifted the lid of the box, expecting to see a red velvet dress of her own. Instead it was a cotton gingham dress. She blinked back tears. She pulled it out for others to see.

"Oh," she heard Momma utter.

Aunt Michelle's forehead was furrowed.

Kay Lynn swallowed and forced out a thank-you.

"You're too old to match the little girls. This color will bring out the blue of your eyes," Yaya remarked. "That's why I chose it for you."

Micaela opened her package next, also a dress, but in the latest fashion in a cream silk, cut with a dropped waist.

"Oh, Yaya," Micaela said. "It's wonderful!"

Yaya beamed. "A beautiful dress for the beautiful young lady you are becoming."

Kay Lynn swallowed hard. She should be grateful for her present, but the other dresses were fancy while hers was ordinary. She pushed down her jealousy while the family continued opening gifts.

After presents and dessert, Kay Lynn and Micaela played jacks on the floor of the living room. Kay Lynn was very adept. She was so used to doing most things with only her right hand that she had a distinct advantage over her older cousin. On one of her tosses, Micaela knocked her ball under the Christmas tree.

"I'll get it for you," Kay Lynn offered, and scampered across the hardwood floor.

When she reached far under the tree, she saw a disturbing scene: Poppa quarreling with Yaya in the back corner of the dining room.

Poppa hissed, "You have gone too far this time. We won't come here for Christmas if you keep treating her differently. You won't see Kristine and Lenny as you have. Do you understand me?"

Yaya glared at him. "I do not understand why you care for that cripple so much," she stated, then quickly she added, "but I agree to your terms."

"Exactly the same," he emphasized each word.

She replied, "Outwardly it will be the same, but in my heart . . ." She looked at him and shrugged.

He shook his head and walked away.

Kay Lynn felt sick in her stomach.

"Did you find it?" Micaela called to her.

"Yes," she replied, her voice high and tight. Kay Lynn took in a deep breath, blinked back her tears, pushed herself out from under the tree, and returned the ball to her cousin.

"I got it. I'm fine. It's fine. You can take that turn over," Kay Lynn said, hoping Micaela didn't see the pain in her eyes.

That was the day she lost her innocence. She'd known she was different before then, but didn't think the difference mattered. After hearing that conversation, she knew better. It mattered, a lot, to some people—including Yaya.

Kay Lynn rolled over in her bed. Hazel resettled herself against Kay Lynn's belly.

She looked at Mitch. Had he ever had such a conversation with his parents, defending her place in their family?

She'd never asked him, nor had she asked him how much he regretted that he didn't go to UCLA. He'd *wanted* to be a college man, a fraternity brother. He spoke of it constantly as graduation grew closer; instead he was forced to become a husband and a father. Kay Lynn didn't regret becoming a wife and mother sooner than she expected, but whenever he made comments like the one tonight, she feared that he resented her and regretted their life together.

"I'm sorry, Mitch," slipped out. She didn't know what she was apologizing for, but the tension from their argument weighed on her. Now that she wasn't mad, she wanted to apologize while he slept and simply move past the disagreement without discussing it. Hopefully he wouldn't bring it up in the morning and they could both ignore her fit of emotion.

CHAPTER 18

July 1944

She'd been sound asleep when Hazel's barking interrupted her dream. It was hard to swim back up to reality, but once Kay Lynn surfaced, her heart thumped hard in her chest. Mitch had started working overnights in June, so she wasn't concerned about disturbing him—a small benefit of his new schedule.

As often happened when she woke in the night, her mind fixated on a picture from the newspaper, causing her to be afraid, sad, angry, or a mixture of all of them—making rest impossible. Kay Lynn recognized this fearful feeling; she wasn't going back to sleep anytime soon. Instead, she got up, dressed well enough for the dark, and set out with Hazel.

The air was clear and cool, with only a touch of fog. Kay Lynn ruminated on an image of a bombed town from the paper.

All will be well, she reminded herself, but that landed flat. *It isn't in your hands.* That felt true. *Not in my hands. Not in my hands.*

Ambulances screamed in the distance. Or fire engines or police cars. She couldn't distinguish between them; but there was more than one vehicle racing to help someone, somewhere.

Kay Lynn turned on Telegraph Avenue and walked toward the White Horse. At the corner of Sixty-Sixth, the dog ran up to a man who greeted her, "Hazel! It's been too long!" He looked at Kay Lynn. "You must be sleeping better."

She laughed. It had come to this, being recognized by soldiers outside of a seedy bar. Maybe it wasn't so unsavory, but it was a bar, and it was late.

In her peripheral vision, two people walked out of the bar; they brushed their arms against one another in the way that secret lovers do. Kay Lynn smiled to herself. Life and love went on, despite the killing and destruction in the world. She turned her head and looked up to see the faces of the young lovers.

Kay Lynn stared right into her sister's eyes. Her heart leapt. Kristine wouldn't like being caught with her beau; but this was her chance to learn more about her sister's private life. She glanced at the person by Kristine's side.

Darting between the two faces, Kay Lynn took a moment to understand what she was seeing. The other person was female. Unaware that she was being observed, the tall, dark-haired woman leaned in, her lips right at Kristine's ear, and whispered something with a sly smile.

The sisters made brief eye contact; then Kristine turned her back to Kay Lynn and walked down the sidewalk. Kay Lynn watched them go, happy to pretend they hadn't seen one another. The two women separated into a respectable distance so quickly that Kay Lynn almost doubted what she'd seen, but now she understood—this woman was Kristine's secret.

Long ago she'd confirmed this was a bar for homosexual men. *But women? She'd never heard of such a thing. Kristine?* Of course, her sister would hide this from their mother. *What would Momma say?*

Her thoughts jumped like a scared rabbit being chased by a wolf. *What does this mean for Kristine's future? Will she scamper into the* shadows? *Live a double life? Leave our family altogether? Lizzie and Timmy will be crushed if Kristine abandons them. What will Mitch say? Carolina already disapproves of my family; this will only add more fuel to her fire.*

By the time Kay Lynn got home, she was more agitated and exhausted than when she left. She turned to reading *The Wonderful Wizard of Oz* to push away thoughts of her sister, though the story about being lost in a strange land and wanting to go home felt too familiar. Hours later she fell into a sleep with troubled dreams.

"Mommy!" Lizzie shook her. "Poppa Leo and Nana May are here."

"What?" She blinked her eyes against the bright light. "What time is it?"

"Nine," Lizzie said.

"Why didn't you wake me for breakfast?"

"I can make us breakfast," Lizzie responded, sounding indignant.

"Of course you can." Kay Lynn smiled at her competent daughter. "Did Poppa Leo and Nana May say why they're here?"

Lizzie shook her head. "But they looked scared and sad. Do you think Uncle Lenny . . ." Her voice broke.

Adrenaline shot through Kay Lynn. She squeezed Lizzie's hand. "We won't borrow trouble," she said, while keeping the rest of her thoughts to herself: *When there is so much freely given to us.*

She considered getting dressed, but instead threw on a robe, prioritizing haste over looking presentable.

"Is Mitch here?" Momma asked without greeting Kay Lynn. Grammy Sadie was here too. Her three elders looked terrified.

Where's Mitch? He was normally back from his shift before eight o'clock; Lizzie said it was nine o'clock.

She shook her head. "They're very busy. Sometimes he works a double shift," she explained. "You can tell me the news without him."

"Lizzie, please go be with your brother," Poppa Leo instructed.

"I'm old—"

"Lizzie!" Kay Lynn barked. "Do not talk back to your grandfather. Go!"

They watched her walk away. When she was out of earshot, Momma whispered, "You haven't heard about the explosion? At Port Chicago?"

"What?" Kay Lynn was confused. She'd been expecting to hear that Lenny had been found dead.

"The *Tribune* says two ships exploded; hundreds are dead." Her momma's voice broke. "Was Mitch working last night?"

Kay Lynn's knees gave out; she sank onto the couch. She stared between the three faces.

"We have to go . . . We have to go . . ." Her mind couldn't form *How? Where?* Was her dreaded nightmare about to be true? She looked at her door. Was a soldier on his way to knock on it right now?

"The radio says the injured soldiers are at several hospitals," Poppa explained. "We can drive to the base, or the hospital in Martinez, or the naval hospital in Oakland. Someone should stay here."

Kay Lynn started to cry. "Do I have to tell the children? What do I tell them?"

"Hide the newspaper and keep the radio off until we learn more. They don't need to know anything yet," Momma said.

"Lizzie thinks you're here because of Lenny," Kay Lynn replied. "We have to tell her we have no news about her uncle."

Kay Lynn's chest tightened. Gasping for air, she sucked in jerky breaths.

"What do we do?" Kay Lynn asked again. They'd just made a plan, but she couldn't remember it.

What if Mitch was dead? They hadn't entirely made up from their fight. He must know that she loved him. Was he injured and alone? How could she find him?

"We'll go look for him," Momma declared. "Grammy Sadie can stay with the children."

"I can't face them, the children," Kay Lynn sobbed, tears streaming down her face. She bit her hand to stop herself from crying out. The pattern at the edge of the rug moved in and out of focus. Like childbirth, she was so overcome that she couldn't stop her body's response. She folded over and sobbed into her hands. A hand or two rested on her back until her tears ran out. Kay Lynn took a deep breath and sat up.

She let out a huge exhale and stood. "I'll get dressed, and we can go."

Kay Lynn's hands shook as she sorted through her clothes. She had to concentrate to remember what month it was. *July.* Foggy mornings, but not in Martinez. It would be hot out there.

Lizzie peeked through the doorway to her bedroom, her expression seeking permission to come in. Kay Lynn nodded. Lizzie quietly approached her and gave Kay Lynn a hug.

"Is Uncle Lenny . . . dead?"

Kay Lynn looked down at her daughter, whose face was filled with fear.

"We don't have any news about Uncle Lenny." She stroked Lizzie's hair. "There's been an accident at Port Chicago."

Keeping her voice light, Kay Lynn continued, "Nana May, Poppa Leo, and I are going to see if we can be helpful. Grammy Sadie is going to stay with you and Timmy."

"Is Daddy hurt?"

Kay Lynn froze. She didn't want to lie, but there was no reason to upset Lizzie until they knew more information.

She replied, "We don't think so, but we're going to find out for certain. He most likely had to stay to help too."

Lizzie nodded. "Can we make a treat for when you come home?"

"Grammy Sadie will be in charge; ask her." Kay Lynn sounded gruffer than she wanted to. But any hint of sorrow would cause her dam to break. "Be helpful," she instructed.

"Yes, Mommy. I will."

On her way out the door, Kay Lynn grabbed her knitting, to keep her hands busy and her mind focused during the long drive.

Poppa Leo drove the route through the Caldecott Tunnel. Route 24 got more and more congested until they were finally at a standstill in Concord. Kay Lynn knit furiously, her needles clinking at a rapid and agitated pace. Horns honked around them, but there was no point. No one could move forward, like the images of traffic jams in New York City. As far as she could see, there were cars ahead of her, and the base wasn't in sight. *Are all these people looking for news about their loved ones?*

After they inched along for an hour or so, a black car cut around them from behind, driving on the left side of the highway. *Could they actually get through that way?* Kay Lynn rolled down the window and leaned out to watch it travel down the road.

Way ahead she saw a large military truck parked across both lanes, blocking the highway. The black car stopped at the barricade where two soldiers stood sentry. Eventually, it turned around and sped back in her direction, heading toward Walnut Creek.

Car after car stopped at the checkpoint; only an occasional one was let through.

A few cars ahead, an arm waved out the window, signaling to a driver heading back toward Walnut Creek. The truck stopped. The drivers had a brief chat, then the vehicle continued forward. Kay Lynn waved down the truck.

An older colored man leaned out of the old, rusty door.

"Hello, sir, what did they tell you?" Kay Lynn asked.

"Only the military are being let through," he replied politely. "Least that's what he said to me."

"My husband was working last night!" she implored, as if this man could assuage her fears.

"My son was as well," he said in a hoarse voice, and then shrugged. "I'll say a prayer for your husband."

"Do you think they'll let me through?"

He studied their car.

"Is he an officer?"

She shook her head.

"I don't see the harm in you asking," he replied. "Good day, ma'am."

He'd been so kind that she wanted to repay him. "I'll pray for your son."

The man smiled. "Thank you. That's all we can do now—pray and wait."

The crawl up to the blockade was interminable. Momma hummed songs from the church hymnal. It was comforting . . . and poignant. Kay Lynn tried to join in, but her throat was too tight.

When it was their turn, Kay Lynn leaned out the window from the back seat.

"Hello, sir," she said to the man who looked to be barely twenty. "I'm here to find my husband, or news about him."

"He worked at the ammunitions depot?" the guard asked.

"Worked?!" she challenged.

"Works, sorry, ma'am." He turned red. "Is he civilian?"

She shook her head.

"An officer?" he asked.

"No."

"I'm sorry, ma'am. There is no information about enlisted men."

"Where have the injured been taken?" Poppa asked.

"The naval hospital in Oakland, and the civilian hospital in Martinez. A few were taken to the hospital in Concord."

"And the . . ." Kay Lynn couldn't say the word *dead* out loud.

The soldier exhaled hard, and he swallowed. "Ma'am, once your husband's status has been determined, you will be notified by the usual navy channels. Good day."

"Is there—"

He interrupted, "We have a long line of cars here. Please return home and be patient."

"Thank you, young man," Poppa replied. "This is a hard day for you. It will be behind you soon enough."

The guard stared off for a moment, then gave a nod. He suddenly looked like a scared boy.

"I hope so, sir," he replied. "Good day to all of you."

They were home in less than thirty minutes, greeted by a batch of thumbprint cookies on the dining room table.

"Is Daddy still working?" Timmy looked disappointed. "We made his favorite with the plum jam. Mr. Cuthbert gave us half a cup of sugar so we would have enough."

"*Lent* us sugar," Lizzie corrected her brother. "I promised him we would return it. We will. Right, Mommy?"

Kay Lynn closed her eyes. All the sentences and questions were too much.

"I have a headache." It was a half truth. "I'm going to go lie down."

"Grandma Carolina called to ask about Daddy after she heard about the accident. She must have been really scared to make a long-distance call. I told her he's still working."

Kay Lynn looked at Grammy Sadie, who gestured with her head toward the kitchen and said, "I'll get us plates for our cookies."

Alone in the kitchen, Grammy patted Kay Lynn's arm. "What did you learn?"

"Nothing." Kay Lynn blinked back her tears. "We wait for the knock or the call."

"Or him walking through the door," Grammy Sadie said.

"Hope for the best; prepare for the worst, right, Grammy?"

The worst kept running through her mind: *Mitch gone, forever.* Imagining life without him was devastating.

"Thank you for being here, baking cookies, and somehow making today calm for Lizzie and Timmy." She teared up. "I don't want them to be scared and sad until they need to be."

Grammy nodded.

"Go rest. We'll stay as long as we're helpful." Grammy Sadie turned away and then back. "Kristine called for you as well. She didn't say what she wanted to speak about. She hadn't heard about the explosion and was very upset when I told her."

Kristine. Kay Lynn had forgotten about seeing her at the White Horse last night. It felt like a dream, or more of a nightmare. Hopefully, she would wake up soon and her life would return to normal. But what was normal anymore? They'd already lost Lenny to the war. What if they lost Mitch to the explosion or Kristine to this? She might simply disappear, unable to tell Momma and Poppa. It was too much to think about.

Instead Kay Lynn lay in bed, and willed the telephone to intrude on her rest. *Ring. Ring. Ring.* She pictured walking into the kitchen and hearing Lizzie speaking of thumbprint cookies into the handset.

I'm safe, she imagined Mitch's voice saying once Lizzie handed her the phone.

A chill ran down her spine as she conjured the scene. She didn't allow herself to imagine a knock on the door or a voice other than Mitch's coming through the telephone.

Momma roused her with a cup of tea. She must have fallen asleep. No phone had rung. Kay Lynn stretched as she sat up. "Thanks, Momma."

"Dinner will be ready soon." Momma sat on the edge of the bed. Dinner? *How long had she slept?*

"Poppa Leo and Grammy Sadie will head home after supper. I'd like to stay here with you tonight, with your permission of course."

Touched at Momma's care, Kay Lynn teared up. "Would you?"

"I'll sleep better knowing you can go right to him when they call," Momma replied.

Kay Lynn smiled. That was the dream scenario: Mitch was in a hospital, being tended to. As much as she hoped for that, she also knew he would have called by now if it were possible. She kept making excuses for his silence. Perhaps there were no phone lines working or he was too busy caring for others. She wasn't ready to abandon hope that he was alive.

That evening Lizzie was restless. For the third time that night, Kay Lynn tucked her into bed, kissed her forehead, and wished her sweet dreams. Timmy was sound asleep.

"Hazel," Kay Lynn called. She pointed to the bed. The dog jumped up to Lizzie's side, curled up by her leg, and cast a calm spell. Lizzie's hand traveled across Hazel's soft fur.

Lizzie whispered, "Do you really, really know Daddy is helping? Or are you just saying that so Timmy isn't scared?"

Kay Lynn sighed. "We don't really, really know, because I haven't heard from Daddy."

"I thought so." Lizzie bit her lip. "I'm going to only think the best thoughts, okay?"

"Yes. That's a very good choice if it helps you to feel better."

"It does," Lizzie replied. "If the phone rings in the middle of the night, is that good or bad?"

"We won't know until we hear the news on the other end of the line," Kay Lynn said.

"Can I get up if I hear a knock or the phone rings?" Lizzie asked.

"Yes. But please do your best to sleep. Don't try to stay up like you used to for Santa."

"Santa was pretend; this is real."

Kay Lynn understood. Still, she instructed, "I am going to do my best to sleep well because that will help all of us. Please do the same."

She saw the disappointment in Lizzie's eyes.

"I promise I will wake you if we get news."

"Good or bad?" Lizzie pleaded.

Kay Lynn nodded; her throat was too tight for words.

Kay Lynn picked up *Little Town on the Prairie* and handed it to Lizzie. "Read; let Laura and Mary's story drift you off to sleep. There is no need to borrow trouble."

Kay Lynn hugged her daughter once again. It was an ordinary part of their day, but during this particular embrace, she savored the magnificence of their love.

Nearly a year ago, the night before Mitch left for basic training, she felt the poignancy when he hugged the children in their beds. She was so mindful that it might be their last that her heart hurt. Yesterday, she hadn't given a single thought to their good-night hug, which may have been . . . their final one? Her chest was so constricted it was hard to breathe.

Kay Lynn could hardly bear the fragile nature of life. If she allowed herself, she would see each day as the potential last of something—because it might be. When was the last time she carried Timmy? He'd grown too big for her to lift, but when exactly? Every day brought beginnings and endings, often going unnoticed until much later, if ever.

CHAPTER 19

July 1944

The phone's ringing cut through her sleep. Kay Lynn bolted awake and ran to the kitchen.

She grabbed at the receiver too quickly, knocking it to the ground. She bent over to get it. "Hello, I'm here," she spoke into the black plastic.

"He's alive." Kristine's voice rushed through from the other end.

Exhilaration raised the hair on Kay Lynn's arms.

"I just saw him," her sister continued. "My friend who works at the naval hospital let me in to confirm it's Mitch. He was admitted with burns in the late afternoon yesterday. His eyes were closed, but he squeezed my hand when I told him it was me. I think he knows I was there."

"Oh, my God. Thank you, God. Thank you, Kristine!" Tears streamed down Kay Lynn's face.

Lizzie and Momma rushed into the kitchen.

"He's alive!"

Lizzie wrapped her arms around Kay Lynn and buried her face in her mother's side. Hazel rested against her other leg.

"Can I see him?" Kay Lynn asked Kristine.

"I'll check," Kristine replied. Kay Lynn heard a muffled conversation. She looked out the window; it was still dark. *What time is it?* The clock on the oven read three fifteen.

"Tomorrow night." Kristine was back. "Kelly already bent the rules in letting me come tonight; I hope you understand."

"Of course, I understand. Tomorrow is . . . such a gift. Tell her I'm so grateful," Kay Lynn said. "And, Kristine, thank you for finding him. We were so worried."

"Me too, Sister. Me too. I'm happy for all of us. Our family without Mitch would have been . . . awful."

Kristine's words hit hard. *Without Mitch.* It had been so close. She sank to the floor. Her hand raised above her head, still clinging to the handset.

Momma took the phone from her hand. Lizzie climbed onto her lap, barely fitting. They hugged each other and rocked.

Lizzie pulled back to look her in the face. "He's alive, Mommy; isn't that great?!"

"Yes, it is, Lizzie." Kay Lynn felt her chest loosen. "Now we can breathe again."

She closed her eyes and felt Lizzie against her. She took in a slow, deep breath. Mitch was alive. Her greatest fear hadn't come true. Relief melted her shoulders, only to be met by a new thought.

Burned. His injuries must be severe since he hadn't called himself or even arranged for her to be called. Tears of fear and relief joined together. She let them come. It *was* good news. And she was anxious for what was to come.

Eventually, they returned to bed with Lizzie in hers and Momma in Lizzie's. Kay Lynn never returned to a sound sleep, but she followed her own admonishment to Lizzie to lie quietly. The line between dreams and her imagination was hard to demark. Would their lives be forever different because of Mitch's injuries? There were so many unknowns.

Give me strength for whatever comes.

She found comfort in the prayer, imagining her hand on the redwood.

Every hour of the next day crawled past. She was so exhausted she lay down for a nap, but her mind wouldn't release her to sleep. The children were quiet, sensing the somber mood. She wanted to make the day normal, upbeat, but it was hard to muster the energy. Today *was* a celebration, but she was also bracing for an unknown future.

"Should we have a picnic at the Marina? Walk the pier?" Kay Lynn asked the children.

"Without Daddy?" Lizzie asked.

"We can go again when he's home," Kay Lynn replied.

"Tomorrow?" Timmy asked.

"No. He's too injured to be home tomorrow."

"When will he be home?" Timmy asked.

"We don't know."

"When will we know?" Lizzie asked. "After you see him tonight?"

"We don't even know when we'll know, so stop asking," she scolded. "I'll pack a lunch; you two get yourselves ready to go."

Lizzie slunk away to get her shoes on.

It was beautiful at the Marina, so clear that they had a great view of the Golden Gate Bridge in the distance. The picnic passed the time, and kept the children occupied, but did nothing to soothe Kay Lynn's agitation. What if Mitch had brain damage and wouldn't remember them? Or shell shock? A severe injury might mean he could never work again, walk again. When she thought of the worst, a shell of her husband, she reminded herself not to borrow trouble. She hoped that seeing him would be a comfort more than raise further concerns. She checked her watch. Only an hour had passed. She had to wait five more hours before leaving for the hospital.

Momma and Poppa came with a simple dinner. Kay Lynn had no appetite, and sat through the meal with her mind gummed up. Her parents tended to the children, allowing her to sink into a thick, confused fog.

After supper, Kristine arrived to take her to the Oak Knoll Naval Hospital. Momma would get Lizzie and Timmy to bed. Kristine's friend started her shift at eight o'clock, so they were leaving now, though they didn't know how long they would have to wait before she could take Kay Lynn to see Mitch. She didn't care if she had to wait for hours; she wanted to see him the very first moment she could.

Lizzie kissed both of Kay Lynn's palms. "Those are for Daddy. Make sure he knows they're from me."

Timmy followed suit.

"Do you have the drawings? And the flowers?" he asked.

She looked around. *Where are they?* She just had them.

Kristine said, "They're in your hand. Would you like me to keep track of them?"

Kay Lynn handed them over.

"What does he look like?" Kay Lynn asked her sister as they drove.

Kindness in her voice, Kristine responded, "The right side of his face is entirely covered by gauze. The left side is puffy like Mitch would look if he had the measles, perhaps; his right shoulder and wrist were covered too. It's not as alarming as you might think, but Kelly said the burns are severe under the gauze."

Kay Lynn tried to picture it. He might be asleep, she reminded herself. Would she be allowed to wake him? What if he was in a coma? She shook herself away from that thought by looking at her sister.

It was strange to see Kristine driving with such confidence. When had she learned? Kay Lynn hadn't even noticed.

It was sad they didn't confide in each other. They were close until Timmy was born. If Kay Lynn was honest with herself, she hadn't taken an interest in Kristine after she'd grown into a young woman. Sure, she attended her school concerts and some of her bowling matches, but Kay Lynn didn't even know if Kristine still bowled. She was ashamed to realize her disinterest had contributed to the distance between them.

And now she knew about a huge secret. She didn't have either the energy or the courage to bring up what she'd seen at the White Horse. The unmentionable traveled between them in the car, dividing them like a hard stone wall. They drove the rest of the way in silence, each lost in private thoughts.

Kay Lynn gazed out the window at the scenery that was as blurry as their lives. She took in a deep breath. *This moment. Don't borrow trouble. This moment.*

The hospital was a converted country club, built in the 1920s in the art deco style that was so popular back then. The entryway of the building wasn't designed to be a reception, more like a hallway, but there were cold metal chairs to sit on.

Kristine gave a note to an orderly to bring to her friend, and then they waited. And waited. And waited. It felt an eternity, knowing Mitch was a few floors away. Perhaps lonely. Perhaps in agony. She wouldn't allow herself to think that he might be dying. She telegraphed a message to him, *I'm down here. I'll be there soon.* She wished she had brought a book or her knitting. It hadn't crossed her mind as she prepared to leave, but a distraction would have been welcome.

A young woman with brown hair cut short, maybe pulled into a tight bun, spoke from the open doorway, "Kristine and . . . Kay Lynn?"

Her sister stood up, "Kelly, thank you for doing this again." The two women hugged hello; they knew each other well.

"This way." Kelly looked at Kay Lynn.

"Here." Kristine handed Kay Lynn the pictures and the small bouquet of carnations and statice.

She would have forgotten entirely. "Thank you."

"I'm sorry, I can't allow you to bring any flowers. They're a contamination risk."

Kristine took back the bunch and sat down. Of course she would stay; letting in one person was more than enough, but Kay Lynn hadn't imagined being alone when she saw Mitch.

"Did you injure yourself?" Kelly asked, noting Kay Lynn's limp.

"At birth, apparently," Kay Lynn replied. "I have palsy on my left side."

"I'm sorry." Kelly sounded embarrassed.

Kay Lynn shrugged. "I've never known anything else. Though two fully functioning hands would be handy." She laughed at her own joke.

She asked, "How is Mitch . . . how's my husband doing?"

"We keep him sedated using morphine grains," Kelly told her. "Otherwise, he would be in excruciating pain. Third-degree burns are unbearable."

"Where?"

"The right arm and hand have the most severe burns, but much of his right side has been afflicted. Fortunately, he was facing down, so there are burns on the back of his head, but he was spared burns on his face, and there isn't a risk of losing his sight."

Fortunately. That word was jarring. It was hard to feel lucky when Mitch was sedated in the hospital.

"Will he lose . . . lose his arm?" Kay Lynn asked.

"So far, the sulfa drugs are doing their job," Kelly explained. "They are a true miracle. Have you heard of them?"

Kay Lynn had. Scientists had discovered that beneficial bacteria could halt the infections that once necessitated amputations. The violence of the war had compelled modern medicine to advance significantly in its efforts to preserve lives.

"Here we are." Kelly stopped at an open door, and dropped her voice. "Be very gentle on his right side because his skin is fragile. And don't be concerned if he doesn't rouse. Morphine is a powerful sleep agent."

Kay Lynn looked at the bed. *This is my husband?* Mitch wasn't recognizable in the slightest. His face was just wrong: swollen and misshaped.

"Not that one, sorry," Kelly interrupted. "Two down."

Kay Lynn looked over to the man by the wall. Relief raised the skin on her arms. She recognized her dear husband's face immediately, despite the swelling and the redness. Her heart leapt, with love and fear in equal measures. Mitch looked as Kristine had described, his face partially covered in gauze and his eyes closed. His mouth hung open.

"Can I take his hand?" Kay Lynn asked. "The left one?"

"Yes."

She crossed to the left side of his bed and leaned over. "Mitchy, it's me . . . Kay Lynn."

His hand was clammy and limp. She leaned over and kissed it.

"We love you. The kids made you pictures; they send kisses and hugs—" Her voice broke. He didn't react in any way. She squeezed his hand, hoping to feel him squeeze back as Kristine had. Nothing.

"Has he spoken to you?" Kay Lynn asked Kelly.

"No."

"Nothing?"

Kelly explained, her voice kind, "We haven't allowed the morphine to wear off. The current protocol is to give him seventy-two to ninety-six hours of continuous sedation. As I said, the pain is going to be excruciating."

"How long has he been here?"

"Less than thirty-six hours."

It had seemed an eternity, but the explosion was less than forty-eight hours ago. Kay Lynn took in a deep breath, reminding herself to be patient. She had to endure the uncertainty.

"I'll give you a few minutes while I check on my other patients," Kelly said.

Kay Lynn nodded. "Thank you . . . so very much." Tears burned at the back of her eyes.

"I'm glad I could be helpful. So many families . . . so many men don't have the opportunity to be comforted by a loved one."

Alone with Mitch, Kay Lynn searched for words. She wished the Lord's Prayer meant something to her, but it didn't.

Give me strength; give Mitch strength; give Lizzie and Timmy strength. Was she asking the tree? God? Herself? She didn't know, but it felt right.

Kay Lynn put her hand on Mitch's chest. His heartbeat was slow, steady, and strong. It gave her true hope that inside he was fine. Her Mitch would come back to her and the children.

"I love you, Mitch. I'm grateful for our home and our family. You rest and heal, knowing we're waiting for you, and whatever happens we'll face it together.

"These kisses are from Lizzie." She kissed the fabric over his heart twice.

"These kisses are from Timmy." She did it again.

"These are from me." She pressed two long kisses on his chest.

Kay Lynn rested her right palm over his heart, telegraphing love and strength.

Kelly interrupted her prayers. "I'm sorry, but I have to take you back to Kristine." The young woman looked near to tears.

"You have given me such a gift; please don't feel bad that it has to end. Can I leave these for him?" She held out the papers with drawings and birthday wishes from Timmy and Lizzie.

Kelly took the sheets and looked between them, her head moving from side to side as she studied them for some time. When she eventually looked up, there were tears streaming down her face.

The young woman spoke, "Sorry. Sometimes the reality for these soldiers hits me hard." She cleared her throat, but her voice was still tight. "I don't know what's worse—remembering the loved ones who are worried about my patients or not thinking of them at all. I will put these in his file now, and in the morning I'll ask the doctor if we can tape them on the wall."

She led Kay Lynn down the stairs and back to the waiting area. Kristine and Kelly hugged goodbye. A handshake seemed cold given their interactions. Kay Lynn opened her arms to offer a hug; Kelly seemed to welcome it.

Kay Lynn paused before they broke entirely apart. She took hold of Kelly's arms and looked the nurse in her eyes. "Thank you. For what you do for my Mitch, and for the care you give to all of these soldiers. I can see it's painful to you, but you're saving their lives. What a treasure you are."

Kelly took a deep breath and nodded. Like the young man at the checkpoint, Kay Lynn suddenly noticed Kelly's age—early twenties, perhaps, just like Kristine. Too young, Kay Lynn thought, to bear the weight of this heartbreaking duty for the nation.

CHAPTER 20

July 1944

Three days later the knock came. Two young men in uniform handed her a note. If Kristine hadn't found Mitch, she would have been desperate to read it, but she already knew what it said: Her husband had been burned in an accident and was recovering in a military hospital. A full recovery was expected, and she would be notified when he was released.

Kay Lynn hadn't visited Mitch again, though Kelly called that morning with a brief update. They'd lowered the morphine, and he was aware of his situation. Kelly had told Mitch about Kay Lynn's visit, and he got emotional when she showed him the pictures the children had drawn for him. He knew he wasn't forgotten, which gave her a measure of comfort.

She should be typing up a manuscript, but she kept making too many typos, causing her to waste paper. There was no point in attempting to work when she was this upset, though she really needed the pay to buy groceries. It was impossible to live solely on the salary the navy paid Mitch. Military wages might have been sufficient for a family in other parts of the nation, but not in San Francisco and its close neighbors.

Kay Lynn told the children she was going shopping, and she would, eventually, but first she went to her parents' house on Woolsey Street. She wanted to be somewhere safe and comfortable, where she would be taken care of.

The warmth and smell of her childhood kitchen was immediately soothing. Kristine left after a cursory greeting.

"Are you two still at odds?" Momma asked.

"I have no quarrel with Kristine. I'm forever grateful to her and feel I owe her a debt I can never repay," Kay Lynn said. Her voice raised with more anger than she wanted to express to her mother. "I told her as much, but I can't force her to stop avoiding me. I'm sorry, Momma."

Momma sighed. "I thought we were a family that came together in hard times." Her voice broke. "But I'm wrong."

"Oh, Momma. Kristine supported me in the most important way she could: she found Mitch."

Momma teared up.

"Maybe sometimes support is being with each other and sometimes it's giving each other privacy," Kay Lynn ventured.

"I fear she's pregnant and isn't telling us," Momma responded.

Suddenly, Momma's concern took on a whole new meaning.

"Like you were?"

Momma nodded. "I thought I was so grown up, able to fix my error on my own. Well, with my cousin's help . . . Elena and I were so young . . . we thought we were adults."

Hearing she was a mistake cut deep. They'd never spoken about it directly, but she knew Momma didn't want her. She swallowed a ball of shame, and uncertainty.

Should she tell Momma what she knew about Kristine? She wasn't hiding a pregnancy. Kay Lynn weighed her choice heavily. If she told her mother, she'd feel like she was betraying Kristine. On the other hand, it might reassure her mother to know Kristine might be . . . Kay Lynn didn't even know the word. Homosexual, perhaps? Could Momma accept her, or would this revelation cause a rift that could never be healed?

Suddenly Momma's hand flew to her mouth. "I'm sorry." Tears glistened in her eyes. "*You* are not a mistake. You're one of the best parts of my life, from the moment you were born, and yet being pregnant with you felt, well . . . it's complicated." Momma took Kay Lynn's hand. "I hope you can understand."

From the moment she was born. That wasn't true. Momma was trying to make her feel better, but she knew she *wasn't wanted.* Nevertheless, she didn't want her mother to regret her honesty. "Complicated. Momma, I do understand complicated. When I missed my monthlies last year right after Mitch enlisted, I desperately wanted my menses to come, and then when it came, I was sad. That child would have been three months old. Is it strange that I know that?"

"Not at all." Momma shook her head. "I miscarried after Kristine, in 1925. She was two. You were past nine."

"Momma, I had no idea!"

"Of course you didn't. I wouldn't tell such a thing to a child. He would have been nineteen in February. I made up a birthday for him and a name: Benjamin, Benny."

A wave of memory swelled. "Did you light a candle for him on his birthday?!"

"I did for a few years. It seemed Catholic, but it also felt right. You remember?"

"There was a time I thought lighting a candle was part of Valentine's Day, but then it wasn't, so I thought maybe I dreamt it. Strange what I remember from childhood."

Momma agreed. "I wonder what our Timmy and Lizzie will remember from this war?"

"May it end soon," Kay Lynn said, her words carrying a tone that resembled a prayer. "The paper predicts it's coming to a close, but I've read those words too many times to believe them."

Kay Lynn's voice tightened. "I don't think Timmy will remember Mitch without injuries. Perhaps it won't matter, but somehow that seems heartbreaking. And he only knows Lenny from a photo."

"It's going to be difficult to bear this and act as if nothing has changed," Momma replied.

"Are you two speaking philosophy this early in the morning?" Grammy Sadie asked, joining them in the kitchen.

"What do you think, Grammy Sadie?" Kay Lynn asked. "How do we bear life's sorrows and act as if nothing has changed?"

"We don't," the elder replied.

Kay Lynn must have looked confused.

Grammy Sadie said, "It is a dishonor to love to pretend you are not hurt by the changes—the losses. Don't dishonor love." Her voice was filled with sorrow.

"Has something happened, Grammy Sadie?" Kay Lynn asked.

"Maggie's son was killed in the explosion at Port Chicago." Grammy sounded tired, angry.

Momma sucked in her breath. "Billy?"

Grammy nodded. "The funeral is tomorrow at their new congregation: Saint Paul AME in Berkeley."

"What time do we need to be there?" Momma was on the verge of tears.

"Eleven."

Momma put her head down on the table. Kay Lynn searched for words, but none came. She patted her mother's arm. Grammy Sadie took Momma's hand. Momma reached for Kay Lynn's, and they completed a circle of sorrow. All over their nation, and the world, horrid news was being borne. She imagined for a moment how Maggie and Naomi were feeling. Her heart clenched in empathy.

Kay Lynn had barely dodged the worst outcome imaginable: a slight change in circumstances, and it would have been Mitch's funeral tomorrow. Kay Lynn's heart hurt so much it was as if she were being stabbed, but it was only her own bodily reaction to the tragic complexity of life in the midst of a terrible world war. As if there could be any other kind of war.

Kay Lynn left her parents' home feeling worse than when she had arrived. She walked up to *her* tree, a necessary detour before shopping at Star Grocery. Resting her hand and head on the sturdy trunk, she asked for strength. *And patience* popped into her mind? Soul? Heart? She didn't know where these urges came from or where they landed. She knew only that they were true. She needed patience—and the perspective of a redwood tree that had been growing for longer than her grandmother had been alive.

In the market Kay Lynn walked past shelves dotted with voids where supply couldn't keep up with demand. At the meat counter she asked for a pound of chuck. At least she could make a nice meal for the children.

"Sorry, ma'am," the butcher replied. "We're all out."

Kay Lynn felt her anger rise up. "It was in the paper *this morning* that you had a special on chuck!"

"Yes, ma'am. And we kept to our promise of only one pound per customer, but we've sold out."

"You shouldn't promise something you can't deliver!" she hissed.

Kay Lynn stormed out of the store empty-handed. *Had people heard her?* She was embarrassed to be so upset. Rationing and low stock was commonplace; it was petty to let it affect her so deeply and shameful to take it out on the butcher. They had plenty of food; it didn't matter that there was no meat she could afford.

Kay Lynn forced herself to take deep breaths as she walked, and by the time she got home, she'd settled her body.

She opened the door, looked down expecting to see Hazel in the entryway, but it was empty. She scanned the space between the entryway and the living room, her gaze landing on the flower pattern on the edge of the carpet. She flashed on the day of the explosion. Her heart raced once again.

Mitch is fine, or fine enough, she thought, trying to calm herself. *Hazel is out with the children. They will all be home soon.*

CHAPTER 21

July 1944

The children returned home for lunch, but Hazel wasn't with them. They'd left her at home when they went out, and she must have gone to find them. After eating, they scoured the neighborhood for her. Kay Lynn could hear them calling out, their voices fading into the distance as they walked further afield. They returned an hour or so later without a canine companion.

"She always comes back eventually," Lizzie reassured Timmy with the same words and in the same tone Kay Lynn had spoken to her many times.

That night Kay Lynn slept poorly, feeling Hazel's absence in addition to Mitch's. It had been months, maybe even a year since Hazel had been away overnight. She ached for the comfort of her companion resting at her side and was horrified to think of her scared and alone. If the small dog tried to get across Grove or Ashby, she may have been injured or killed. Each time she pictured her whimpering in pain by the side of the road, she forced herself to imagine a child taking the dog into their safe home, excited to have a new pet. But even the thought of her living with a new family was sad. She'd grown to love Hazel and appreciate her steady companionship. The mere thought of writing to the Fujiokas to tell them they lost their beloved dog was stomach turning.

The next morning Hazel was still at large. Timmy suggested they make signs to post around the neighborhood. Lizzie helped her brother form letters, with just the right touch of instruction and encouragement. He was getting the hang of holding a pencil. They left with their signs and some thumbtacks to post them on the telephone poles.

Oh, God, please bring Hazel and Mitch home soon. Kay Lynn was shocked by her specific request of a god she wasn't sure about, but it was the deepest longing of her heart. She scanned the headlines in the newspaper, hoping for a distraction from her own life. The good news was that the government was guaranteeing easy credit for homes, autos, and appliances, a sign the war was ending. Otherwise, the paper was filled with disheartening news about the explosion.

It had only been a few days since the incident, but the navy already declared they would build a larger, permanent weapons depot. So much for the war coming to a close. Would Mitch have to return if he recovered? The military was investigating the reasons for the Port Chicago explosion. Would Mitch be part of the investigation?

She was borrowing trouble again. *This day,* she reminded herself. *Just face this day.*

On this day she would be grateful her husband was alive, she would prepare for the hour when he came home, and she would count her many blessings even among the pains.

"Are you *sure* it is a kindness?" Lizzie challenged. "Maybe Hazel will be back, and then we will have caused them hurt for *no* reason!"

"Lizzie, it's been a week. Hazel would have come back by now if she could. We must tell Donna."

Lizzie burst into tears. "Right now, she thinks Hazel is happy with us. This letter will ruin her life."

It's already been ruined, Kay Lynn thought.

Lizzie read Kay Lynn's face and succumbed to the inevitable. She put her pencil to the paper and wrote word after word quickly, ending each sentence with a hard dot.

She pulled her head up; red-eyed, she read,

> Dear, dear, dear Donna.
>
> I am so, so, so, so (thousan times) sorry.
> Hazel is missing. We tride so hard to
> find her. We called around the naybor-
> hood as soon as she was gone, but she
> didn't come back. Then we made signs
> and put them evrywhere, but she is still
> gone. Mommy even went to the Berkeley
> Humane to see if she was there. We love
> her so much, and I know you do too. We
> like to think a nice family has her.
>
> My daddy is heeling and will be home
> next week we think. I hope your dad is
> fine in AFRICA!!!!! He will have sum good
> storys for us when he comes home.
> Love (a thousan times),
> Lizzie

"That's a very sweet note. Well said, Lizzie."

"I still don't want to send it to her," Lizzie replied, pouting like she was three.

"Me either, but it's only right that they know. Where's Timmy's picture?"

Lizzie handed over the five-year-old's drawing. The patch of dark scribble on the shoulder made it clear it was Hazel, but the proportions were what you would expect from a boy who was about to start kindergarten. His crooked heart was especially endearing.

"Thank you. I will write my note to Mrs. Fujioka, and we can walk this to the postbox this afternoon."

She sat down at her desk.

> Dear Kimiko,
>
> I write with sad news upon sad news. It is entirely unfair that I have to burden you with anything disturbing. But I just told Lizzie that it is a kindness to let you know, even though we are ashamed and embarrassed.

Kay Lynn felt tears form. She was glad her children could only see her back.

> Somehow we lost Hazel. We love her so much. She is very dear to me and a comfort. I hope you know that. I would never ever want anything bad to come to her. Every night I pray we will hear her scratch at the door or bark in the front yard. It's a constant longing of my heart. But after a week, I fear she's dead. I couldn't even fulfill my promise to take care of her. I don't know how you can forgive me, and I understand that you may never trust me again.
>
> It's just that I have been so distracted by Mitch. He is still in the hospital. They don't know

when he will be home or what he will be able to do.
He's still at risk of a stroke from blood clots. I'm not
allowed to visit or speak with him. I make up stories
in my head about how it will be when he gets home.
He has both legs? He has one leg? Will he use a
wheelchair? For a short time or forever? A walker?
Canes? If he can walk, can he climb steps? Will he
be able to work? I have so many questions, and no
one has the answers. So it is left to me to plan for
an unknown life.

Which leads me to my last sad news. I am closing our business. I wish I could say it was a well-
thought-out choice, but I looked up one day and
realized I hadn't typed any summer session papers
and I hadn't given any thought to advertising at
all. Most of our old clients have graduated, and I
have done nothing to cultivate new ones.

I am desperate for money. I don't know how I
lost track of it. Mitch's military salary doesn't go
far enough AT ALL. The government is lying when
they say it is enough for frugal women. I am frugal.
Truly I am.

Somehow we—I—am down to only one cli-
ent: Richard Cousineau. Our annoying, but loyal,
geologist. I'll type any papers he sends my way, but
I can't face what it takes to get more clients. I can't
be nice to people. Is that the saddest thing you've
ever heard?

I had a terrible visit with Mitch's parents last
week. They criticized everything about my home
and children. His mother suggested that he go con-
valesce in Santa Monica rather than come home to

Berkeley to "take some of the burden off" me. As if I can't take care of him. I'm well aware of how severe his injuries are. His wounds will need constant monitoring, and his bandages will need to be changed. I'm fully capable of taking care of my own husband despite what his horrible mother believes. If she really wanted to be helpful, she would provide us a loan or move here for a time. Can you imagine that she actually thought he and I would agree to him being away from our family for even longer than is necessary?

I told her not to mention the possibility to Mitch when she wrote to him, but she did. I was so furious that I said to her face that she was no longer welcome to stay in our house. If she wants to see her son, she can stay in a hotel, but I don't need her attitude in my home.

My parents have been marvelous. Not only have they helped with the kids, and told us to pause payments on our car loan, but they offered me a job. The pay is consistent, and I won't be responsible for drumming up any work. I don't have to be nice to anyone, which is good because I have such a short fuse.

As you well know, I never, ever wanted to join their accounting business. Never say never. My words from five years ago are being thrown back in my face. I hate being so dependent on them, but it is for the best. They SAY they need me because they have lost SO many men since the war started.

I can't believe I'm asking you to feel sorry for me. I have a house. My children are safe. Mitch is alive.

*I think the saddest part about my life is that if
someone were making a book about it, I wouldn't be
the main character. Does anyone remember Ma in
"Little House on the Prairie"? She's just there, kind
and stable, but invisible compared to charming Pa.*
    *I am way too full of self-pity. Please don't tell
anyone.*
    I miss you.
    Kay Lynn

She exhaled when she finished writing. She could hear the kids
playing Go Fish at the dining room table. She reread what she wrote.
It was all true—and pathetic and self-indulgent.

Kay Lynn held up the note in her left hand; with her right she
tore it down the middle. She took those two halves and tore them
into little pieces. She swept the bits of paper into her trash can and
then wrote another letter.

Dear Kimiko,

*I am sad to add any burden to your life. I've come to
have such great affection for Hazel that I'm heartbroken for myself as well as you that she has gone missing. The kids called for her, put up signs, and I even
ventured to Berkeley Humane to see if she had been
rescued by them. We have had no luck in finding her.
I comfort myself and the children with the hope that a
family has taken her in to love her as we have.*
    *I expect you have heard about the Port Chicago
explosion. Mitch was severely injured, but not killed.
I fluctuate between gratitude for his life and despair
at his long recovery. His right side is terribly burned.*

*Before sulfa drugs they would have amputated, but
he seems to be fending off infection and regrowing
healthy skin. I am grateful for advances in medicine.*

*We expect he will come home next week. The
time in the hospital has been exhausting, but caring for him here will be its own challenge.*

*My other sad news that I must share with you
is that I will be ending our business. My mother
and father have offered me a position that will be
more consistent and pay better. I never wanted to
be a bookkeeper. I left that to Mitch and them. But
they are in need of workers, and I am in need of
income. I delivered my final typed paper last week
to our fussy Richard Cousineau. Perhaps when the
war is over, and we have returned to our lives, we
can open our business again.*

*I pray for you, Ken, Donna, George, and Missy
(in my Unitarian way) every night. I wish we could
have kept Hazel safe until your return. But please
know that she was in no way a burden to me. I've
surprised myself by coming to love her dearly.*

Kay Lynn

Kay Lynn folded up the letter, added it to the addressed envelope,
and walked out the back door to mail it. Ever since Hazel had disappeared, she couldn't bear to use the front door. The living room was
an unbearably painful reminder of the day Mitch was injured and
her missing companion, and she didn't need her emotions to be any
more stirred up.

CHAPTER 22

August 1944

Kay Lynn sat at the edge of their bed. She entwined her fingers with Mitch's. Their strong hands connected; their weak ones lay across from each other. It was strange how they were a type of mirror now.

"What?" he asked.

"I can't just take delight in my husband being home after he was nearly killed?"

"You can, but . . ."

He was right: she did have something to tell him.

"Your commanding officer is on his way. That call was to confirm you were home."

One blue eye got wide; the other was still covered to protect the burns on the back of his head.

"What does he want?"

She shook her head. "Did he visit you at Oak Knoll?"

"Not once," he replied. "I imagine he wants to speak about the investigation."

Kay Lynn nodded. "Would you like to be in bed when he comes?"

"Absolutely not," he replied. "I don't care how hard it is; I am meeting that man in the living room."

"Get to work, seaman!" Kay Lynn said, rising to get his uniform and sounding more cheerful than she felt.

After he was dressed, Kay Lynn guided Mitch to the living room. He leaned hard on Kay Lynn as he sank down onto the couch. He fell the last six inches, just as she had when she heard about the explosion. Between his feet she saw the red flowers on the edge of the rug, setting off an alarming aftershock in her heart. She saw herself leaning over, sobbing like she was watching a movie.

She wished she could go back and tell her past self, *It's okay. He lives.*

But she'd also have to tell herself that he'd been changed and they didn't know if he would ever be the same again.

Patience, she reminded herself. He was in their living room, which was true progress and a joy when she considered the alternatives.

Kay Lynn patted his shoulder. He wiped his brow, sweaty from the effort of getting to this room. He tried to smile at her.

She went to the kitchen to prepare . . . *coffee?* Coffee was dear, but this was an important visitor. Before she made a final decision, she heard a knock at the door and went to answer it.

"Hello, ma'am," the tall man greeted her.

Irrationally, her heart raced. She flashed back to the day two men in uniforms stood in the doorway with an envelope. She swallowed her fear.

"Come in." She pointed to the chair by Mitch.

"Would you like some coffee?"

"No, thank you, ma'am," he replied. "I won't be here long enough to enjoy your hospitality, but thank you for the offer." She was glad she hadn't used some of their precious beans.

Her husband struggled to stand. She didn't help him, knowing her assistance wouldn't be welcome.

"I'll leave you to it," she said, and left the room.

She strained to hear their conversation from the dining room, but couldn't make out any words. After a few sentences there was silence. She waited; when no voices resumed after a minute or so, she peeked into the room. The CO was gone.

"He left already?" she asked Mitch.

He nodded. His neck was glossy. From pain? Fear?

"What does he want?" she asked.

"I think he came to threaten me."

Her stomach dropped.

"He said, 'When you're asked about work conditions, I'm sure you will say that safety was our top priority at all times. I'd hate for you to lose your GI benefits when you're injured like this.'"

"Why would you lose your benefits?" Kay Lynn asked.

"I believe he was threatening a dishonorable discharge if I testify that I was concerned about safety and expressed that concern to *him* as far back as last fall." Mitch's voice was shaky.

"I see. Did you ask him what he meant?" she asked. "What else did he say?"

"That was it." He exhaled hard. "Except to say he'd show himself out."

"What are you going to do?"

He leaned his head back and sighed again. Eventually, he asked, "What do you think?"

She teared up. Those benefits were dear. They were struggling to make ends meet with them. Then she thought about the fifty Negro men who refused to go back to loading ammunition without better training and safety measures. She thought of Cousin Naomi's grandson killed by the explosion.

"I think if those Negro men can risk being court-martialed and sent to prison for speaking up, then you can keep your honor by telling the truth even at the risk of a dishonorable discharge."

"Me too," he replied.

A few hours later the call came ordering Mitch to testify the next day. Kay Lynn's hand shook hard as she wrote down the Oakland address where he needed to appear.

The jostling of the covers woke her the next morning. It was still dark outside. She felt Mitch struggling to sit up.

"Good morning," she croaked, still lying on her pillow.

"Sorry to wake you early," he replied.

"Better early than late on a day like today." She put on a false cheer.

She rose, brought his crutches to his bedside, and started their morning routine. She was glad to get Mitch out of bed and ready before the kids awoke.

"Where's Daddy?" Timmy asked as he came into the kitchen, his eyebrows high and his voice panicked.

"He's in the living room," Kay Lynn told her son. His face relaxed.

Mitch was dressed in his uniform, resting on the couch from the exertion of getting ready.

"Can we eat our cornflakes in there with him?" Lizzie asked.

Kay Lynn shook her head. "Let him rest."

Lizzie nodded without arguing. She poured cereal and milk into a bowl for Timmy and then another for herself. They sat close together, their heads nearly touching. Timmy was explaining something to Lizzie, maybe a dream.

Kay Lynn's heart filled with love and a fierce sorrow. She desperately wanted to protect her children from feeling scared, but danger lurked so close that fear was their first response to any change. They no longer feared being attacked in Berkeley, but the potential danger to those they loved was constant. She swallowed down her emotions.

Timmy and Lizzie would stay with her parents at their office while Kay Lynn drove Mitch to the hearing. Mitch scooted down the stairs by sitting on his bottom and lowering himself tread by tread. She'd never been more grateful to have a car and her driver's license. Mitch couldn't take a streetcar with his injuries, and she didn't have to go begging for a ride or to borrow a car. She was ashamed that they'd stopped payments to her parents, but they said they could make do without the money for now. Their business was steady enough that she believed them. But it weighed on her, and she was determined she would make good on their agreement as soon as possible.

Despite her nerves, the building was easy to find, and she parked close. Mitch hobbled up the stairs using her arm and the handrail for support. She returned to the car for his wheelchair and lugged it to the entrance at the top of the stairs. She pushed him along the corridors to the hearing room guarded by a single young soldier.

Mitch gave his name. The blond man in uniform nodded and told them to wait by the doors.

She sat down on one of the folding chairs, the cold metal made a chill run up Kay Lynn's spine. Down the hall, a clock read nine fifty.

"We made it on time," she exhaled.

Mitch nodded. He ran through his hand exercises, barely moving each finger on his right hand in turn like he was considering playing a piano. His ring finger and pinkie wanted to move in unison. He held his pinkie with his left hand and wiggled the ring finger alone.

She wished she had brought her book or her knitting to pass the time.

"I'll wait here while you're in the hearing. How long do you think you'll be there?"

"You know as much as I do." Mitch sounded annoyed.

Kay Lynn closed her eyes and took in a deep breath. There was nothing to do but wait. *And pray,* Grammy Sadie's voice echoed in her mind.

What could she pray for? She took in a deep breath again. *Give me patience. And faith.* Another chill ran through her. *Faith.* She didn't know exactly what that meant, but her body longed for it.

She opened her eyes and looked at Mitch. She wanted faith that they could protect their children and be loving through whatever came next. Mitch had come so far. He could have died if he'd been standing four feet in any direction. They should be grateful, but they were each impatient in their own way.

Mitch was frustrated by the limitations of his body. It hurt for him to bear weight on his right foot. He wanted his right hand to function as it had. He worked at his exercise constantly, but no one could tell him if he would ever be able to write with his dominant hand again.

She longed to know what to expect in the future. Would he recover enough to work? Would he need caretaking for weeks? Months? Forever? The doctors said it was too soon to answer those questions.

Both of them were deeply unsettled, uncertain they could manage whatever was to come and looking for answers that didn't exist.

Faith. Give me faith that we can manage whatever the future holds.

The door opened. A soldier walked out, looked at Mitch, and cocked his head with an audible tsk.

"Good luck," the stocky man said.

"Thanks," Mitch replied.

The guard held the door open. Kay Lynn started to stand, but her husband waved her away. He maneuvered the wheelchair, using his left hand back and forth on each wheel, slowly pushing himself through the doorway, determination on his face.

Kay Lynn glanced at the clock. It was just past ten o'clock. They'd only been waiting for ten minutes, though it felt much longer. If he finished by eleven o'clock, they might get home in time for her to do an hour of bookkeeping before lunch. Since Mitch had returned, her parents gave her work to do from home. Most days she managed to get in three or four hours of paid labor.

To save on cooking time, she'd taken to making a large casserole for them to eat over many days. Cold cereal for breakfast and sandwiches for lunch reduced time in the kitchen. Lizzie was old enough to wash dishes, and Timmy took out the trash. All the other chores fell on her. She was exhausted by the work, but more so by her fears about their future and their finances.

The door opened again. Mitch slowly rolled himself out. Kay Lynn looked at the clock; it was ten thirteen.

"How . . . ?" she started to ask, but stopped when he shook his head.

She helped him to the car in reverse. Once they were alone she asked about his interview.

He sounded tired. "Fine. Terrible. They were more focused on the events of the day than the training and practices that might have led to the explosion. I was honest about my concerns, but it didn't lead to more questions. It seemed they were looking for certain answers."

She patted his arm and said, "Whatever happens, we'll be glad you were honest."

She hoped she was right.

"And now we wait," he replied with a sigh.

She nodded. *Waiting.* She'd had enough of waiting. She feared it would never end.

A week after his interview the paper reported that the investigation into the explosion had been concluded. The navy determined there was no malfeasance or neglect on the part of the military. The accident was due to the carelessness of the loaders.

Kay Lynn felt bile rise in her throat as she read the article. She knew that the soldiers had insufficient training because Mitch had shared more than she wanted to know about the practices at the depot. Hundreds of men had died, and even more were injured. Businesses in Contra Costa were shut because of damages from the explosion. But there were no recommended changes to the practice of loading ships because the navy concluded that loss of life and property was simply the cost of war. *The cost of war?* Perhaps it was, but she didn't know what was right anymore.

In late August the paper reported that the House of Representatives approved five-thousand-dollar payments to each soldier injured at Port Chicago. That news would have assuaged her fears about their immediate finances if she were confident of Mitch's good standing. But she wasn't.

A few days later the Senate lowered the amount of compensation from five thousand dollars to three thousand dollars because most of the injured were Negro. Their potential safety net was being frayed. If Mitch received it, three thousand dollars would see them through a few years, but wouldn't replace Mitch's wages for the rest of his life. To be realistic, she had to plan for a future where he never worked again.

Each time she looked through the mail, her heart pounded because she feared she would find a letter from the navy saying Mitch was dishonorably discharged. She breathed in relief each time an envelope came with Mitch's disability.

The close proximity of the machinery of war was a two-edged sword. Kristine was able to build ships while living at home. And Mitch had been assigned near enough to commute. But the military's presence in the Bay Area had driven up the cost of food, housing, transportation, and goods well beyond the national rise in prices. Kay Lynn was less and less confident each month that they would be able to make rent or buy healthy food, even with her work.

When the mutiny trial against the Port Chicago 50, as the newspaper called the Negro soldiers who refused to return to work loading munitions, ended with convictions, she felt sick once again. Those men were going to jail because they wanted to be safe. Was she entirely naïve to want her government to protect soldiers? Perhaps not on the shores of other nations, but was it too much to want that in the boundary of the United States?

Kay Lynn was a constant jumble of emotions. Mitch was alive. For that she was thankful every day. But she was so tired. She remembered being patient and kind to her children and feeling joyful and safe. It was hard to imagine ever being that way or feeling those things again.

CHAPTER 23

Fall 1944

Somehow Halloween had become a complicated day in Kay Lynn's life. In addition to her daily responsibilities, she had to concern herself with costumes for her children and treats for the children who would knock on their door that evening, visit Nana Lisbeth's grave with Grammy Sadie and Momma, and volunteer at the Halloween carnival at school. She could push off cleaning, laundry, and shopping, but Mitch's medical care couldn't be postponed for a day.

"You're certain you'll be fine by yourself?" Kay Lynn asked Mitch again.

"Stop asking me," he snapped. "I've told you, I want to stay here alone. Even if I fall to the ground and can't get up, I won't die."

"I'll come back in time to get you lunch. Then we'll do your shower and change your bandages before I go to the Halloween carnival."

"You should have told them no when they asked you to volunteer," he said. "Don't you have enough to do today without the burden of handing out candy at a children's carnival?"

"It means *so* much to Lizzie that I'll be one of the mothers there, helping out," she replied.

He shrugged.

She teared up. "Last Halloween was one of the best days of my life."

"Me too," he replied.

She'd been so naïve with no idea of the danger that lurked stateside.

Kay Lynn left through the back door to pick up her mother and grandmother for their visit to Nana Lisbeth on the anniversary of her death. She was halfway down the block when she realized she hadn't said goodbye, let alone given Mitch a hug. She was so lost in her own worries that she often forgot the social niceties.

With a car, they were parked near Nana Lisbeth's grave ten minutes after they left the Grands. How had she managed to fit everything in when she was using streetcars for transportation?

Kay Lynn hid her impatience as best as she could. Rushing Grammy Sadie through the visit with her mother was unkind. She'd forewarned them she wasn't able to stay long enough for a picnic lunch. While she would have welcomed sitting on the ground, soaking in the sun, she didn't have the time for that luxury today.

As always, they stopped at Jordan Wallace's grave before heading home. Kay Lynn's heart flew into her throat when she saw the new headstone.

WILLIAM HAYS

HE GAVE HIS LIFE FOR OUR FREEDOM

AUGUST 20, 1925–JULY 17, 1944

He was not yet nineteen.

Grammy Sadie touched Jordan's gravestone and said a private prayer, repeating the ritual with Billy's. Kay Lynn felt compelled to follow suit. Her hand rested on the corner of the granite stone. She opened up her heart: *Bless you. Thank you. I'm sorry.*

A nagging question bubbled up.

"Grammy Sadie," Kay Lynn asked, "if Naomi is your cousin, is Jordan your aunt?"

Grammy Sadie gave a sad smile. "Our two families have many complicated ties. Naomi married my first cousin Willie. Your mother and Maggie are second cousins."

"So Billy is my third cousin?" Kay Lynn asked, not certain why it mattered to her.

"Yes," Grammy Sadie replied.

It could have been Mitch's headstone they were visiting instead of her distant relative. She swallowed hard. They stood, soaking in the bright sun, each lost in her own rumination.

"We were so hopeful that racial prejudice would not follow them to Oakland." Grammy Sadie's voice shook as she said, "I fear harmony and respect between the races is much further away than I'd believed."

Grammy Sadie's sad, true words sunk Kay Lynn's spirits even lower. She wanted to argue or reassure, but there was no point in platitudes.

"It's up to us to honor their memories by keeping that hope alive," Momma replied. "Nana Lisbeth and Miss Jordan wouldn't want us to do any less."

"Grateful for the strides they made and hopeful for the strides to be made," Grammy Sadie replied.

"Indeed," Momma replied.

Grateful. Kay Lynn considered the word as she walked back to the car, but she wasn't able to conjure that emotion; instead, she only felt overwhelmed by the complexity of it all. Was it right to have a children's costume parade when young men were killing each other and families were being bombed? Was it harmful to continue with the small joys in life while such horror was reigning in other places? What was she doing for the strides that needed to be made?

As she drove to the Grands house, her thoughts turned to Mitch. They'd been gone longer than she expected. Had he been able to care for himself for so long? By the time she got home, she feared what she might find.

When she opened the front door, she was instantly faced with Hazel's absence. She'd been so focused on Mitch that she forgot to go in the back to avoid the pain of not being welcomed home by her dear dog.

Mitch was in the living room, listening to the radio, a pen grasped in his fingers and a pad of paper resting on his lap. His forehead shone with perspiration. She glanced at the paper. She could make out his name and their address. His letters were coming along.

"As you can see, I'm alive," he said. "I only had to call the fire department twice to get me up off the floor."

"Very funny." She smiled. "Look at you, getting a glass of water from the kitchen to the living room."

"Call me Mr. Competent," he replied. "My next trick will be showering all by myself."

"No rush," she replied. She leaned over and kissed him, her hand cradling his warm cheek. She looked into his eyes. "I'm glad it went well."

"Me too," he replied. "No need for constant companionship anymore. I survived nearly two hours on my own." He shrugged.

"That's a big improvement," she said. "The doctors say we have to be patient."

Truly he had come far, but he had a long way to go before he was able to contribute to the running of the household. It was hard on both of them.

"There was a call while you were gone," he said, his voice carrying the weight of distressing news. "Your grandmother is quite ill."

"Oh." Kay Lynn's heart tingled. This news wasn't surprising, but it hit hard. "I can't . . . I don't . . . How can I possibly go to San Francisco for a visit with . . ." She waved her hand around the room.

"You'll regret it if you don't," he replied.

She considered, weighing the options. Driving to San Francisco, leaving him alone for hours. She could go while the kids were at school, but what if Mitch had an emergency? But missing the final chance to pay respect and love to Grandmother Barrow felt wrong too. Maybe Mitch could go with her even though it was a lot of work to get him out of the house and into the passenger seat. Could he wait in the car for her?

"You know I'm able to work the phone, don't you?" he said. "I can walk to the kitchen by myself. Your parents are five minutes away and would come at a moment's notice."

She stared at him. It would be hours. Would he really be all right? It was scary to imagine, but also liberating, and perhaps a necessary step.

"Tomorrow?" she asked.

He nodded.

"I'll tell my parents. That I won't be working . . . and that you'll call if necessary."

"Please thank them for me," he said.

"My family may be 'complicated' but we do take care of each other," she shot off as she walked into the kitchen.

"You're never going to let me live that down, are you?" he yelled across the house.

"Don't know why I would," she yelled back as she stepped on something wet. There were splashes of water across the floor. She wiped it up before calling her parents.

She drove away soon after the children had left for school. Lizzie had argued that she should get to visit Grandmother Barrow too, but Kay Lynn stood firm in the face of Lizzie's pleas. She wanted to say good-bye to her grandmother without being concerned about her child.

Before hitting the bridge she stopped at the service station. Kay Lynn studied the map while the attendant filled the tank with gas, put air in the tires, and checked the radiator. She knew the route, but wanted to be certain. She kept the map spread out on the passenger seat, reminding herself that if she made a wrong turn, she would pull over and get back on track. Her toll money sat in a cup where she could easily reach it.

It was smooth driving to the Bay Bridge. She ignored the view as she drove, since it wouldn't be safe to glance away from the road, but it was a beautiful fall day. The fog had even burned off in the city.

When she reached San Francisco, she parked on a flat street and walked up Nob Hill to Grandmother Barrow's home. The house was cool, dark, and eerily quiet. Hannah led her up creaky stairs to the old woman's bedroom.

"I told her you were coming, though I'm not certain what she understands," Hannah explained.

Kay Lynn crossed to the side of the bed. The room was so dark that she barely made out the small, still figure under the old silk bedspread. The door closed with a click. Kay Lynn looked back at it. Hannah was gone; they were alone.

Did Grandmother Barrow want her here? Where was her family? Should she sit? She looked around; there wasn't a chair, and sitting on the bed would be too intimate, so she stood.

Kay Lynn studied the thin, drawn-in face. She wasn't recognizable. She reached out to touch the woman's . . . heart, arm, hand? She was uncertain. She didn't want to intrude or make her uncomfortable. She imagined putting her hand over Grandmother Barrow's heart, but even over the blanket, this gesture seemed too familiar.

Finally she touched her thin arm ever so gently. Her grandmother's raspy breathing didn't change.

Kay Lynn leaned over and whispered by her ear, "Grandmother Barrow, this is Kay Lynn. I came to tell you I love you." Her voice caught, and her heart raced. She'd never said those words to Grandmother Barrow. It felt wrong, too emotional.

She stood back up, uncertain and scared. It was a mistake to have come.

Kay Lynn stepped back from the bed. *Goodbye. Thank you for . . .* Kay Lynn thought about Grandmother Barrow. *Thank you for your steadfast care. I do love you. And I will miss you. Farewell.*

She stepped away to leave.

She heard her name in a hoarse whisper, "Kay Lynn?"

Grandmother Barrow's hand shook at her. Kay Lynn moved back to the bedside and took it. It was freezing, like life had already left it.

"You came," the old woman said.

"Of course," Kay Lynn answered, as if she hadn't debated it with herself.

"Thank you," her elder said, her voice clear now. "Anne says thank you too."

"Anne?" Kay Lynn asked.

"Your aunt Anne is right here, waiting for me to go with her."

Kay Lynn looked around the empty room. Should she correct the dying woman?

"Get your gift from Hannah before you leave," Grandmother Barrow said, her voice raspy, but strong. "It is for *you*. Promise me you will keep it, and pass it on to Lizzie." Her milky eyes were insistent. "Promise!"

Flustered but wanting to comfort the old woman, Kay Lynn readily agreed. "I will. I promise."

The tension poured out of the old woman. She closed her eyes and turned her head. "You have always been such a precious girl." Then she mumbled, "I wish . . . urgh . . . yes, but . . . blhrr . . . fie . . ." Kay Lynn listened for coherent words, but no more came. Deep, raspy breathing signaled sleep. Their conversation was over.

She leaned over, kissed Grandmother Barrow's cheek, placed her hand over the woman's heart, and said, "I love you. Goodbye. May you go in peace."

Kay Lynn wiped a tear as she left. This was likely the last time she would ever speak to Grandmother Barrow. Hannah waited for her at the bottom of the stairs, a small bag in her hand.

"These are for you," Hannah said.

Whatever she had promised to pass on to Lizzie was small.

She pushed the bottom edge of the bag into her left hand and pulled it open. She gasped, and her heart squeezed when she beheld the string of pearls inside. Doubtful, she looked at Hannah. "Truly? For me?" She'd never seen Grandmother Barrow without this necklace.

"She was insistent. She called me into the room to bear witness when she informed the Barrows. 'For the firstborn daughter,' she said. Since Miss Anne passed without a daughter of her own, it falls to you."

Kay Lynn held them against her heart. "I will . . . treasure these and pass them on to Lizzie. Please give her my deepest gratitude."

"If she wakes again, I will."

Kay Lynn left the house, but she needed to compose herself before she could drive home safely. She found a resting spot on a retaining wall, and looked out at the view. Ferries crossed the sparkling water, disappearing from her sight before they reached the iconic Ferry Building. She could make out part of the Bay Bridge but none of the Golden Gate. More of the bay used to be visible, but the new construction blocked much of it now.

Kay Lynn pulled the pearls out of her purse and studied them. They were absolutely stunning, practically glowing. She looked around, suddenly self-conscious to have them out in public. A thief would make a pretty penny from a strand of pearls. She poured them back into the bag and held it against her heart.

Profoundly touched that Grandmother Barrow wanted her and Lizzie to have this family inheritance, Kay Lynn teared up. She held her grandmother's love and acceptance in her hands.

The wall around her heart cracked. She looked to the right and left. No one was in sight. Grateful to be alone, she let her tears fall.

She cried for Grandmother Barrow, who was leaving the world and heading into the mystery, for Mitch and all that he might never be able to do again, and for herself because most days she wanted to stay in bed and have someone take care of her, but that was not to be. Regardless of how she felt, she rose each day, faced the world, and took care of her family.

CHAPTER 24

November 1944

"Aunt Kristine!" Timmy shouted when they arrived at the Grands for Thanksgiving dinner. He beamed at his only aunt and ran to embrace her. Blessedly the tension between Kay Lynn and her sister had not harmed Timmy and Lizzie's relationship with their aunt.

"Can we go play at John Muir?" Lizzie asked Kristine about the nearby school playground.

"After dinner. Now you must help me set the table."

Kristine rushed through hugs with Kay Lynn and Mitch and herded the kids into the kitchen.

Mitch stood close. "Do you know why she's so cold to you?"

Kay Lynn looked at her husband, weighing what to tell him. She finally replied, "She wants space to have her own life. Privacy."

"It's hard to be living with your parents and grandmother when you're twenty-one." Mitch asked, "Does she have a beau?"

Kay Lynn shrugged. Lying, even by omission, to Mitch went against her morals, but she didn't want to sully his feelings about Kristine. How would he react? He'd never spoken disrespectfully about homosexuals, but they'd never had any reason to speak about them. Would he avoid Kristine, or want to keep the children from her if she . . . ? Kay Lynn couldn't abide by that. Their family could be torn apart.

"Not that she's told me." That was the truth, if slanted.

"There you are," Momma declared as she walked in carrying a large bowl of stuffing. "The mashed potatoes can go right on the table. Put the pumpkin pie in the kitchen for now."

"Happy Thanksgiving, Momma," Kay Lynn said.

Momma's lips pulled into a tight, sad smile. Lenny's absence covered every family gathering with a blanket of sorrow, but today it was suffocating.

Grammy Sadie came in. "Happy Thanksgiving."

She carried a pitcher of lemon water in one hand and greens in the other. The children and Kristine followed with plates, cups, and cutlery. Soon, the table was well laid, and the family gathered around with their hands joined in a circle of connection.

"Holy creation," Grammy Sadie prayed, "thank you for this glorious day with our beloved family. Let our most beloved Lenny know he is missed, though he is in our minds and hearts. Give him strength to make it home to us." Her voice caught. She cleared it and continued. "Thank you for Mitch's healing. May this war end soon, and may all people, all over our Earth, be home safe with their families. Amen."

Amens traveled around the table.

This was their third Thanksgiving without Lenny. How many more would there be? Kay Lynn had stopped predicting when this war would come to an end. Lizzie didn't ask anymore. Timmy never had since he didn't remember any other life.

Kay Lynn looked at Mitch. Gratitude poured into her. Somehow they hadn't been apart for any of the holidays. His injuries were so severe that he'd been discharged back to civilian life. The threat of the government sending him far away was behind them, though their lives were still far from being back to normal.

Momma asked, "When are your parents coming?"

"December 15," Mitch replied. "They booked a room at the Claremont Hotel, but said to pass on their thanks for your kind offer to let them stay in Lenny's room."

Momma looked relieved, but replied, "They are welcome, of course, and they must be where they feel most comfortable."

Kay Lynn and Momma exchanged a look, and Kay Lynn mouthed, *Thank you.* Offering for them to stay at the Grands home had been her way of keeping Carolina out of their home while also being gracious.

"My job is ending at the New Year," Kristine blurted out. "No more liberty ships means no more weld inspectors."

"I'm sorry, Kristine," Poppa said. "What will you do now?"

She shrugged. "What's a woman to do? The trade unions aren't letting us in. I suppose I'll find work as a secretary." She looked upset, but then a flash of anger crossed her face. "You don't need to feel sorry for me," she snapped.

"Kristine, you know we would welcome you at Stevens Financial Services," Poppa said. "Your name is already on the awning."

"Absolutely no—" she started to exclaim. She caught herself. "Thank you, Poppa. I don't think it's for me."

Kay Lynn understood Kristine's attitude. She'd felt just that same way, until she didn't. Working for her parents, with her parents, was a blessing.

"There was no harm in reminding you," Momma chastised.

Mitch spoke up. "If you'll have me, I believe I'll be ready in a few months. I can work the adding machine quite well."

"Truly?" Momma asked.

Mitch and Kay Lynn nodded together. He'd been practicing on some of her bookkeeping work.

"We need accountants more than we need bookkeepers," Poppa replied.

Kay Lynn's hopes fell in the mud.

"Modern companies want degrees and credentials," Poppa explained. "I have no interest in going back to university at my age. We'd love to have you back of course, in any capacity."

Momma added, "But with a degree in business, as a certified public accountant, the business would be on more solid footing."

She and Poppa kept glancing at each other, making it obvious they had planned this conversation.

"It's the future," Poppa said.

"You can use the GI Bill to pay for it, right?" Momma asked.

"I'll look into it," Mitch replied. He looked at Kay Lynn. "We'll talk and get back to you."

They'd already decided he'd be ready to work again in January, and she'd imagined life settling into a satisfying routine. Her parents' suggestion threw an unwelcome fork into their road.

Mitch go to Cal? It seemed out of the question. Tuition was easily covered, but it meant Mitch would be out of the workforce for four years. They were already in debt. The thought of taking on more was disturbing. She'd hidden their financial straits from him because there was nothing he could do to change it and there was no point in further dampening his spirits.

If Mitch started college in January, he'd finish in December 1948; Timmy would be nine, and Lizzie would be thirteen. Mitch had been prepared for university when he was eighteen, but did he have the mind and stamina now?

Tension filled the room. Kay Lynn searched for a response, but before she came up with one, Poppa changed the topic entirely. "I believe *Korematsu* will be decided soon, perhaps in a way that we see as favorable."

He referred to the Supreme Court case about the relocation of all residents and citizens of Japanese descent from the West Coast. It took years to get it through the courts. There was a possibility Executive Order 9066 would be deemed unconstitutional and the

Fujiokas could come home. Kay Lynn's hope skipped down that welcome path.

Mitch said, "You know I wish it would be so, but the Supreme Court is not going to side with the ACLU."

Her short-lived optimism stumbled.

The conflict *was* winding down. There was evidence in all the layoffs and plans for a postwar economy, but no one could say how long it would go on, so she couldn't pin her hopes to any timeline. Just as the machinery of war had ramped up for years before the declaration, it seemed the wind down would take years as well.

"Excuse me," Timmy interjected.

"Yes, dear." Kay Lynn looked at him, grateful for the intrusion.

"Can we go to the playground now? With Aunt Kristine?"

Kay Lynn looked around the table at the mostly empty plates. She looked at Mitch, who nodded.

"Is everyone finished?" he asked.

"How about we all go for a walk, and have the pie when we get back?" Momma asked.

The group readily agreed, not even clearing the table before they left for the playground at John Muir School.

Kay Lynn walked behind with Mitch, who held a cane in his right hand to keep him steady.

"You're excited, aren't you?" she asked. "At the idea of attending Cal?"

"Of course," he replied. Then asked, "What about you? Do you want to get a business degree?"

"Uncle Sam isn't going to pay for *me* to go to university," she replied. "But how can we afford to live on my income for years? Even with your injury payment?"

"There's a stipend for students. I don't know how much, but it would help."

He looked excited and calm. She admitted, "It would be an investment in our future, I suppose."

"Before you say no, can we find out how much the monthly payment will be if I'm admitted?" he asked.

"You'll be accepted. The paper says they're putting out the welcome mat for GIs."

Kay Lynn didn't understand her annoyance, but the thought of Mitch attending Cal put her in a foul mood. It wasn't only the money. Cal had been her domain. As a typist, yes, but she was the one who strolled along Strawberry Creek on the campus. Perhaps she was jealous.

"Can I go to the veterans administration to learn more details?" he asked.

No, you may not, Kay Lynn thought to herself, and then said out loud, "Of course."

She smiled at him, but felt anything but generous.

CHAPTER 25

December 1944

A few weeks later Kay Lynn stared down at the newspaper on her dining room table. Two headlines, nestled against each other, jumped out:

> Army Approves Return of Japs: Pacific Coast Exclusion Order to be Revoked to Loyal Effective Jan. 2: No Mass Move from Homes Seen
>
> Court OKs Jap Exclusion

Joy surged as she read the top article. Kimiko and the children could return anytime they wanted. They were free.

Then her joy was tinged by the Supreme Court's ruling, explained in the second article, that Executive Order 9066 was a war necessity. However, they ordered that those residents and citizens of Japanese ancestry that proved they were loyal to the United States must have an unconditional release and be allowed to return to the West Coast.

January 2. In two weeks they could return.

Kay Lynn finished scanning the newspaper and then wrote to Kimiko.

> *Dear Kimiko,*
>
> *I have tears of joy in my eyes after reading the headline today. You can leave that wretched place in the new year. I can only imagine the excitement in Topaz, Utah. Though it must be daunting to think of leaving all on your own with three children. The newspaper mentions fear of violence, so please be very careful.*
>
> *You will return here, won't you? I like to think you'll be safe in Berkeley. Let me know if there is anything I can do to be helpful. You are welcome to stay here if you need a place. It would be crowded, but we'll happily make room for you four.*
>
> *Mitch is so much improved that he'll be attending UC Berkeley at the start of the next term. My parents suggested it, arguing that their business needs more accountants. The GI stipend for students is more than he earns from them as a bookkeeper. Four years seems such a long time, but we are fortunate to live near a university eager to enroll returning soldiers. The admissions director assures him that most of his fellow freshmen will be older than eighteen.*

She considered writing, *I must admit that I am jealous,* but stopped herself. Did she want to tear up this note and start again? She took out a fresh piece of paper and wrote without censoring herself:

I admit only to you that I'm jealous. I never knew I wanted to go to college, but when my parents said he should, I thought, Why not me? I could be an accountant. Not that I want to. I just would LOVE to be a student again. Walking on campus, meeting new people, talking about ideas. I would choose psychology or sociology, not business.

Instead I'll be at home washing dishes and using a ten-key machine to add up numbers for hours on end. I should be grateful for this opportunity for Mitch. Carolina might actually make peace with our family. No, that's too much to wish for.

Mitch and I had a terrible quarrel last night—about Christmas presents for the children. He thinks I'm silly to spend so much money on Little Golden Books for Timmy and Lizzie, but I imagine the look on their faces when they open their presents, and it will be worth it. "The Poky Little Puppy" and "The Lively Little Rabbit" will make a magical Christmas morning.

The day is going to be so sad with Lenny and Hazel gone. I want there to be one moment that is only joyful. I know it is silly. I know I am silly.

I am silly.

She stopped writing and felt sadness surge through her body. As much as she hoped they could, presents could not make up for all the absent people or the missing dog.

Life was just sad.

She tore up the lone page and finished her letter to Kimiko.

The news that you can leave Utah will bring joy
to our holiday table. Though we'll feel the absence
of Lenny—and Hazel. We have not forgotten
her. I know you miss Ken. I pray this is the last
Christmas you will be apart. The war is winding
down, at least in Europe, so he should be home
soon.

If you need temporary accommodations when
you return, our door is wide open to you, though
you understand we are not the Ritz.

Your friend,

Kay Lynn

CHAPTER 26

January 1945

She slowed to a stop at a red light, looked at her watch, and exhaled relief; they had plenty of time. Kay Lynn glanced at Grammy Sadie next to her in the passenger seat, and then peered in the rearview mirror at Momma and Lizzie in the back seat. They were in San Francisco for Grandmother Barrow's funeral.

Kay Lynn was grateful Momma asked to attend the worship service. Mitch had offered as well, but she didn't feel it was important enough for him to miss two classes in the first weeks of university.

Kay Lynn shouldn't have been surprised that Grammy Sadie wished to pay her respects or that Lizzie had wanted to attend as well. At first it seemed excessive, four of them going, but she didn't see any harm—and Lizzie was old enough to attend her first funeral.

Kay Lynn was a jumble of emotions as she walked into the dark stone sanctuary. It had high Gothic arches, like a European church built in the Middle Ages, but was so new that it was yet to be completed. It was one of the many building projects curtailed by the Great Depression. The largest Episcopal church in San Francisco had been destroyed during the 1906 earthquake. This building was meant to be a cathedral for the Episcopal church, Grace Cathedral, large and important. For now it was Grace Chapel. Functional as a church, though in an awkward stage. Many cathedrals took centuries to be built; perhaps this one would only be decades in the making.

Lizzie clung to Kay Lynn's hand as they walked down the center aisle. The first third of the sanctuary was scattered with congregants. She found a pew in the middle with room for four.

After they slid in, she looked around.

"Momma." Lizzie tugged at Kay Lynn's arm.

Kay Lynn looked down at her daughter. Lizzie's eyes were wide, the back of her hand covered her mouth with one finger pointing.

Kay Lynn followed the line of her daughter's finger.

A crucifix.

Lizzie had never seen that gruesome symbol before.

"Why is that in a church, Momma?"

"I'll explain it to you later," Kay Lynn said. "Don't look at it." Kay Lynn pulled out *The Book of Common Prayer.* "Look at their hymnal to learn how they are the same and different from Unitarians."

"Kay Lynn," Hannah interrupted.

Kay Lynn stood to greet Grandmother Barrow's maid.

The young woman waved her over. "Come with me. There's a seat saved for you in the front."

"I have my . . ."

"All of you come," Hannah insisted, and rushed them down the aisle toward the closed coffin. Grandmother Barrow was in there. Sorrow crashed over Kay Lynn.

Hannah stopped at an empty pew in the second row. Kay Lynn immediately recognized Jonathon Barrow sitting in the front row with his head bowed. Another huge wave of emotion, perhaps fear or maybe anger, hit Kay Lynn.

The three women who sat next to him turned and stared at her. Kay Lynn's breath caught. They must be her half sisters and his wife, officially her stepmother. She hadn't prepared for meeting them for the first time.

She froze, wanting to rush back up the aisle and out the sanctuary doors. Grammy Sadie slid into the pew and pulled Lizzie behind her. Momma followed, guiding Kay Lynn to her seat by the hand. She wanted to curl up in a ball and hide, embarrassed to be so rattled when she knew they would be here.

Momma looped an arm through Kay Lynn's and patted her with her other hand.

The service began with organ music and a processional. The words of the priest sailed by. Momma held up *The Book of Common Prayer*, turned to the right pages, but Kay Lynn didn't recite with the congregation. The unfamiliar words and ritual held little meaning or comfort. When the priest invited the congregation to take communion, Lizzie stood. Grammy Sadie pulled her back down and whispered something in her ear. The four of them sat while the entire congregation stood in line in the center aisle. There was no eulogy specific to Grandmother Barrow, other than lifting up her devotion to the church.

When the service ended, Hannah invited Kay Lynn to be in the receiving line, but she refused to stand with Jonathon Barrow and his family. She didn't belong with them and wasn't going to pretend otherwise.

Instead, she led the line of people shaking hands with the mourning family.

"Thank you for coming," Jonathon Barrow said to her. He looked old and tired. Death had a way of aging people.

"She was very dear to me," Kay Lynn said.

He teared up. "You were dear to her, you know."

"Yes, I do."

She paused for a moment, considering what more to say to him, but nothing came to mind. He stared at her, looking self-conscious and confused, struggling for something as well. She ended the uncomfortable moment by moving on to shake his wife's hand. The world called her stepmother, but they'd never met, so the name "stepmother" was too intimate.

Next were the two daughters, her half sisters. Did they know who she was? Their striking resemblance to her was at once unsettling and intriguing. She considered introducing herself, but didn't want to start a conversation in this line. She shook the older one's hand.

The younger one, with the combs and netting but no hat, took her hand, leaned in, and whispered, "I wanted those pearls."

She sounded like a pouty child. In truth she wasn't more than twenty, so she was hardly an adult.

"Clara!" her mother scolded, and then said to Kay Lynn, "I'm sorry for my daughter's rude behavior. Grandmother Barrow made it very clear to all of us that she wished you to have them."

Kay Lynn smiled at the woman, took back her hand, and walked away. The girl was rude, but Kay Lynn appreciated her honest and feisty spirit. As she distanced herself, the fear and anger she initially felt melted away, replaced by a poignant ache. This might be the last time she ever saw her seed father or her half-sisters. Although she looked like them, the realization lingered that they were not truly family in any meaningful way.

Kay Lynn had no desire to stay for the reception to make small talk with strangers. After walking away from the incomplete church, they got in the car to join the traffic heading back to the East Bay.

From the back seat, Lizzie asked, "Momma, that was Jesus, right?"

"Yes," she replied.

"Now can you tell me why they would hurt him in a church? I thought they liked Jesus the most?"

Kay Lynn took in a deep breath and replied, "There are many, many kinds of Christian churches. What they have in common is that they believe there are three parts to God: the father, the son, and the

Holy Spirit. We call them Trinitarians. They believe they go to heaven because Jesus died in the way that he did, because he was crucified, killed on a cross."

"Who killed him?"

"The Romans."

"Why?"

"They thought he wanted to overthrow the Roman government, become king, maybe. I know he fought for the poor and the people who were being mistreated by the Roman Empire."

"When?" Lizzie asked.

"Two thousand years ago."

"What do we believe about Jesus?"

Kay Lynn replied, "Jesus was an important man who taught us to make the world more fair, but he isn't more God than any other person. He's an example—to be loving and kind to all people even if you don't agree with them."

"I'm glad I don't have to look at a . . . what's it called?"

"A crucifix."

"Yeah, that."

"Me too. Thanks for being a Unitarian, Grammy Sadie," Kay Lynn said.

"Can you imagine thinking God wanted someone to be tortured so you can go to heaven?" Grammy Sadie replied. "That just never made any sense to me."

"Why didn't we get to eat a cracker like everyone else?" Lizzie asked.

"That was called communion," Kay Lynn explained. "They only want people who are members of their church to have communion."

Kay Lynn considered saying more.

"That's not very nice," Lizzie said.

"It's a special ritual for them," Kay Lynn said. "We want to respect their religion even if we don't believe the same things. For them it's a ritual that makes them feel closer to Jesus, and they only want people who are close to Jesus the way they teach to do the ritual. Before the service the priests bless the crackers, and they believe it turns the crackers into Jesus's body. And the wine in the cup is Jesus's blood."

Kay Lynn expected to hear a response from the back seat, but Lizzie was quiet.

"What do you think of that?" Kay Lynn asked.

"I'm being like Jesus, and being kind even when I don't agree."

Her three elders laughed. Lizzie had learned something from Kay Lynn's spontaneous religious education lesson.

Sitting next to Grammy Sadie, Kay Lynn looked in the rearview mirror at her mother and daughter. She and Lizzie exchanged a sweet smile. They were all so precious to her, each representing a crucial piece of her life: her past, her present, and her future. She was filled with gratitude that the three of them were by her side at the funeral.

CHAPTER 27

February 1945

The long march of celebrations that started in November with Thanksgiving ended with Lizzie's birthday in January. In February there was nothing to look forward to, and the constant rain dampened Kay Lynn's spirits further.

Mitch, newly enrolled at UC Berkeley, was entirely occupied by his schoolwork. When he wasn't studying, he was sleeping because the effort to be a student was exhausting.

Kay Lynn couldn't remember the last time they did something for pure enjoyment like play a game or read out loud. With many days of being cooped up inside, Kay Lynn wanted to get out and have an enjoyable time as a whole family.

After they finished breakfast on Saturday morning, she declared, "Family, let's picnic at the Marina for lunch. My scientific analysis of the sky leads me to predict it won't be raining."

"Hooray!" Timmy squealed.

Mitch looked at Kay Lynn and shook his head. "I need to study, and I don't want—"

"Kids, you may be excused," Kay Lynn interrupted him.

She waited until Lizzie and Timmy were gone before she said, "Please, let's do something nice as a family." She hated to nag, to be unsupportive, but all of Mitch's time and energy was going to his classes. He had little time for the children and no time for her.

She also suspected that he avoided going out in public because of his injuries. Not because it was difficult to walk, but because he was self-conscious of his limp and the scar on the back of his head where his hair had never returned.

"Please, Mitch," she practically begged.

He looked at her.

"You've stopped going to church with us, you're barely ever home for dinner, and when you are here, you're either sleeping or studying," she said.

"You don't understand how hard this is for me," he said. "School at my age."

She concealed her frustration by standing to clear the table.

Two plates in her hands, she said, "One picnic, two hours. That's all I'm asking." She teared up. She didn't want to fight with him. "The kids miss you." *I miss you.*

He nodded. He didn't look enthusiastic, but he agreed to her request. She got the dishes cleaned and put away and made them a lunch.

A few hours later, Mitch was ready to go on time, a cap on his head, as they walked out the door.

Lizzie stopped along the pathway and shouted, "It's here, at last!"

"What?" Timmy looked where she pointed.

"A crocus *flower*, not just the leaves."

Sure enough, a bright-purple crocus popped out of the ground. Cousin Naomi's suggestions had worked. Or perhaps it was the weather pattern. Whatever it was, she was glad to have them back.

"There's another." Timmy pointed to a bright-yellow flower.

"They are beautiful," Mitch said.

"Even in February," Kay Lynn agreed. "I must have known in my bones we were going to see a crocus today. Good thing we already have a picnic ready to go, to celebrate this sign of spring."

As usual these days, Kay Lynn drove. Mitch had yet to figure out how to safely work the shift. It was one of the many things that they had to be patient about. In time he might have the dexterity to drive, but he might never recover that ability.

Many people shared her idea to visit the Marina on this beautiful day. The parking spaces were full when they arrived, and she had to drive in circles until she spotted a car leaving.

They walked to a rise, spread out plastic sheeting and covered it with an old blanket. Kay Lynn admired the view of the Golden Gate Bridge. In other parts of the country, snow blanketed the ground. But this was one of her favorite times of the year: a season that seemed to embrace all the others at once. Colorful dried leaves still clung to the branches of Japanese maple trees, evoking the essence of fall; the bare wisteria and plum branches echoed the starkness of winter; the blooming crocus added a touch of spring; and it was as sunny as any summer day in Berkeley.

Kay Lynn closed her eyes and drew in a deep breath. She allowed a wave of joy to sweep over her, despite, or maybe because of, Mitch's accident. Life had left her so weary that she forgot to be grateful for what they still had and what they'd escaped. Just imagining Mitch gone raised her heart rate, so she pushed the idea aside.

He survived the explosion—he was alive. He'd come so far in the seven months from the accident. He was in school. Money was a struggle, but their financial situation was no worse than it was during the Depression. His student stipend was greater than his wages when he was in the navy.

She should feel grateful, but she was angry or disappointed far too much of the time. Mitch had been changed by the accident. He was tired and moody, and distracted.

She didn't want to burden him with household demands, so she continued taking care of the household and the children without his help and was working as many hours as possible for her parents. Mitch was kind to the children, but was withdrawn from her. They didn't speak of it, but they went through their days like the two proverbial ships passing in the night.

She'd asked about the night of the accident once, but he told her he couldn't remember it and preferred it that way. He wanted it to stay in the past, but his shouts and whimpers in his sleep revealed that it still haunted him.

Suddenly a cold and wet object assaulted Kay Lynn's cheek. She flinched and batted at it.

"Hazel!" Lizzie screamed.

The dog—their dog—stopped licking her and ran to the kids, greeting each of their faces in turn, her tail flying from side to side. She returned to Kay Lynn, licking her cheek again; this time Kay Lynn savored the sensation. Kay Lynn hugged Hazel, feeling her soft, warm body. Hazel plopped down close by her side as if they'd been apart for a few hours rather than a few months.

"Hello, Hazel," Mitch said. "Do you remember me?"

She got up to sniff his outstretched hand. She licked her approval and returned to rest against Kay Lynn's leg.

Hazel's coat was shiny, and she was well fed. Clearly, someone had been caring for her. Maybe multiple people. Kay Lynn stood up and scanned the wide field of grass. She turned in a full circle, looking and listening for a person who might have kept Hazel for months, but didn't see anyone searching for a dog. The dog's reappearance was as much a mystery as her disappearance.

"This is the best day ever!" Timmy declared.

"Second best," Lizzie said. "Halloween when Daddy came home was the very best, but you were too little to remember."

"Best enough," Kay Lynn said as she sat back down. Hazel rested her head on Kay Lynn's leg. Kay Lynn petted her soft fur while she ate a sandwich, apple slices, and cookies. Delight added to her bath of joy. She reveled in this gift of grace.

"Mommy, are you sad?" Timmy asked.

"No, sweetie. These are happy tears. Tears of joy."

Timmy drew in his eyebrows.

Kay Lynn nodded at him. "Happy tears aren't so common."

"I can't *wait* to write to Donna!" Lizzie squealed.

Kay Lynn shared her sentiment. "Me too!"

A few weeks later Kay Lynn woke with a start. She instantly thought of the rent payment, and fear flooded her body. She had most of the money but would need to get an advance on her next check from her parents. Rather than lie in bed fretting, she got up to walk off the rush of adrenaline. She'd been wanting to take Hazel by the White Horse since her return. Her fans might not be there anymore, but they might be.

Outside, Hazel trotted close by her side. Ever since her homecoming, she'd shadowed Kay Lynn through every room of the house, never leaving her sight. At Telegraph, Hazel automatically turned right. Kay Lynn spotted a few people leaning on the outside of the building. As they walked closer, she recognized one of the young men.

"Hazel, you're back!" He crouched down to give her a good pet. "We missed you . . . and you had your mama worried, but it seems you had yourself a good time while you were gallivanting around!" He gave Kay Lynn a knowing look, his eyebrow raised.

She looked back at him quizzically.

"Miss Hazel is in the family way," he explained.

"What?"

He nodded. "These teats are a dead giveaway." He felt around her belly. "Three or four more weeks until they come, I'd say."

Puppies? How many? Her face must have shown her concern.

"You don't need to be scared," the young man said. "She'll know what to do and when to do it. It is as natural as losing a tooth."

"Thanks . . . Uh," Kay Lynn replied. "We've never exchanged names. I'm Kay Lynn."

"Isn't that a beautiful and unusual name . . . I'm John, plain old John. Like a toilet."

Kay Lynn laughed. "I'd never describe you as plain. Thanks for making my midnight walks a bit friendlier."

"This is my last night in Oakland. I'm glad I got to see you and Hazel one last time."

Kay Lynn's heart fell. *Would he be sent to danger?* "Where are you headed?"

"Back home. Uncle Sam is done with me. He thanked me for my service and is busing me back to Iowa."

"Do you have a farm?"

"Yes, ma'am. That's why I know about teats!"

"Good luck as you journey home. You've seen so much that it won't be easy, will it?"

His face contracted in a mixture of sorrow and longing. "I really love it out here—the freedom and the weather can't be bested. And I love my family. I hate to choose between them."

Kay Lynn thought about Kristine. She didn't know if this young man was homosexual, but that might be the freedom he was referring to. *Did Kristine have to make the same choice between family and freedom?* It was easier to empathize with this kind young man than her angry, distant sister.

CHAPTER 28

April 1945

Kimiko's last letter indicated they would most likely return to Berkeley today, though nothing was guaranteed. She'd graciously turned down Kay Lynn's offer of accommodations. Her cousin Misako's house had stayed in the family, so they would stay there until they found a new home.

"Please, Mommy. Please, please, please. Please a thousand times, ten thousand times!" Lizzie begged after school.

Kay Lynn consented with a nod. "Pick some flowers from our yard and put them in a jam jar with water and make a card. We'll leave them on the porch. I doubt you'll see Donna, so please prepare your heart for that likelihood. We don't know what time they're getting to Berkeley, or for certain it will be today."

"Thanks, Mommy. I'll be happy if flowers are waiting for her when she gets here. Miss Brown agrees it would be nice to have her in our class . . . you know, to make her feel welcomed back."

"We can suggest that to Principal Bartley. He makes the assignments."

Lizzie and Timmy each made a card. They went into the garden with shears and a jar of water. The children scampered in the yard, collecting a lovely bouquet of scarlet carnations and purple statice that contrasted beautifully with the white Queen Anne's lace.

"I wish we had wisteria in our front yard." Lizzie pointed across the street. "I'd put a big bunch in the middle bouquet."

The vine was glorious in full bloom. Kay Lynn's breath caught. She flashed back to the bare vine and the fallen petals on that gloomy day when they walked the Fujiokas to the buses that took them away. It seemed poignant and fitting that bright-purple blossoms celebrated the day they returned home, or rather, most of them returned. Ken was somewhere in Europe, and wouldn't be with his family.

"It's beautiful. Perhaps one day we will plant one of our own. But for now, we get to enjoy the beauty of the one Mrs. Hori planted."

"Donna's grandmother planted that tree?" Lizzie asked, her eyebrows drawn together in confusion.

"Yes, when she was a very young woman just come to California."

Lizzie eyes grew wide. She emphasized each word, "It is very, very, very old!"

Kay Lynn laughed. "It is. Put your flowers in the jar."

They walked the four blocks to Misako's house.

Kay Lynn directed, "Leave the flowers on the porch. They'll feel obliged to invite us in if we knock, and we don't want to be a burden."

"But, Mommy," Lizzie whined.

Kay Lynn snapped. "Elizabeth Carolina! Do *not* talk back to me!"

Lizzie hung her head and walked up the wooden stairs. Hazel followed close. Lizzie set down the flowers and walked back to Kay Lynn's side, but Hazel didn't return with the girl. Instead, she barked and scratched at the door; her belly hanging nearly to the ground. Her puppies were coming any day.

The door opened.

"Hazel!" Donna screamed. She dropped to the ground to greet the dog. George and Kimiko appeared in the doorway. Hazel ran between them, barking with joy, her tail wagging from side to side.

"May I?" Lizzie asked from Kay Lynn's side. "Pleeease."

Kay Lynn nodded. They all walked up to their dear friends. Kimiko looked the same, except for a weariness in her eyes, but the children were utterly transformed in the three years they were away.

"It's so good to see you," Kay Lynn told her friend, tears burning her eyes. "We don't want to be a nuisance."

"You aren't. We've missed you so much. Please visit with us."

Kimiko opened the door wide. Kay Lynn appreciated the warm welcome and was well aware this wasn't Kimiko's home.

"Don't offer us hospitality. Though we very much want you to come for dinner as soon as you're ready."

"Tonight, Mommy," Donna begged. "Please?!"

Kimiko shook her head. "Tonight, we must eat here. Tomorrow we can eat on Prince Street."

Kay Lynn's heart twisted in empathy. Had it been a kindness to invite them to have dinner at a house next door to their old home? The painful self-consciousness she felt when writing to Kimiko filled her body.

"Hooray!" the kids yelled in a high cacophony as they jumped up and down. Their delight was contagious.

Kimiko and Kay Lynn settled on the couch, and the older children played on the rug. Hazel curled up at Kimiko's feet, and Missy clung to her side, staring warily at Kay Lynn.

"Mommy, what's wrong with her eyes?" Missy asked.

"Has my mascara run?" Kay Lynn wondered.

"Missy, that's rude!" Kimiko admonished her. "Your mascara is fine," she assured Kay Lynn. "I'm sorry for her rudeness."

Confused, but not hurt, Kay Lynn replied, "Three-year-olds ask the strangest questions. I find it endearing, but peculiar. But I don't understand her . . ." The question suddenly made sense; a chill traveled through Kay Lynn's body. "Oh, my! She's never seen hazel eyes before, has she?"

"I suppose not," Kimiko replied. "You are the first Caucasian she's been this close to."

Kay Lynn sucked in her breath. A tear slid down her cheek.

She tried to smile, but it was tight. "I'm not insulted for me; I'm just stunned by the reminder of what you've been through." Kay Lynn took in a breath to stop her emotion. She didn't wish to be a burden to Kimiko.

"Not that I've forgotten where you were . . . oh."

This reunion was uncomfortable. Was it better to speak directly about what had happened or let it remain behind them? Like Mitch, Kimiko might prefer to leave the unpleasantness in the past.

Kay Lynn decided to move on. "How was your journey home from Utah?"

"Long and uneventful. The bus was comfortable enough. April is a good month to travel."

"Have you heard the news?" Kay Lynn asked, referencing President Roosevelt's death.

"Yes, Cousin Misako told me when we arrived. It's unbelievable that he's gone. He's been the president for most of my life," Kimiko said. "All of the children's lives."

Kay Lynn started to say, *He was a great man.* He *was* a great man. He'd done much good for their nation and the world, but he had also signed the relocation order. She wouldn't blame Kimiko if she despised him.

Donna stood up and came to Kimiko's side, waiting to speak. Kimiko nodded in permission.

The girl spoke. "Lizzie wants me to be in her class. Can I go to school tomorrow?"

Kimiko bit her lip and nodded again. "We don't know what they will say, but we can ask."

Donna clapped and trotted back to Lizzie.

"You have so much to do. Please let me know how I can be helpful. The children are welcome at our house anytime. I'm sure Missy will accept me soon enough. Do you have any leads on housing?"

"None. Berkeley is so crowded and expensive. For every home listed for rent in the paper, there are twenty ads for people looking for housing. We may have to move to El Cerrito."

"What? No, you can't mean that," Kay Lynn responded. She didn't expect they would be next-door neighbors again, but she imagined Kimiko would live nearby once she returned.

Kimiko shrugged. "I remind myself to take each day as it comes. Please, let me know if you hear of any available rentals. Even an apartment will do."

"Two bedrooms?"

"Ideally, though we can make do with one. Simply having a kitchen of my own will be luxurious after Topaz. I don't know when Ken will be home," Kimiko said.

Another wave of empathy crashed through Kay Lynn.

"Do you know where he is?"

"It sounded like Italy from his last letter. I can't decide if that's better or worse than North Africa." She shrugged.

"I'm so tired of predicting this war. I was certain Mitch would be safe if he stayed stateside," Kay Lynn replied.

"How's the recovery?" Kimiko asked, concern in her eyes.

"He's so determined," Kay Lynn replied. "Learning to write legibly and type with his left hand is daunting, but he works at it constantly. He says I'm his inspiration. If I can do everything with one dexterous hand, he can as well. I don't remember any different, so I know he has the bigger challenge. School keeps him very occupied," Kay Lynn added. She didn't say that he was tired and withdrawn, his body in their house but his mind and heart seemingly elsewhere.

They continued chatting, navigating around the complex emotional land mines that were affecting each of them.

"Before you left Topaz did you get our letter telling you Hazel is pregnant?" Kay Lynn asked.

Kimiko shook her head. She ran her hand around Hazel's belly. Her eyes widened, and she teared up. "Life continues, even in the midst of our pain and loss. We marveled at that in the camp. So many beautiful babies were born. Each day I could focus on the ugliness of the barbed wire or beauty in the dramatic landscape behind it. The beauty and the ugly were right there at all times."

She shook her head as if to fling away memories, like a dog shaking off drops of water. Kay Lynn took that as a cue to give them family time.

"Thank you for our visit. We'll see you tomorrow at Lincoln School, 8:00 a.m. on the playground?"

Kimiko smiled. "That would be very welcome. Thank you."

Kay Lynn rose. "Children, it's time to leave."

She saw Lizzie was about to ask for more time and gave the girl her sternest look.

Her daughter nodded. "Come on, Timmy." Her daughter stood and reached out a hand. "We have to go home now."

She and Kimiko watched the children hug goodbye. Their heads rested on each other's shoulders for a moment, clinging as if to a raft. When had they learned such sweetness? George and Timmy hadn't had contact in years, and yet somewhere in their cells, they knew each other. When Kay Lynn hugged Kimiko, a surge of love and gratitude poured through her.

"I'm glad you're home," she said. *Can you forgive us?* she wondered. *Will you find a welcome here?*

"Let's go," Kay Lynn called out. Timmy and Lizzie followed her out the door, but Hazel stayed at Kimiko's side. Kay Lynn started to call her and then resisted the mistaken impulse. Hazel wasn't their dog. She'd done what Kimiko had asked of her—cared for Hazel when her family could not—and now they had returned to her.

Hazel looked directly at Kay Lynn, her caramel-brown eyes asking for understanding. Kay Lynn smiled at Hazel and nodded. She was too choked up to speak. So she mouthed the words, *Good girl.*

"Hazel?" Timmy asked.

She turned away quickly to hide her tears from Kimiko.

"Hazel is home now," Kay Lynn said to her son in a high voice.

It was as right for Hazel to stay with the Fujiokas as it was heartbreaking.

In the morning, Principal Bartley's eyes widened as he saw them walking toward him. A wave of emotion—fear . . . sorrow, it was hard to be certain—crossed his face. Kay Lynn understood his feelings.

He made a small, awkward bow, and said, "Welcome back, Mrs. Fujioka. Are you Donna? So grown up?"

Looking proud to be remembered, Donna nodded with a tiny curtsy. Kay Lynn found herself tearing up again. She hadn't realized this would be an emotional morning.

"Principal Bartley, can Donna be in my class, please? Miss Brown told me, 'It will be splendid to welcome her back.'"

The tall man nodded. "She mentioned the possibility to me yesterday. I didn't realize we would have this wonderful opportunity so soon. Donna, line up with Lizzie. She knows where you need to be. And this must be—" His voice broke. He cleared his throat. "You must be George. I remember when you could hardly walk. Would you like to be in class with Timmy?"

George nodded, though he likely didn't know what he was agreeing to.

"Mrs. Fujioka, come with me, and I will introduce you to Miss Chinn. She's new to the school since you . . . You do not know her, but I'm confident she'll welcome George into her classroom."

Once the children were settled, Kimiko, Missy, and Kay Lynn left the schoolyard together, but instead of walking home side by side, they paused at the gate to part ways.

"I have a lead on an apartment; wish me luck," Kimiko said.

Kay Lynn wanted a home for her friends right next door to hers, but she didn't have one, so she conveyed her support by raising her right hand with her first two fingers crossed, offering the symbolic blessing that Lizzie so often used.

A few weeks later Lizzie yelled as she ran in the door after school, "Mommy, Daddy, guess what?!"

"What?!" Mitch asked, mirroring Lizzie's excitement.

Timmy declared from Lizzie's side, "Hazel had her puppies!"

"Timmy! I wanted to tell them," Lizzie scolded.

"Sorry," he replied.

"Four! She had four babies last night. Donna watched three of them be born. Can we go see them today, please? Mrs. Fujioka invited us, so it's fine with her. She asked us when she came to school for pickup because Donna and George can't cross Ashby by themselves."

"Please, Mommy," Timmy begged.

"Go get a snack while Daddy and I decide," Kay Lynn replied.

As soon as the kids left, Mitch said, "I want to see Hazel's puppies, don't you?"

Kay Lynn nodded. "Let's hope I don't fall into a puddle of tears. I get so emotional around them it's embarrassing."

"It means you care; that's not something to be embarrassed about."

"Sometimes, I think I care about other people too much. I want to make everything better for them, but I can't find Kimiko a new home . . . or bring Ken home . . . or Lenny home . . . or end this war."

Or encourage Kristine to be honest with me.

"There's something I haven't told you." Her heart beat hard. It had been weighing on her for months. She hated to betray Kristine, but even more so, she was uncomfortable being less than forthcoming with Mitch.

"What?!" He looked alarmed.

She inhaled. "I saw Kristine, in a romantic situation . . . with a woman."

His eyes rounded in surprise. "Are you sure? Where?"

"Nearly certain. At that bar on Telegraph, the White Horse. It was brief, only a momentary glance and finger brush, but you know that look. She's in love," Kay Lynn explained. "It was the night of the explosion. I saw her; she saw the surprise on my face. She turned away, and we both rushed off. It's been nine months, and we've never spoken of it, but it's a giant moat of rattlesnakes between us. She's kept her distance even more since that night, so I think that's her secret. Last year, Momma thought she was pregnant, but that was all wrong. Why doesn't Kristine trust us?"

"You can't possibly want that life for your sister. She can't want it for herself. Living in the shadows. Hiding from the police?"

"Can women be arrested for it too?"

"I believe so, but I don't really know."

Kay Lynn shook her head. "This is why I've avoided thinking or talking about it. Talking about it won't help, and it could be harmful. If Momma lost sleep imagining her being pregnant, can you imagine how hard this would be for her? Grammy Sadie?"

"You're right to keep it from the Grands. It's Kristine's private business. Forcing her to speak about it isn't wise, but I'm glad you told me." Mitch pulled in his eyebrows. She wanted to smooth them out. This was why she hesitated to tell him. They had no choice in the matter, but it convoluted their relationships.

She said, "I don't know anyone who speaks directly about such things, though we all know it exists."

Kay Lynn thought of Mr. Navias and Mr. Grant from their Unitarian church. Somehow she believed them to be a couple, though she had no recollection of anyone ever telling her so. Somehow she just knew that they were family to each other though they were not brothers.

She asked, "Do you think less of her?"

"I don't know what to think," Mitch replied.

She expressed her biggest fear. "Would you . . . if she were . . . would you want her to stay away from the children?"

"Oh, my gosh." He looked stunned. "Kristine?" Mitch stared at her. He thought before he answered. "No. Kristine is not going to harm our children. Her private life is her own."

Relief spread through Kay Lynn. That was her concern, that she and Mitch would have a rift—that her family would be torn apart by Kristine's secret.

"You didn't know my family could get more complicated, did you?"

His face pulled in. "Do you have any more secrets you've been keeping from me?"

She took in a deep breath to calm her heart. "We owe my parents almost two thousand dollars."

His eyes went wide.

"That much?" he said, looking utterly ashamed.

She nodded. At first she kept it from him because of his injuries, but then she kept not saying anything. She was embarrassed she hadn't managed their money well, but also didn't want to add any burden to him. It became harder and harder to tell him.

"I wasn't blind to our finances, but I didn't imagine so much. I thought the settlement would go further," he replied.

"I tried to make do, but . . ." She trailed off.

Sheepish, he said, "I'm sorry."

"It's not your fault," Kay Lynn reassured him. "It's . . . I don't know? Mine? The government? Hitler? The emperor? Who can we blame? I just don't know how to stop being in debt to my parents."

"We're ready." Lizzie stood at the doorway, a bread-and-jam sandwich in her hand. "We can eat our snack on the way."

"Did you clean up in the kitchen?" Kay Lynn asked.

"Yes, Mommy," Lizzie replied.

"Let's go meet some puppies!" Mitch exclaimed, putting on a good face for their daughter.

When Lizzie left, Mitch turned to Kay Lynn. "I'll do my best not to blame myself, and you do the same. Somehow, someday, we will get back on solid ground."

Nothing had actually changed. Kristine was still hiding and they were still in debt, but somehow she felt better after being honest with Mitch. It was their burden to share, not hers alone.

Hazel lay in a large cardboard box on a heap of tattered towels with four tiny balls attached to her belly. Looking weary, she lifted her head when they entered the room. Her tail beat against the floor when she saw it was Kay Lynn. She started to rise; Kay Lynn stopped her by immediately crouching down by her head.

"Hazel, you deserve to rest. Look at your beautiful babies. Well done," Kay Lynn assured the dog. Hazel licked her hand. "Don't touch the puppies, children, not until their eyes open."

"That's what my mother told us," Donna whispered.

"Where are the puppies?" Timmy asked.

Mitch pointed and spoke softly into Timmy's ear. "They're suckling right now. For many days they will stay very, very close to Hazel.

It's like they took the tiniest little step away from her body. That's how Mother Nature designed it for dogs."

Timmy stared where his father pointed and asked, "Do they have tails? Or ears?"

"Think about how curled up they must have been inside her. Those parts are tucked in tight. It'll take a little time for them to learn they have room to expand."

The two families clumped together staring at the new life; awe and delight filled their faces. A surge of love and gratitude took over Kay Lynn. She didn't care that tears ran down her face, revealing the depth of her feelings. She kept stroking Hazel's sweet ears. Her love for Mitch, her children, this dog, and these friends was as thick and sweet as honey.

"Those are happy tears, aren't they, Mommy?" Timmy whispered.

"Yes, they are," Kay Lynn assured him. "Very happy tears." her voice broke. "I love all of you, very much. Including Miss Hazel. And these puppies."

"You have *five* dogs now," Lizzie spoke to Donna. "What are their names?"

The adults laughed.

"What?" Lizzie looked hurt.

"We won't be keeping the puppies," Kimiko said, "not even one of them."

Donna and George's faces fell.

"They'll stay with us until they're weaned," Kimiko explained to her children. "You know we are fortunate that we found an apartment that allowed us to have one dog."

Donna nodded. "How long?"

Kimiko looked at Mitch. He shrugged and replied, "Eight to ten weeks, if I remember correctly from my childhood. The puppies were the best, and the saddest. I hated saying goodbye to them, but the families that took them were so happy."

"You mean . . . Can we?" Timmy asked, so excited that he sucked in his breath. "Can we . . . can we . . ." He continued stuttering. "Can we have one of Hazel's babies be *our* dog forever?"

Kay Lynn looked at Mitch. He raised an eyebrow and gave a slight nod. Kay Lynn looked at the four little beings. Did one of them belong in their home? In a flash she thought of the comfort and joy Hazel brought to her life for three years. Certainly, it had been a lot of work, but Hazel's companionship had been so welcome. She still missed her every day. It didn't make sense in her head, but her heart longed for a dog of her own.

She smiled and nodded. Looking at Kimiko, she said, "It would be an honor to have one of these puppies join our family."

Kimiko smiled back, her eyes bright like the day Missy was born. Kay Lynn flashed to the memory of Hazel curled in protection around Kimiko. Life sure was beautifully strange.

"Hooray!" Timmy squealed.

"Shhhhh," Lizzie corrected her brother with a firm whisper. "They need to rest. They are little, tiny babies."

Kay Lynn reached her hand up to Mitch. He took it and rested it against his leg. She studied the precious puppies. *Which one would they pick?* The one on the far left drew her eyes, again and again. It was caramel brown, with a necklace of white. Kay Lynn didn't know much else about this little being, but she knew this was her beloved dog.

CHAPTER 29

In June, the school year ended for Mitch and the children. In a strange but lovely twist of events, Kay Lynn left for work each morning while he minded their home, the children, and their puppy, Lucie. They'd found dog-training books at the library and were using the tools faithfully to teach her to be a good companion. Coming home to Lucie was a reliably delightful part of Kay Lynn's day.

Kay Lynn found solace in leaving her family at home to make their way without her while she added up numbers in neat columns. Her former reluctance to work for her parents seemed childish now. A stable and accommodating job was a godsend. So many women were losing their jobs to accommodate returning soldiers that Kay Lynn was all the more appreciative to have employment.

Most of the country celebrated the end of the fighting in Europe and the effort to form the United Nations to prevent future conflicts. But for Kay Lynn, the ongoing war in the East was personal and alarming.

Each day the paper reported US air strikes on Japanese soil. Kay Lynn understood that was a sign the war could be coming to an end, but bombing those established cities meant that women and children, little babies and the elderly, were being attacked. How could that be moral?

Her concern wasn't only abstract. Lenny might be in the place they were dropping bombs. Their letters to the Red Cross hadn't resulted in any information about where he was being held.

In addition, Kimiko's grandparents lived in Nagasaki, one of the common targets of air strikes. Were they in harm's way?

Kay Lynn had taken to adding them to her quick prayer for Lenny and Ken each morning: *Keep them safe.* It wasn't much, but it was something. She imagined their faces from a photo taken decades ago. Grammy Sadie was right, somehow it helped her to feel better to plead for her deepest hope.

On August 6 the paper reported a new kind of weapon had been used on a military base in Hiroshima, Japan. That night Kay Lynn and Mitch listened with horror to President Truman's speech about the atomic weapon that "harnessed the power of the sun." He declared it to be a two-billion-dollar gamble that had worked beyond their hopes.

We are now prepared to obliterate more rapidly and completely every productive enterprise the Japanese have above ground in any city. We shall destroy their docks, their factories, and their communications. Let there be no mistake; we shall completely destroy Japan's power to make war.

Obliterate. That word pierced Kay Lynn's heart. She imagined the terror and shock of the families in Hiroshima. Had they been warned it was coming so they could get somewhere safe?

Please surrender, she begged the Japanese emperor.

The following day there was no such headline, but there was speculation that Tokyo would be the next target of an atomic bomb. Millions of people lived there. Was Truman truly going to obliterate them along with their docks, factories, and communications? Kay Lynn felt ill.

On Wednesday a large headline screamed "Russia Declares War on Japan," and the paper reported that sixty percent of Hiroshima had been destroyed by the atomic bomb. It also had an article praising the UC Berkeley scientist that created a bomb that could destroy more than half of a city. There was no hint of caution or concern about the invention of such a devastating weapon. Had they ever been working on it when she was on campus? A weapon of that scale could have destroyed all of Berkeley. Could it still? Were their safety precautions better than at the naval weapons depot?

On August 9 Kay Lynn read the headlines and then locked herself in the bathroom with the newspaper. She didn't want the children to see her dismay. Another atomic bomb had been dropped, this time on Nagasaki, and yet there was still no surrender. Tens of thousands, perhaps hundreds of thousands, were dead. That had to include babies and children and the elderly. She was overwhelmed and furious and sad. These men wanted power at any cost. *Surrender,* she shouted in her mind to the Japanese emperor.

She thought of Kimiko and Mrs. Hori reading the news. She imagined Mrs. Hori's pain knowing that the place she was born, her parents' hometown, had been attacked with an atomic weapon. She felt as overwhelmed and helpless as she had on the day she read about the relocation order. She let her tears flow.

"Mommy?" Timmy's voice came through the door.

She put on a cheery voice. "Yes?"

"I have to go," he pleaded. "Real bad."

She cleared her throat and wiped her face. "Okay."

Kay Lynn turned the knob, and he rushed past her.

It had been weeks since they visited with Kimiko and the kids. Time just got away from them. With school out, there was nothing that brought them together, but today she would make the time.

"Lizzie, get me six lemons. We are going to make lemon bars for the Fujiokas and deliver them," Kay Lynn directed her daughter.

"Did something bad happen to them?" Lizzie asked.

Kay Lynn took in a breath and considered her answer. "Mrs. Hori's parents and cousins live in Japan, in the places the United States is bombing. I know Mrs. Hori loves and supports the United States, but she has to be sad and scared for her family too."

"So we will bring them lemon bars to show them we love them," Lizzie said. "And we aren't mad at them."

"Right," Kay Lynn replied, pleased that her daughter understood her gesture.

It wasn't much, but it was something.

CHAPTER 30

Fall 1945

Kay Lynn planned the menu for Thanksgiving dinner as she walked toward the office on College Avenue. Lucie, her near-constant companion, trotted by her side. She was fortunate her parents were willing to have a dog in the office, so long as she was quiet. At seven months old, she was starting to act like a teenager with a mind of her own, but interacting with Lucie, playing fetch, walking, or cuddling with her, was the best part of Kay Lynn's life.

She had so much to be grateful for this year. Mitch was at the top of the list. He was alive. His stamina and confidence had returned. She didn't know if it was physical or emotional healing, but this term he had time for the family. He'd even taken to making dinner when he got home before her. She'd stopped being protective of him, and had become more honest about her fears as she grew more confident in his strength.

They'd paid half of what they owed to her parents with her inheritance from Grandmother Barrow, and were making payments on the rest. It would take a while, but they were eliminating debt rather than taking on more.

The war on *all* fronts was over. Many soldiers were working on the aftermath, but even more were returning to civilian life. The Fujiokas were in a small two-bedroom bungalow in Berkeley. Ken returned from Europe a few weeks ago and was considering enrolling at Cal for the winter term. Like Mitch, he could use the GI Bill to pay tuition and get a generous stipend for their living costs.

But life wasn't all good. As long as Lenny was missing, an enormous pall sat over their family. He might be dead, injured, or starving. The information about the treatment in the prisoners of war camps in the East was nauseating. She didn't even allow herself to imagine what it was like for him. She just knew that if he was still alive, he'd been living through horrid conditions.

Most of the men returning to San Francisco were injured, angry, or both. They were having difficulty finding work and housing because of the droves of people who'd moved to the East Bay during the war and weren't leaving. The appealing social and physical climate had won people over, and now they wanted to stay.

Whole communities were being built to meet the demand for more houses. The push was to make everything in life—cars, stores, streets, appliances—modern. The urgency of the war effort that had filled life with a frantic energy was not coming to an end.

Kay Lynn was unsettled, foolishly waiting for a routine that would never return. She missed the life she had before the war, working with Kimiko and taking care of their young children. She wasn't yet thirty, but she felt like an elderly woman pining for the simple, good-old days. Would she ever feel safe, or at least content, again?

When she walked into the office, Momma was bent over her desk, sobbing; Poppa hovered over her. The corner of a telegram poked out of her tight fist. *Lenny!*

Kay Lynn's heart stopped and then raced hard. She rushed to her momma's side, crouched down with an arm around her. She looked at her dad.

"He's alive," Poppa croaked.

Kay Lynn gasped. "Thank you, God!" A chill ran down her spine.

Momma grabbed her hand and squeezed hard. Her face still buried in her own arms, she whispered, "He's on his way home."

Tears streamed down Kay Lynn's cheeks. *Lenny is coming home. He's alive. And he's coming home.*

"Oh, Momma! This is the best news ever!"

Momma raised her head and hugged Kay Lynn tight. She cried so hard her shoulders jerked up and down. Poppa wrapped his arms around them both. Tears—of joy and sorrow, relief and fear—poured out of them.

Everything was going to be all right. Lenny was alive and on his way to Berkeley. Perhaps now she'd be satisfied.

At the end of the workday, Kay Lynn rushed home to tell her family the fantastic news. The maple trees, dressed in their best fall colors, celebrated as well. Some endings were the most beautiful part of life. This one certainly was—the end of the war for their family. The children would be beside themselves with joy. Timmy didn't actually remember Lenny, but he cared because they did.

"I have great news!" she declared as soon as she found her family in the kitchen. Mitch had started dinner, and the children were playing Go Fish at the table.

Three beautiful faces stared at her.

"Lenny is on his way here!" she declared, giving herself a chill just by saying it out loud.

Those faces cracked wide with joy.

Lizzie screamed. It pierced, but Kay Lynn didn't scold. Timmy, captivated by her excitement, joined in the cheering. Mitch added a shout of joy of his own.

"Wahoo!" Kay Lynn tipped back her head and let herself yell at the top of her lungs. *"Wahoo!"*

"When will he be back?" Mitch asked, putting an end to the loud chorus.

Kay Lynn shrugged. "The telegram didn't say."

"Let's make him a welcome-home sign," Lizzie said to her brother. She grabbed his hand, and they ran off.

Mitch hugged Kay Lynn. She melted into his embrace. Except for Kristine, absolutely everything had fallen back into place—at least the most important things. She exhaled and felt her body begin to release years of fear.

"I'm very happy for your mother. For the whole family . . . all of us," Mitch said.

There was something strange in his voice.

"What?" Kay Lynn asked.

"I have bad news, or not-so-good news," he replied.

Her lungs tightened.

"Mrs. Jacobs stopped by. They're selling the house."

"How is that bad news? We can buy our home!"

"Eighty-five hundred."

"Dollars?" Kay Lynn exclaimed. "Is she crazy? I know prices have gone up, but she's insane."

He shrugged. "I don't know what she can get, but I know we don't have that much money, and she won't take payments over time. I asked."

Kay Lynn's heart fell to the floor. "When?!"

"She'll give us a week to decide. Then she'll advertise it in the newspaper. She claims it's less than she can get on the open market."

Kay Lynn sank into a chair. Move? She looked around her beloved kitchen. She didn't want to leave the only home the children had ever known.

"I can't," she stuttered. "I don't even know how to think about this."

Mitch nodded. "We don't need to panic. The real estate men in my department can advise us."

"I'll go into the realtor's office on College Avenue. They'll know about prices in this neighborhood."

Moving into action she opened the paper to the real estate section. She turned past the many pages that had column after column listed under Housing Wanted. She finally got to the Houses for Sale section and found the listing for Berkeley. She counted eighteen for the whole city.

The first listing was a three-bedroom for fifteen thousand dollars in Arlington. That neighborhood was way out of their price range. Eleven thousand dollars for a duplex in a commercial area.

A two-bedroom at Dwight and Sacramento was listed for seven thousand five hundred dollars. Her heart sank. That was smaller and only a few blocks away; it would be the same price as this neighborhood or less. Mrs. Jacobs wasn't crazy. She pointed to the listing. Mitch read it over her shoulder.

Two bedrooms. They had three upstairs plus the office downstairs.

"It appears she's offering us a good price," he said.

"This might work for us. 'Open Sunday, ten to five, 1442 Sixth Street. Lovely two-bedroom home, very clean. Large lot. No racial restrictions. Special attention veterans, one thousand eight hundred fifty dollars down, balance thirty dollars per month,'" she read. "Maybe we can manage that?"

He stared at her.

"We'd have to borrow back all the money we paid my parents and then some," she mumbled. She shook her head. "It's never ending. How can we possibly get out of this debt?"

Mitch shrugged. "We'll manage," he said, but he looked as stricken as she felt.

"I was *so* happy when I knew Lenny was safe and on his way to us. I thought that would settle everything and I could relax. Now I have to solve this before I'll be at peace."

Once again she believed she was on a clear path to the Emerald City and she was forced off it. This time by the evil flying monkeys of housing. All she wanted was a nice home for her family. Was that too much to expect from life?

CHAPTER 31

December 1945

A week later Kay Lynn greeted Missy on the playground at Lincoln School. "Happy fourth birthday!"

Working for her family had its challenges, but also benefits. Her parents had been kind enough to give her Friday afternoon off so she could spend time with Kimiko.

"How did you know it's my birthday?" Missy asked.

"I was there when you were born."

"Mrs. Brooke is the first person who ever touched you," Kimiko explained to her daughter.

Missy looked at Kay Lynn, surprise widening her beautiful brown eyes.

"You plopped out onto a towel on the floor right in front of me. I scooped you up and put you in your momma's arms. It was so exciting and so scary. You were beautiful and tiny and perfect."

Missy beamed and then ran off to the jungle gym to join the older kids.

"That was a lifetime ago, in so many ways," Kay Lynn said.

Kimiko nodded. "How was the reunion with Lenny?"

Kay Lynn welled up. "Beautiful. Horrible. He's like a shell of his former self—so thin and fragile. The children could sense it right away; they were quiet and serious, as if we were attending a funeral. I could see him struggling to speak, trying to smile. It's like he has a memory of knowing how, but he's lost the ability to interact with others."

Kimiko sighed. "So many men are coming back like that. It's them, but not them."

"Is it still battle fatigue if it comes from being a prisoner of war?" Kay Lynn wondered. "That was a long time to be locked away and uncertain."

Shame poured over Kay Lynn. Kimiko had been locked up and uncertain for nearly three years. She was being insensitive.

"I'm sorry," Kay Lynn stuttered. "Our family problems are nothing compared to what you've been through."

"In the camp I realized that diminishing my pain didn't help anyone. Some people had it worse; some had it better. But better and worse was individual. I stopped trying to understand why some were sad and others furious; some organized and some took to bed. We all coped in our own ways. I settled on doing my best to be kind and to withdraw when I could no longer be kind to those around me."

Kay Lynn took in the wisdom of Kimiko's words. Too often just being kind was difficult. And judging, herself and others, came too easily.

Kimiko teared up. "Kenji's regiment liberated Dachau."

The word *Dachau* was a giant wave crashing over Kay Lynn. The reports in the paper were sickening; the pictures of emaciated men, the stories of systematic murder and forced labor entirely changed her understanding of what horror humans were capable of doing to one another. The two women sat in silence, each lost in her own emotion.

"April 29, 1945," Kimiko said.

Kay Lynn sucked in her breath. "The day Lucie was born," she murmured. "Is this what life is from now on? Anniversaries that connect the very best with the very worst. Missy's birth and Pearl Harbor? Dachau and Lucie? Such beauty and such brutality right next to each other is dizzying."

"*Dizzy* is the right word," Kimiko agreed, her voice somber. "I too have been dizzy. I wait for the world to stop spinning, which is foolish because science tells us spinning is what keeps our feet firmly on this planet."

Kay Lynn felt something give inside her.

"I just didn't know, none of us did, that this war would change our world so fundamentally that we will not be going back. For months, then years, I waited for a return to normal. Years later I'm still struggling to accept that there is no going back"—Kay Lynn's voice broke—"but perhaps we will move forward and eventually arrive at a new normal."

She choked up, cleared her throat, and blurted out, "We have to move because we can't afford to buy our home."

"That's very sad," Kimiko replied. "I'm sorry."

"Mitch's colleagues are confident our landlady can get more than the price she's asking of us; there's been bidding wars. I don't understand how people have such incomes. They told him we should look in Contra Costa. The new houses out there have three bedrooms and large lots with guaranteed low-cost funding for GIs so they can close quickly."

"Is that what you're going to do?" Kimiko asked.

"No." Kay Lynn shook her head. "I have no desire to leave South Berkeley or North Oakland. A realtor is showing us houses west of Sacramento tomorrow. He says he has a small selection, and they sell fast. I'll miss being able to walk to my parents' home, but we hope to get permission to keep the kids at Lincoln School."

Kimiko replied, "Principal Bartley has been very understanding about the turmoil the low housing stock is causing. I'm sure he'll make accommodations for you like he did for us."

It was hard to fathom that she was now one of the people struggling to find a home in this terrible "seller's market," as the real estate men called it. If only they had bought something before the war. It was water under the bridge, but she kicked herself for getting so comfortable in her home that she'd didn't realize it wasn't her house.

CHAPTER 32

December 1945

"Momma, Timmy and I talked about it, and we don't want to hug Uncle Lenny," Lizzie informed them as they were walking to Sunday supper.

Her children exchanged nervous looks.

Kay Lynn exhaled hard. She understood why they were making this request. Lenny was stiff and vacant. It was hard to know that he welcomed hugs from them. He hardly spoke, and when he did, it was about something that already passed or that didn't seem to make any sense except to him. But they all had to make him feel loved, including the children.

She shook her head. "He's your uncle. He's been through something so horrific that we don't want to even imagine it. Our job is to make everyone coming back feel welcomed."

"Momma . . ." Lizzie started to whine.

"You are not talking back to me, are you?!"

"No, Momma."

"Thank you," Kay Lynn snipped. Unsettled, she let herself walk behind the rest of her family until they got to the Grands. She sounded confident, but she was torn. Normally she would let her children decide who to hug, but Lenny was their uncle and he needed to be embraced by family.

"Aunt Kristine!" Timmy ran to greet her, showing her the bouncy ball he'd brought. She rocked him side to side in a big embrace.

Lizzie gave her aunt a less energetic but still enthusiastic hug.

They gave quick hugs to Lenny, clearly dutiful to meet Kay Lynn's demand. He allowed it, but he didn't look at either of them, nor did they exchange any words. That was fine.

She hugged Lenny next, his arms stiff at his side. When she pulled back she looked at him. He made eye contact.

"I'm so very glad to see you," she said.

His deep-brown eyes watered up. "Really?" he asked.

Tearing up, she nodded. "Truly. Our family isn't complete without you."

He pulled in his eyebrows, considering her statement, and finally gave a small nod. As if he were considering if she could be correct. He turned and walked away without saying more.

She exhaled. Then hugged the other members of her family in turn. She was in the dining room before she realized that somehow she'd hugged everyone in the house except Kristine. Had Kristine avoided her, or had she avoided Kristine? She didn't know anymore.

"How was your tour of homes? Did you find one?" Momma asked after they said grace.

Kay Lynn looked around the table. They were all there: Grammy Sadie, Momma, Poppa, Mitch, Timmy, Lizzie, Kristine, and Lenny. She teared up again. She was so grateful and so disturbed that it was hard to contain all of the conflicting emotions within her. The tension between her and Kristine and the awkwardness with Lenny were awful, but the war was over and they were here, alive and well.

Her face must have revealed her complex emotions, because Poppa said, "That bad?"

Mitch replied with a sigh, "We can scarcely afford houses in Berkeley or Oakland that are less than one thousand square feet *and* need repairs."

Kay Lynn added, "Which we can't afford."

"Will you continue to rent?" Poppa asked.

"Rents have gone up so much that it's more than a mortgage payment. It seems wiser for us to buy if we can," Mitch said.

He looked sideways at Kay Lynn, and she nodded her consent.

"My fellow students in real estate say the smart move is Lafayette or Orinda," Mitch said. "GI loans are already approved for use in those new tracts. Redlining means that we can't use the GI housing benefit in many neighborhoods in Berkeley. Ironically, we could afford those neighborhoods if they allowed us to use the favorable terms in the GI loans."

"Redlining?" Grammy Sadie asked. "What's redlining?"

"During the Depression the government made maps indicating what neighborhoods are going up in value and which ones are going down. They don't guarantee or give loans in neighborhoods where prices aren't going up because they didn't want to be left with bad investments."

"That makes good business sense," Poppa said. "I'm glad Uncle Sam isn't wasting our tax dollars."

Kay Lynn burst out, "I'm not glad that Uncle Sam thinks he knows enough about Berkeley to know where to invest. The real estate agent assures us prices will keep going up. But how can those houses go up in value if all of the best loans aren't available there? It isn't fair. It seems to me the federal government should help those of us who can't afford larger, newer homes."

"Are you going to buy in Lafayette?" Momma sounded scared.

Kay Lynn replied, "I've agreed to look at houses out there before we make a decision, but we only have a few weeks to decide. Our house was in the paper this week."

"The tunnel and highway make it a fifteen-minute drive from Lafayette to Berkeley," Mitch said.

Kay Lynn heard a sniffle and looked at her daughter. A tear ran down Lizzie's cheek. Kay Lynn opened her arms. The girl accepted the offer of a cuddle. Lizzie curled up, only half succeeding. It was bittersweet to hold the ten-year-old on her lap.

Lizzie understood moving through the tunnel would mean a new school for her. Kay Lynn hugged her tight but didn't reassure her of anything she couldn't deliver. Mitch's arguments for moving made logical sense. Once he was finished with school, she wouldn't need to work to pay their bills if they lived in Lafayette. The new, large high school had all the latest amenities, unlike Berkeley High, which was showing its age. He assured her they could still go to church in Oakland if she wanted to and come to Sunday dinner. He could commute to university, and eventually to work, with the car or by bus, and it would hardly take more time than her walk to work did now. She could even drop him off and keep the car to spend time in Berkeley or Oakland.

But it wouldn't be the same. She just wanted to live in their home, but staying wasn't an option. They had to move.

After dinner, Kay Lynn was alone with her father in the kitchen, washing up the dishes.

"Poppa, will Lenny be okay? I know it's only been a few weeks, but he seems . . ." She searched for the right words. "Gone? Like he doesn't want to be here, or maybe he can't?"

"He's living in two worlds. When you've faced what he faced, it's hard to believe this world is real," Poppa said.

"What do you mean?"

"There are rules and kindnesses here that are hard to trust once you learn firsthand the lengths a man will go to survive." He looked up at her with his deep-brown eyes, red and shiny. "Knowing what lies in other men's hearts is hard to live with."

Kay Lynn nodded. She waited while her father wrestled with something from his past.

"It was even more terrifying to discover what I was capable of." His voice broke. He cleared his throat. "I promised myself to live a gentle life after what I did. To make up for . . ." He shook his head. "I will take it to my grave, but I see it in Lenny's eyes. Perhaps he hasn't learned about the depths of his own depravity, but he's no longer naïve about what men are capable of."

Kay Lynn spoke gently, "Will you speak to him about your experiences? It may help him to know that you understand."

He stared at her, panic in his eyes. More silence filled the room. Apparently she was asking too much of him.

"I don't want him to think less of me," he finally confessed.

"Oh, Poppa," she countered, "knowing this causes me to think *more* highly of you."

He shook his head.

"Truly," Kay Lynn insisted. "Even if I imagined you doing the worst that humans are capable of, and I've read and heard entirely too much of it for the last four years, I'm impressed that you chose love and kindness. If you felt anything like Lenny seems to feel." She teared up. "You never treated me differently—"

"You are my daughter, no different," he interrupted.

"Most men would not feel that way. You are a good man. Despite what harm you did—were forced to do."

He looked straight into her eyes. "Kay Lynn, *you* transformed me—made me want to be a loving poppa instead of a scared and hurt boy."

Kay Lynn's heart swelled; tears burned at her eyeballs. She smiled at the only father she ever wanted to please.

"I know you stood up for me with Yaya," she confessed. "That year, with the dresses. I was so ashamed, but you . . . Thank you."

"You heard me? Speak to her?"

Kay Lynn nodded. "I was retrieving a ball from under the tree, hidden from your view, but I saw you."

"My mother did not choose kindness." He shrugged. "I don't know why she was petty and bitter, to the end, but she was."

He blinked; lost in his thoughts. Kay Lynn waited.

Eventually he pushed out through a tight voice, "I cannot imagine how we will move forward as a world, as a country."

Kay Lynn thought for a moment and finally replied, "The Buddhists say peace starts in each human heart, spreads to families, then radiates to a town, a nation, and finally, perhaps, a world. I think we will move forward one heart, one family, at a time."

He got quiet and then asked, "Will you make up with Kristine?"

"Is it that obvious?" She'd thought they'd been successful at hiding the tension between them.

"Yes. Your mother is concerned. She frets over you two, nearly as much as Lenny. What's the problem?"

Kay Lynn hesitated. "It started with a small confusion. Right before Mitch's accident I learned something she meant to keep private." That was all Kay Lynn was comfortable saying. "We didn't speak of it then, and soon we stopped speaking about anything of consequence. I know she would *do* anything for me, and I hope she knows that is true of me. I didn't set out to invade her privacy. And now so much water has passed under the bridge that I can't tell if she isn't speaking to me or I'm not speaking to her. It's very confusing."

"Kristine is one of the most private people I know," Poppa said with a shrug. "We can't force her to confide in us."

Kay Lynn nodded. It felt impossible to bring up what she saw with her sister, but she had to at least try to repair their breach—for their parents' sake, if not for each other's. Kay Lynn assuring Kristine she was keeping her confidence might make ease between them again.

Kay Lynn left the kitchen, resolved to broker a peace with Kristine. She was done being a coward. Their standoff was not serving anyone, and it was harming all of them.

"Kristine, can we please speak?"

Her sister's brown eyes went wide. She shook her head. Panic in her face, she replied in a low voice, "I have nothing I want to discuss with you."

"I can talk with you here, or we can go for a walk around the block, but I have something I need to say to you," Kay Lynn insisted, despite the pounding in her heart.

Fury replaced the fear in Kristine's eyes. Her sister rose and hissed, "Walk around the block."

Kristine turned and left immediately out the door, down Woolsey. She walked at a clip, forcing Kay Lynn to rush to keep up.

"I'm sorry I saw what I saw," Kay Lynn started.

"You didn't see anything!" Kristine responded.

Kay Lynn took a deep breath. As much as she wanted to argue, to insist that she saw what she saw, to understand what she saw, Kristine wasn't ready to explain.

Kay Lynn stopped walking. She watched her sister fly down the sidewalk. Kristine was at once a woman and a child.

Kristine stopped, spun around, and yelled, "What? What do you, Miss Perfect, *have* to say to me?"

Kay Lynn walked up to her sister like she approached Lizzie when she was on the edge of a tantrum.

"We do not have to speak of that night ever again. I love you. You're my sister, no matter what—do you understand?" Kay Lynn felt tears sting the back of her eyes.

"You don't know what it's like!" Kristine growled.

"I don't," Kay Lynn agreed.

"I think I would kill myself before letting Momma and Poppa . . ."

"No!" Kay Lynn's heart squeezed tight. "Don't say that. They love you. I've never heard Momma say a bad word about Mr. Navias and Mr. Grant from church."

"I *do not* want to talk about it," Kristine insisted.

Kay Lynn nodded and took in a deep breath to calm herself. They resumed their walk, slowly moving forward, turning on Eton, then Claremont, and back to Woolsey, making the triangle they walked so often when they were kids. Kristine stayed next to her. Both silent; both not discussing it. Perhaps agreeing not to talk would make Kristine talk to her again.

CHAPTER 33

December 1945

Kay Lynn checked the clock on the dashboard the moment they drove away from their house: ten forty. They were heading to Lafayette to meet Mr. Sweet, the realtor. He represented three different tracts, and each tract had more than one home currently available—some were brand new. Timmy and Lizzie begged to go too, so the four of them set out together. She'd marked the route to the first home on the map that lay on her lap. She navigated, her finger following the path on the paper while Mitch drove the car on the highway. When he pulled into the driveway on Sunnybrook, it was 10:53. Mitch was correct, these homes were less than fifteen minutes from Berkeley.

This house was at the end of a cul-de-sac, set back from the road. Before she could study the neighborhood, a man walked up to the car and opened the door for her.

"Mrs. Brooke?"

She nodded.

He reached out a hand. "How do you do? I'm Mr. Sweet. Let's find you the home of your dreams!"

She shook his hand politely, keeping her retort to herself: *Then let's head back to Berkeley.*

The children skipped up the walkway to the wide brick porch, large enough for two chairs and a bench. The man opened the door with a flourish, as if they were entering a grand estate instead of a good-sized living room. Though Kay Lynn was impressed by the beautiful box-beamed ceilings. It added an unexpected warmth and style to the modern architecture.

"The fireplace works well but is mostly ornamental. The furnace is fabulous and has ducts in every single room. Unlike Berkeley, all of the homes I'll be showing you have adequate heat."

He led them to the dining room with a lovely view of the back-yard through a large picture window. To the right was the kitchen, which also had a view of the garden from the sink. He opened the back door and gestured for the kids to go out with a wave of his arm.

"Pick a lemon if you like," he called to the children and pointed to a tree heavy with fruit.

"As you can see"—he pointed through the window over the sink—"you can easily keep watch over your children while you cook and clean."

Kay Lynn had never worried about her children in the yard while she was in the kitchen, but she did see the attraction of being able to see them, and it was a nicer view than the stucco on the side of her neighbor's house. The children ran in a big circle on the grass, each grabbed a lemon, and returned to the kitchen.

"What's that?" Lizzie pointed to a flap in the door.

"It's a pet door, for a dog or cat. They can come and go without you having to let them in or out."

"Lucie would *love* that, don't you think?" Timmy said.

She would, as would Kay Lynn. Letting her in and out was tiresome.

"Come see the three bedrooms, and the two baths! You'll be amazed at how delightful and practical it is to have two bathrooms, one for the parents and one for the children. There's no fighting in the morning between fathers and children getting ready for their days."

They walked down a small hallway and peeked into two good-sized bedrooms with large built-in closets. Mr. Sweet slid the doors of the closet from side to side.

"These sliding closet doors don't intrude on the room, so you can use more of the space, unlike a hinged door." They were more than double the size of the closets in their current home. It would make keeping their room tidy more practical.

He moved on to the last bedroom. The third and largest also had a view of the backyard and a doorway into a private bathroom.

"I want this one," Timmy declared.

"This is the master bedroom, young man, for your parents. One day, you will earn the right to have your own master bedroom."

Timmy nodded, taking in the words of this salesman as if he were Moses himself. Kay Lynn was at once impressed and annoyed by his tactics. She wanted to hate this home, but it *was* wonderful. Her heart sank.

The realtor walked them back to the kitchen. He pulled papers out of his briefcase and lay them on the peninsula between the kitchen and the dining room; a map of Lafayette was on top.

"Let me give you an overview of this neighborhood, your neighborhood." He pointed to a dot. "Here is this home. The elementary school is right here, the reservoir is right here, and your nearest grocery store is here. The reservoir is one of the loveliest recreational facilities in the entire San Francisco Bay Area. When we finish with our tours today, you must drive around before you make your final decision. We only want the finest families who want to be a part of this community to buy here."

He turned to the next piece of paper. "Here are the numbers. This is the asking price. You need only put down fifteen hundred dollars, and the guaranteed financing through your GI benefits means your monthly payment for your loan would be $25. Taxes and insurance are additional, of course, but taxes provide you with the schools you want for your children, so they're an investment in your future. This is the bottom line you'll be paying each month to live in this fine home." He circled a number.

Kay Lynn's stomach dropped. It was less than she had imagined. Mitch looked at her, his eyes wide. She bit her lip and nodded.

Fifteen minutes. Fifteen minutes. Fifteen minutes, she chanted in her mind.

"I have one of these sheets for each home we'll visit today. Ready to see the next one?" the realtor asked. He walked out without waiting for their reply. He seemed to think they were hooked, and he just had to reel them in.

At the end of the morning, they'd seen five homes and reviewed the five price sheets. They were all similar sized and equally afford-able, but the first was beautiful with charming details the others didn't have. Kay Lynn imagined herself in that yard, in that kitchen, and in that bedroom. She would be happy in that home.

"The good news is you have five lovely choices," the realtor said. "The bad news is that I have an appointment at two o'clock with another wonderful family. They will have the same five choices unless you remove one of them by signing a purchase agreement. As you probably noticed, the home on Sunnybrook is unique—custom built. There's no other like it. I can't guarantee it will be available next week-end. Or even this evening."

Kay Lynn felt physically ill. Did she trust this man? If she had to move out here, she wanted *that* house. Did she really have to make a decision today, this morning?

"Can you give us a few minutes to speak?" Mitch asked.

The man pulled out a card. "I'm heading back to my office. I'll be there until one forty-five. Should you settle on one or have further questions, come by. We can have you sign the papers before you head back to Berkeley."

He shook both their hands and left them alone in the front yard of a house.

"If it's no for you, we can drive home," Mitch said.

Kay Lynn teared up. "It's not. I love the Sunnybrook house," she pushed out through a tight throat. "It feels like home."

He nodded.

"I'm afraid I'll regret it if we lose the chance to live there." She shook her head. "I can't believe I'm saying this, but I think we should buy it."

His eyes went wide. "Are you certain?"

Her chin quivered. "I love our house, but we can't keep it. I have to be realistic, think about our future, not the past. Lizzie is on her way to being a young woman; I don't want them sharing a bedroom. As you say, my parents will be fifteen minutes away."

She stopped speaking. She closed her eyes and imagined one of the small bungalows in Berkeley they'd looked at and filled with dread.

She took a few deep breaths. She pictured the house on Sunnybrook. *Is that our home?* She waited for the still, small voice Grammy Sadie spoke of. Her heart started to race; she felt into it— excited. It was a beautiful house; she would be happy there. They would be happy.

Kay Lynn had her answer. "My heart is telling me our home is on Sunnybrook."

Mitch smiled. "I love it too."

Kay Lynn teared up. They were really doing this.

"I'm going to be sad for a few days," she prepared him, "but I do want to do it."

Mitch nodded and pulled her into a full embrace. She rested into him and imagined telling the kids,

We're moving!

Remember the first house? That's going to be ours!

Daddy and I've decided we are moving to Lafayette.

Lizzie glared at them as they broke their embrace. "We're moving here, aren't we?"

Kay Lynn and Mitch nodded in unison.

Mitch said, "Not this house, the first one. With the lemon tree in the backyard."

"Hooray!" Timmy declared, "That was my favorite."

"Shut up!" Lizzie shouted at him, and ran off.

Kay Lynn followed, intending to scold her for yelling unacceptable words at her brother. But Lizzie, collapsed on the clean sidewalk, was sobbing so hard that Kay Lynn simply sat down on the ground next to her.

Eventually, Lizzie spoke. "I hate Lafayette. This is never, ever going to be my home."

Kay Lynn rubbed her back. "I'm sad to leave Berkeley too."

"I won't get to go to Willard, will I?" Lizzie confirmed.

"No."

"Why can't we stay? I don't mind sharing a room with Timmy," Lizzie said. "I promise. I won't ever complain about him, even when I'm sixteen."

"This is a decision that Daddy and I are making. We're thinking about the good of our whole family. Changing schools is hard, and you're strong enough to do it."

"What if I'm not?" Lizzie asked.

"If we have learned anything from this terrible war, it is that people can do hard things," Kay Lynn reminded her daughter. "Donna made a *much* harder move than this, right?"

Lizzie hung her head. "I've been praying they would be our neighbors again."

Kay Lynn smiled. "Me too. Maybe they will be. There are so many houses out here, perhaps they'll move here too."

Lizzie sat up. "Really?"

"Of course," Kay Lynn replied. "I thought it would be terrible until we came here. Mr. and Mrs. Fujioka might decide this side of the tunnel is best for their family as well."

"It's a nice backyard. And I liked the room that Timmy didn't want, so we won't have a fight about that."

Kay Lynn took in a deep breath and exhaled. Just like that, Lizzie's despair had turned into excitement. If Kay Lynn hadn't had the same emotional loop the loop, she'd be concerned about her daughter's well-being. Three hours ago, she couldn't have imagined agreeing to move here, and now she was ready to sign on the dotted line. The complexity of the human heart, even her own, or maybe especially her own, was hard to understand sometimes.

When they walked into his office, Mr. Sweet grinned as if he'd won a bet.

"Let me guess . . . ," he insisted, paused, and declared, "you want to purchase the house on Sunnybrook?"

They nodded.

"I could tell that was your home. A realtor gets a sense for these things. Excellent. Let me get the papers for you to sign, Mr. Brooke. My man will get the loan settled for you. All I need today is your signature on a few pages and a fifteen-hundred-dollar deposit. Mrs. Brooke, you and the kids could get some ice cream down the street while we take care of this boring business."

Kay Lynn asked, "I don't need to sign the papers? We want my name on the deed."

"California is a community property state. Anything either of you purchases belongs to both of you—unless you have a legal agreement in place that I don't know about." He paused for a chuckle. "Mr. Brooke can fill in your name for the deed. We only need his signature."

Kay Lynn looked at Mitch. He shrugged. She shrugged back with a tip of her head.

"Let's get some ice cream, kids!" she declared, excited to explore their new city. It suddenly seemed like the best of both worlds—an adventure in a new place combined with the comfort and security of being close to her family.

CHAPTER 34

December 1945

Kay Lynn took in the majesty of their church sanctuary. The bright sun caused the Sower, the stained-glass window over the chancel, to glow. She loved its colors as well as the message it conveyed from the parable in the Bible: to be fertile soil for the teachings of the spirit.

Mr. Navias and Mr. Grant sat three rows in front of her. No one spoke of it, but everyone understood they were homosexual. They participated in all the church activities as a couple. She scanned the other rows. Were there women in such relationships? She'd never considered the possibility, but after that night at the White Horse, she knew otherwise.

There were several pairs of women who lived together that attended their church. Kay Lynn had never considered they were anything other than spinsters making their way in the world together. She watched two such women, who usually sat in the row in front of her. It was subtle but obvious they were not simply roommates now that the scales had fallen from her eyes.

Momma slipped in next to her. The young Reverend Crompton started the service. Kay Lynn preferred when President Reinhardt led the worship, but this new, young minister was beginning to draw a nice crowd.

Kay Lynn took her momma's hand. After church she would deliver the bittersweet news: they'd bought a house in Lafayette. What a difference this week, these twenty-four hours, had made.

Kay Lynn took a deep breath. She took Mitch's hand with her left hand. Their two weaker hands hooked together, reminding her that difference wasn't a problem unless you rejected it.

Mr. Navias whispered into Mr. Grant's ear. Mr. Grant turned his head and looked at Mr. Navias with pure love. She smiled and leaned her head against Mitch's shoulder. She was suddenly grateful to be part of a church that could welcome these two men. While it would seem tragic if Kristine never had children and had to hide to be safe, Kay Lynn was confident she could hide in plain sight in their church.

Kay Lynn waited for the bell to ring at Lincoln School. She'd left work early once again to catch Kimiko to deliver their news in person. She didn't want Lizzie to keep it secret from Donna, nor did she want Donna to have to keep it from her parents.

She blinked back tears as Missy skipped up to her. "Hello, Mrs. Brooke!" She turned around and pointed to her tall ponytail. "Do you like my new ribbon?"

"That is a beautiful red," Kay Lynn replied.

"Thank you."

The little girl sat close to Kay Lynn on the bench, leaving room for her mother.

"How was your search for a house?" Kimiko asked as soon as she sat down.

"Horrible; wonderful," she said, her voice tight. "We found one we loved in Lafayette. We'll be moving in a few weeks."

"So soon." Her voice was quiet.

"Our landlady offered us one hundred dollars if we leave before the New Year."

"Congratulations," Kimiko said.

"Thank you. It feels like a funeral and a birth at the same time."

Kimiko nodded. "Most beginnings are also endings."

"I'm sadder for Lizzie than for myself," she said. "But sad for me too."

Kimiko nodded.

"We'll come back often. I'll work out here until Mitch has finished with school. I don't know all the details, but I hope nothing will change in our friendship." As soon as she said it, Kay Lynn knew that was impossible. She corrected her statement. "I know our friendship will change; I only hope it will never end."

Kimiko squeezed her hand. "Me too."

Kay Lynn teared up. "As hard as the 1930s were, with the Depression and our very little ones, I sometimes feel as if I forgot to notice how wonderful it was too. Or at least to notice the parts that were wonderful. Do I sound silly?"

Kimiko said, "Not at all. It's like the play *Our Town*. At the end when Emily is a ghost and says how none of us can take it all in when we're alive."

"Yes! That's what I'm trying to say. And you, I just thought you'd always be there, living next to me . . ." She sighed. "I told Lizzie maybe you and Ken would like to move through the tunnel. The price per square foot is so much less, the GI Bill makes financing it easy, and it's only a fifteen-minute drive, but you would need a car."

"And to learn how to drive," Kimiko replied. "Though Ken says he'll learn soon."

"I feared it until I started doing it; now I find driving very liberating."

The doors opened, and the kids ran out onto the playground, ending their conversation. Kimiko sounded like she would consider moving east. Perhaps her dream of them being neighbors again was not so far-fetched.

CHAPTER 35

December 1945

Everything was packed in boxes. Tomorrow they were taking all of their belongings to Sunnybrook Drive.

Kay Lynn considered asking Lizzie and Timmy to help her in the yard but decided to do this alone. She dug in several spots, finding crocus bulbs hidden underneath the earth. Some were large, some were ready to be divided, and others were nearing the end of their lives. Ten healthy bulbs seemed enough. She dug out all the carnations, placing them in three separate containers. And finally, she dug out some of the Queen Anne's lace and flowering rosemary. They weren't as dear as the others, but it would do well in the more arid climate through the tunnel.

She looked over at the wisteria across the street. It was all branches and no leaves. She would miss it. Perhaps she could collect some of the pods next spring and plant one of her own in their new yard. Would wisteria take in Lafayette? If it could, it would likely be years and years before it would bloom.

She left the precious plants on the porch, washed her hands, and called her family to the table for their last meal in that home.

"Let's share memories . . . good and sad ones, from this home," Kay Lynn said after everyone had served themselves. She wanted to imprint this place on her children's memories.

Lizzie's hand shot up. Kay Lynn nodded.

"My first scary memory here turned out to be happy," Lizzie said. "Remember when Missy was born? You had blood on your face and dress when you came to tell us. I thought something really bad had happened, but it was just Mrs. Fujioka having a baby."

Kay Lynn smiled. "That was a beautiful and surprising day."

Timmy followed suit. "I remember all my birthday cakes: four was vanilla, five was spice, and six was white!"

"That's not all," Lizzie retorted. "You don't remember one, two, and three, do you?"

He shook his head.

Mitch said, "I remember bursting with joy walking into the house with an angel and a pirate on Halloween. I was very, very happy to be home."

"That was a really, really, really good day," Lizzie agreed.

"Did you have happy tears?" Timmy asked.

Mitch smiled at their son. "I did."

Timmy nodded, looking proud. He asked, "What do you remember, Mommy?"

"Want to try to guess my memory?"

"Yes!" Lizzie yelled. She loved their memory game. "It had to happen at home, right?" Lizzie confirmed.

Kay Lynn nodded.

"Was Daddy there?" the girl asked.

"Yes."

"How old was I?"

"Yes or no questions, Timmy!" Lizzie corrected her brother.

"Was I older than five?" he asked.

"Yes," Kay Lynn said.

"Were we eating something?" Mitch asked.

"No."

"Were we in the living room? Listening to the radio?"

"No and no."

"Our bedroom?" Timmy asked.

"No."

"Your bedroom?" Lizzie asked.

"Yes."

Mitch smiled. He'd figured out the memory but didn't say so.

Lizzie scrunched up her face in thought.

"When Lucie—" she blurted out.

Timmy interrupted, "Came home!"

"Yes!" Kay Lynn declared.

"That was the best!" Lizzie said. "She was so little and curled up in her cute little box by your bed."

"We sat on the floor and just watched her sleep," Kay Lynn said. "Waiting for her to wake up."

A knock on the door interrupted their reminiscing. Lizzie ran to the entry and returned with a paper bag.

"Mr. Cuthbert gave us some sugar to keep!" she explained. "He said it's in case we don't have neighbors to borrow it from."

Kay Lynn laughed. That was a fitting goodbye from the man who had turned out to be a fine neighbor. Not close, but reliable and kind.

Kay Lynn's parents and brother arrived to help pack up the truck they borrowed from Cousin Alex.

"Kristine is on her way separately," Momma announced before Kay Lynn asked about her.

"Hi, Uncle Lenny," Timmy said, navigating around the packed boxes lining the living room. Timmy wrapped his arms around

Lenny, who hugged him back. Kay Lynn smiled, pleased to see the genuine warmth between them. She had been right to encourage her kids to be welcoming to their uncle.

"I like your shirt," Lenny said to his nephew. "That's my favorite blue."

Timmy smiled. "Me too!"

Kay Lynn embraced Lenny, and he hugged back, holding her close for an extra moment. Then he bent over to give Lucie a long belly rub. Before the war, those small interactions would have been unremarkable, but today they were absolutely beautiful. Lenny was healing.

"Hello, everyone," Kristine said from the doorway. "This is David," she announced, gesturing toward the young, dark-haired man at her side.

He waved at them in greeting and then jumped right into carrying the heavy furniture with Lenny.

Kay Lynn directed from inside the house while Mitch oversaw the loading of the truck. When she reached the back office, Momma followed her in, looking around to make sure they were alone. "What do you know about David?" she whispered.

Kay Lynn shook her head and shrugged. "Nothing."

"He seems like a nice enough young man," Momma said. "Right?"

"I suggest you don't make a fuss," she replied, "or Kristine will pull into her shell."

David and Lenny walked in with Kimiko's trunk.

David said, "Mitch thinks you want to leave this trunk here for your friend."

Kay Lynn stared at it. The Fujiokas' tiny apartment didn't have storage for their treasured family possessions, so she'd offered to keep it for them until they settled into a larger home.

"Tell him we're taking it to Lafayette," she replied.

In three hours, the truck was loaded, with Mitch behind the wheel, ready to take their belongings through the tunnel. The kids piled into David's car with Kristine. He'd won them over when he said of course Lucie could drive with them. Clearly, he was working to impress the family. Poppa Leo drove Momma, Grammy Sadie, and Lenny. Momma offered to drive with Kay Lynn, but she declined. She wanted to say goodbye to her home on her own.

Once they were gone, Kay Lynn walked from room to room, glad to have privacy for this bittersweet ritual. *Goodbye, thank you,* she whispered in each room, recalling the precious moments she experienced there: rocking her children to sleep; lying arm in arm with her husband; soaking in the bathtub; working with Kimiko; opening presents around the Christmas tree; family dinners. It was all so ordinary and yet so beautiful. It was *her* life.

At the front door she held up her hand: *Thank you for sheltering my family in these difficult and beautiful years.*

She pulled the door behind her. Mr. Cuthbert waved from his porch.

"Here's a ball that will get more use in your home than mine," he said, walking over to her.

She took the small ball—one of Lucie's that Mr. Cuthbert was forever throwing back over the fence.

"Thank you." She smiled at him. "For this—and for being a good neighbor."

"I know I was a bit harsh at first. I didn't want to be here any more than you wanted me," he said.

She started to protest, but it was true—she hadn't wanted him living next door.

He continued, "That was the way of this time, wasn't it? Most of us struggling to be kind in a situation we didn't want to be in."

"Yes, it was. I don't know what the future holds, but best wishes to you, Mr. Cuthbert," she said with an outstretched hand.

He took it and replied, "Same to you and yours, Mrs. Brooke."

Kay Lynn let the tears fall as she drove away from her beloved home. These streets held so many memories. They would still be here, but after today her relationship to them would be changed forever. Her markets, Lincoln School, and the Grands house had been her daily life. Now they would be places she visited. She let herself wallow in sorrow on the journey through the tunnel, not wiping her tears until she pulled up into her new driveway.

She got out of the car and looked at her house. A peculiar impulse compelled her to close her eyes. She clicked her heels together three times while thinking, *Take me home.*

Lenny walked out of the moving truck with a large box in his arms. She followed him through the front door, and her shoulders dropped in relief. The living room looked as beautiful as she remembered.

Momma was in the kitchen, setting down a big box on the counter.

"Don't strain yourself," Kay Lynn scolded.

"I know my limits," she replied.

Grammy Sadie was already putting dishes into the cupboards. "Kay Lynn, you have found a lovely house for yourself. Congratulations!"

"It *is* wonderful, isn't it?" Kay Lynn asked.

"You know I have a prejudice against modern architecture, but I see the attraction," Momma said as she waved at the view of the yard.

"I look forward to adding our favorites, but it's a lovely start, just as it is," Kay Lynn replied.

"Did you bring your crocuses and your carnations?"

Kay Lynn nodded. "Yes. They're safe in my car."

Momma and Grammy Sadie nodded approvingly. Like the crocus bulbs, the carnations had been handed down for generations. Some were mottled red and white, others were white, and others were scar-let. You never knew what was going to come up each year.

Kay Lynn said, "I have sandwich makings. Will you help me pre-pare lunch for everyone?"

The three women made quick work of it while the others unloaded the truck. The peninsula between the kitchen and dining room meant they could easily serve buffet style, each person making their own plate. Already Kay Lynn was seeing how the open architec-ture would make this a wonderful home for family gatherings.

After everyone was settled with their food in the newly furnished dining room, Kristine cleared her throat. She startled Kay Lynn by grabbing her hand under the table and squeezing it. Kristine was nervous about something. She took a deep breath and put on a smile.

"I have an announcement," she declared, a bit too loud.

All eyes turned to her. She looked at David, seated on her other side. She took his hand and held it up between them. "David and I are engaged."

"What!?" Kay Lynn exclaimed, and then immediately regretted it. "I mean, congratulations!"

Best wishes rang out around her, but Kay Lynn's mind swirled in confusion. *Engaged? How long had Kristine known this man? What happened to her . . . ?*

Kristine explained, "We've known each other since high school, so it's not as rushed as you might think."

"I've adored Kristine for a very long time," David said. "I was too shy to court her when we were younger, but the war pushed me to find courage I never knew I had."

Grammy Sadie said, "The finest of marriages have been formed that way!"

Momma and Poppa shared a sweet look. Kay Lynn studied Kristine's face. She appeared to be satisfied, though not besotted.

Unlike David, who beamed as if he had won the Irish Sweepstakes. *Should I ask Kristine about* . . . Kay Lynn's thoughts trailed.

"How will you support my daughter?" Poppa asked, only half joking.

"I'm a history teacher at Berkeley High. Not the finest living, but steady," he replied.

"Can we call you Uncle David?" Lizzie asked.

"Yes, please, that's much preferable to Aunt David!" he teased.

"Margie Biblin is David's younger sister," Kristine explained.

A round of ohs went around the room.

Margie was one of Kristine's high school friends from the bowling team.

"It seems you're following in our footsteps," Momma declared. "Are you a bowler too?"

David nodded. "Yes, indeed. You'll find us at the Berkeley Bowl on Tuesdays and Thursdays. Kristine's ladies' team is the best in the league. Now that I'll be on a mixed team with Kristine, I might place." He grinned at his fiancée.

The table laughed.

"We'll have a backyard wedding as soon as we can find a date that works for both families," Kristine explained.

"Can I be a flower girl?"

"Lizzie!" Kay Lynn admonished her. "Wait to be asked."

David asked, "Lizzie, will you be our flower girl? And, Timmy, will you be our ring bearer?" Then he looked at Kristine. "If it's acceptable to you."

She smiled and nodded. "I hope you'll be my matron of honor," she said to Kay Lynn.

Kay Lynn started to answer, but had to clear her voice first. Quietly she replied, "Yes."

She didn't know why she felt so emotional. Was she happy or sad for Kristine? It was all mixed together. She could have a family, and live her life in peace, but was she compromising too much? Could she actually be a good wife to David?

"Where will you live?" Momma asked, trepidation in her voice.

"His family home on Parker between Sacramento and Grove," Kristine said.

"My parents just sold it to me . . . to us," David explained.

A pang of jealousy pierced Kay Lynn's heart. Kristine was going to live in Berkeley, close to their old neighborhood. Her children might go to Lincoln School. She pushed down the green monster, telling herself to just be happy for Kristine, like everyone else in the family.

She stood and said, "Congratulations, to both of you. Welcome to the family, David."

Kay Lynn hoped she sounded only gracious. She started congratulatory hugs, and everyone followed her lead.

David genuinely seemed like a terrific man. His attention to her children alone had won her over. Timmy shadowed him like a love-sick puppy. But Kay Lynn could not shake off her unsettled feelings; it was so fast, too fast.

They finished their meal and returned their attention to the move. Kay Lynn was thinking about arranging their bedroom when she nearly crashed into Kristine carrying a box into the master bath. They were alone. *Should I say something?*

Before she could formulate a statement or a question, Kristine said, "He's a good man. Please don't judge me."

"Oh, you misunderstand," Kay Lynn reacted. "I *only* feel compassion for you. I know you're faced with a very difficult choice."

Kristine bit her lip; she closed the door to the bathroom. "We love each other, but we're not so brave. She's gone back to Indiana."

"I'm sorry." Kay Lynn took her sister's hand. "What's her name?"

"Oh . . ." Kristine let a tear flow. "Kelly."

Kay Lynn gasped. "Mitch's nurse?!"

Kristine nodded.

A wave of emotion caused the hair on her arms to rise. Tears pushed at Kay Lynn's eyes. "Wow. She is . . ." Kay Lynn didn't know what to say. She took a deep breath. "She's a lovely person."

Kristine nodded, tears in her eyes. "She's wonderful."

"I never said anything to Momma or Poppa," Kay Lynn assured her sister.

"But you told Mitch?" Kristine asked, with accusation.

Kay Lynn nodded.

"What did he say?" Kristine challenged, her soft tears replaced by hard eyes.

"Nothing bad. He loves you. He worries over you, like me. I know it takes courage to be"—she whispered the word—"*homosexual*. Whatever you did, I would love and support you, but this *is* easier if you think you can really . . ." She stopped. *Really what?*

"Be a good wife?" Kristine said.

Kay Lynn nodded and shrugged.

"He's a kind man. He'll be a good husband and father. I don't need romantic love to be happy."

Kay Lynn offered, "This might be the brave choice, you know."

"It's not," Kristine insisted, then shrugged. "But this is the decision that I've made, and I will live with it for the rest of my life."

Kay Lynn opened her arms, offering her sister a hug. Kristine accepted it. She leaned her head on Kay Lynn's shoulder and let herself be held. Kay Lynn felt the jerk that went with great sadness. She held her sister until the tears ran out.

"Thank you," Kristine said as she wiped at her face.

"We were each facing so much. I'm sorry I couldn't be more helpful to you," Kay Lynn said.

"I didn't let you. I just wanted to . . . be in love," Kristine said.

"That feeling doesn't last anyway," Kay Lynn replied. "I love Mitch, very much, but the heart-stopping, *I can't be away from you for a moment* kind of love fades away. But I enjoyed it while it lasted . . . and I'm glad you got to experience it."

Kristine whispered, "It still hurts, to be apart from Kelly."

"The pain will go away, eventually. And hopefully only sweet memories will remain."

Kristine looked at her and asked, "Your heart-stopping love wasn't Mitch, was it?"

"No, he wasn't my first love," Kay Lynn confirmed.

"Perhaps you have more secrets than I know," Kristine said.

Kay Lynn shrugged. "I was fifteen, so it was never going to last."

"Eighteen is so much older," Kristine teased.

Kay Lynn laughed. "It sure seemed so at the time, but now: *eighteen*? We were so young." She bit her lip, considering what to reveal. "I suppose you don't know that Mitch and I got married because I was pregnant."

Kristine's jaw fell open, like a character in a comic book. "I had no idea!"

Kay Lynn laughed. "You were in sixth grade, not information we wanted to share with you."

"Little Miss Perfect *does* have more secrets than I knew."

Kay Lynn bristled. "Why do you call me that?"

Kristine sat down on the toilet. Kay Lynn joined her level, balancing on the edge of the tub.

Kristine replied, "I was always jealous of you, trying to get your attention. You were so old and pretty and got to go on special trips to San Francisco with Momma. You came back with beautiful dresses and chocolate you would lord over us."

"Lord over you? Really?" Kay Lynn asked. She considered those trips from Kristine's point of view.

Kristine nodded.

"You know I was going to see my father who never showed up," Kay Lynn said. "Or almost never showed up."

Kristine replied, "I know that now." She shrugged. "But at the time it just made you seem like a princess. And me, well, I'm not a princess, am I?"

"Oh, Kristine," Kay Lynn said.

"Momma loves me," Kristine replied, "but she doesn't understand me like she understands you."

Kay Lynn wanted to deny it, but Kristine was right. Kay Lynn and Momma did have more in common.

"You know I was jealous of you too?" Kay Lynn replied.

"No!" Kristine reacted. "Why?"

"Well . . ." Kay Lynn choked up. She'd never said this out loud before. "Momma and Poppa wanted you, and Lenny, for always. You all belong together, and I'm . . . different."

"What do you mean? They love you!"

"I know they love me, but they didn't *want* me when I was born. Did Momma even hold me?" Kay Lynn wondered.

"What? Why wouldn't she hold you?" Kristine asked, looking sad and confused.

"Would you hold a baby you didn't want and were giving away?" Kay Lynn asked.

Kristine looked stricken. "That's so sad. I never thought about it, it's just been a story."

"Momma was younger than you are right now," Kay Lynn explained. "She hadn't even told Grammy Sadie she was pregnant. Can you imagine?!"

"Ask her!" Kristine said. "You have to ask her."

Kay Lynn pulled in her face. "If she held me?"

"Would it matter to you if she did?"

Kay Lynn felt tears push at the back of her eyes. If Momma had held her, somehow that meant she had loved her from the beginning, even if she was giving her away. She was scared to hear the wrong answer, but also longed to know.

"Maybe," Kay Lynn replied with a tilt of her head, "I'll ask her sometime. Thanks for talking honestly with me. Even though I was jealous, I always loved you."

"Me too," Kristine replied.

The sisters hugged. For the first time in many years, Kay Lynn leaned into Kristine without reservation. At once she was resting in care and giving a caring rest. A flood of love and gratitude mixed into their embrace.

CHAPTER 36

Spring 1946

"Hello, Mrs. Brooke," a voice called out while she was digging in the front yard. She was trying once again to get some of her great-grandmother's carnations to bloom in her new garden. The ones she transplanted in December had died. These she'd dug out of the Grands yard, hoping they would take root and thrive out here. The green stalks of the crocuses were healthy enough, but they hadn't flowered this year. The man at the nursery had said that he'd known them to bloom in Lafayette and suggested she buy some bone meal for the soil.

"Good afternoon, Mr. Sweet," Kay Lynn replied. She hadn't seen their realtor since the day Mitch signed the papers just before Christmas.

"The house next door is for sale, and I thought you might like a hand in choosing your neighbor."

He reached out, not for a handshake, but to give her a slip of paper. She looked it over. Her heart skipped a beat when she saw the price.

Her shock must have shown on her face. He continued, "Your home has increased in value already. Families have discovered the joy of suburban living and are clamoring to come here. Even at that price, it costs less than Rockridge or Claremont. Tell your Berkeley friends I can get them the same excellent funding you have, thanks to Uncle Sam," he said. "The ones that were soldiers, that is." He tipped his hat and went on his way.

Kay Lynn looked at the house next door. She hadn't realized the Hoctors were moving. They'd been courteous neighbors, but nothing more.

She smiled, letting herself imagine the dream of dear friends as next-door neighbors once again. Kimiko longed to move into a larger home. This house was available—and though it was expensive, there was good financing for veterans. After church tomorrow when they met up at Lincoln School, she'd tell Kimiko about it.

"Mommy! You almost forgot the paper for Mrs. Fujioka," Lizzie scolded. Her daughter took the sheet that was sitting on the peninsula and held it out.

"Thank you." Kay Lynn took the paper, folded it in half, and put it in her purse.

"These, Mommy?" Timmy pointed to the bags on the counter she'd asked the kids to carry to the car.

Kay Lynn nodded. Timmy took one, and Lizzie grabbed the other for a canned-food drive. All over the nation, churches were raising funds and gathering tin cans of food to send to the Unitarian Service Committee for the starving people in Europe. Kay Lynn carried their contribution for Sunday supper, still-warm lemon bars.

Lizzie skipped to the car, chanting a little song about Donna moving next door. Eleven was a peculiar, fascinating age, with one foot in childhood and the other in adolescence. Many days it was dizzying to know where to meet her daughter.

"Timmy, do you know that Donna and Georgie can be our neighbors again?"

Lizzie explained the situation with great, if misplaced, certainty to her brother as they drove to church in only twenty minutes. It was faster than taking the Key Route from Berkeley. Kay Lynn was again reminded why they had made the choice to move. While living in Lafayette still felt strange, it was extremely gratifying to know they were making a good, stable home for their children.

The guest minister, Dr. Fritchman, gave a preview of the address he would make on Tuesday night: America's Role in a World at Peace. He warned of never-ending conflicts without a strong United Nations. His arguments and passion were compelling, if somewhat cerebral. Dr. Fritchman reminded the congregation that as Unitarians they must take action to improve things on Earth for all people if they hoped to end the never-ending cycle of war. His conviction was contagious and gave Kay Lynn hope that the United Nations might be the means to bring peace to the world.

After church Kay Lynn left Mitch at the Grands to help Poppa Leo with a project at the house, and then drove the kids to Lincoln School. Between the rain and their schedules, it had been two months since they had visited with the Fujiokas. She and the kids had looked forward to it all week.

Lizzie spotted Donna, George, and Missy as soon as Kay Lynn pulled up. She leapt out of the car and raced across the yard toward them. Timmy ran behind her, his arms pumping hard trying to keep up. Lizzie hugged Donna in a huge embrace, rocking from side to side, and then swinging the girl around. Tears sprung to Kay Lynn's eyes. Lizzie had friends at her new school, but it wasn't the same.

"They sure love each other," Kay Lynn commented as she joined Kimiko on the bench. "That kind of devotion doesn't last forever, but it sure is beautiful."

Kay Lynn took in a deep breath, relishing the misty air. The weather in Lafayette was lovely, but she still felt more at home out here with the touch of moisture from the bay.

Kay Lynn took the realtor's paper from her purse and handed it to Kimiko.

"This house is right next door to ours," Kay Lynn declared. "We can put another gate in the fence!"

Kimiko blinked hard; she didn't look enthused. Her reaction was as disappointing as it was unexpected.

"I didn't relish the idea of moving so far, as you know, but it truly is a fifteen-minute drive."

"We would love to live there," Kimiko replied. Her voice resigned. "The distance is not the problem."

Of course, Kimiko would be concerned about the cost. Kay Lynn was eager to explain.

"The realtor arranged financing through the GI Bill. I was amazed at how affordable our monthly payments would be. If you have money for a down payment—"

"Price is not the concern either."

"Then what is?" Kay Lynn asked. Was her friend angry at her for some reason?

Kimiko looked at her and sighed. "We cannot buy through the tunnel because of the restrictions."

"What restrictions?"

"Racial restrictions," Kimiko replied.

"That can't be true!" Kay Lynn said. She thought back to the showings. The realtor hadn't mentioned it was a segregated neighborhood.

"We know families that have tried," Kimiko responded. "The realtors shrug and say their hands are tied by the deeds."

"We would never have bought a home in a place that's only for . . ." Kay Lynn paused. "Are you saying it's only for Caucasians?"

Kimiko nodded.

A pit hollowed out Kay Lynn's stomach. Kimiko must be confused. She must be thinking of a different area.

"Would you buy the home if there were no restrictions?" Kay Lynn asked.

Kimiko smiled. "It would be a dream come true to be your neighbor again."

Kay Lynn patted Kimiko's arm. "For me too!"

Kay Lynn would look at their deed to prove that Kimiko was mistaken about Kay Lynn's tract. She'd let her know, and then Ken could call Mr. Sweet first thing in the morning to jump on this chance.

Kimiko interrupted her planning with a change of subject. "How is Lenny?"

Kay Lynn's mind was dizzy, switching topics so quickly, but she accepted Kimiko was done speaking about the house and followed her lead.

Kay Lynn pictured her brother and smiled as she thought of the transformation. "So much better. Mitch helped him get a job at the university as a groundskeeper. He'd rather be outside digging, planting, and pruning than doing office work. Poppa was right; we needed to give him time to trust in the goodness of the world."

Kay Lynn asked, "How are Ken's studies going?"

"He's enjoying being a student again. He'd prefer to study law, but he would need a graduate degree and that's too many years. Engineering suits him well enough. Are Kristine and David well?"

"Yes, I have to make an effort to see her now that she doesn't live with my parents. Fortunately, David is devoted to Sunday supper— and he's a wonderful uncle."

"Is he a church man?" Kimiko asked.

"No, but Kristine isn't a church woman, so that suits them both. Their exciting news is that she's expecting."

"You're going to be an aunt!" Kimiko exclaimed with genuine joy in her eyes. "Congratulations."

"Thank you."

Kristine and David seemed to be good companions. When asked, Kristine reported that she was content with her choice. Kay Lynn hoped her report was honest—and she was grateful that their family was growing. Lizzie and Timmy were beside themselves to welcome a baby cousin.

Kimiko and Kay Lynn shared the news of their lives until it was time to leave. Kay Lynn didn't mention the house again, but she was certain Kimiko was mistaken; Kay Lynn and Mitch would have never bought a house in a white-only neighborhood. She would find their deed and prove her friend wrong. By tomorrow night they could be neighbors again.

They returned to the Grands after the park. The children ran in, excited to return to the game of Monopoly they'd been playing for two weeks. Mitch had already finished his house project and was waiting to play with them, and David and Lenny. She left them to it in the living room and found Momma and Kristine in the kitchen. After hugging them hello, she sat at the table to peel potatoes.

Ask her, Kristine mouthed to Kay Lynn when Momma's back was turned at the sink.

Kay Lynn knew immediately what she meant: *Had Momma held me after I was born?*

Just the thought of the question caused her to feel shame. She knew she wasn't wanted, but had there been any love at the moment of her birth? Why would it matter? Momma had loved her well over the years. Would knowing change anything?

Kristine gave her a look. She leaned in and whispered, "Now's your chance."

Kay Lynn inhaled, gathering her courage, and asked, "Momma, did you hold me right after I was born?"

Momma turned around, looking stricken. Then a bittersweet smile raised the side of her lips.

She sat down and took Kay Lynn's hand.

"Your birth was beautiful and complicated. Just like you."

Kay Lynn nodded. Momma hadn't answered the question.

Momma said, "Cousin Naomi was very kind and thoughtful. She gave me the choice to feed you or let someone else give you a bottle."

Kay Lynn swallowed hard. "What did you choose?"

"I held you, expecting it would be the only time. But I wanted to pour as much love as I could into you to give you strength on your way."

Kay Lynn teared up. She hadn't expected that answer.

"I asked Cousin Naomi to say a prayer over you, I wrote you a note and sent your blanket with you," Momma said. She teared up. "I really, really believed you would have a better home with two parents and only wished the best life for you."

"And then." Kay Lynn held up her left hand.

"When that horrid doctor said you were too defective to be wanted by *any* family, I was so angry. You were beautiful, not perfect, but who is?"

"What are you talking about, Momma?" Kristine asked.

"You know I planned to give Kay Lynn up for adoption?"

Kristine nodded.

"That plan changed because she had a seizure and the doctor said she would have to be institutionalized rather than placed with a family," Momma said. "Can you imagine?"

"I had no idea!" Kristine said. She looked at Kay Lynn, her eyes wide with shock. "You knew that?"

"Always," she said. Kay Lynn looked at her mother. "You were very strong to keep me."

"You come from a long line of strong women who do hard things when they have to."

"But you loved me? Even at the beginning?"

"You were the most wondrous thing I had ever seen," Momma replied. She rose and in a somber voice said, "Just a moment."

Kay Lynn and Kristine exchanged puzzled looks. Had this become too much for Momma?

She returned with a card in her hand. Momma placed it on the table in front of Kay Lynn. In Momma's hand it said:

I loved you from the beginning. Your new family will give you a better life than I ever could.

There it was, in writing: Momma loved Kay Lynn on the day of her birth. A chill moved through her, sweeping away insecurity. Momma first loved her by giving her away, and then loved her by keeping her. It was complicated. She was complicated, and beautiful in her own way, perhaps like everyone.

Kristine rubbed her belly. Her little one's start might be complicated too, but he was welcome, very welcome in their family. Kay Lynn and Kristine smiled at each other.

As soon as they walked in their front door, Kay Lynn asked, "Mitch, do you know where our deed is?"

"For the house?"

She nodded.

"In the filing cabinet in the folder labeled Sunnybrook," he replied. "Why?"

"Kimiko thinks she's not allowed to buy in our neighborhood; I want to prove she's wrong."

He started to ask her something, but she walked away to find the file. She took it to the dining table, and stood over the opened folder. On top was the information sheet Mr. Sweet had made. She remembered her excitement on the day they first saw the house and she realized they could make a wonderful home here. This was a different life, simpler in some ways, more complicated in others, but satisfying.

Out here Kay Lynn's life revolved more around the children, and what would make them happy. There were activities after school and endless opportunities for mothers to volunteer. She still worked for her parents, but mostly from home, and was one of the few mothers who did.

Fathers worked or were at the university, retraining after the war. The men took a bus to Oakland, Berkeley, or San Francisco, leaving the cars with the mothers. By necessity, every family had a car for running errands and driving children around. The wide streets were perfect for cars, but made walking impractical and less safe.

Out here, the optimism for a good life—a settled home and happy children—was abundant and palpable. The loss and uncertainty of the war years had been packed away and hadn't moved with them.

Kay Lynn found the deed and skimmed the many pages of the declarations of restrictions. Finally, she found what she hoped not to see. Her throat closed tight, and her heart sank into her stomach. She looked at Mitch.

Seeing her despair, he asked, "What?!"

She pointed. He stood next to her, and he read out loud.

```
    That no part of said real
property shall be used or occu-
pied by any person whose blood
is not entirely that of the
Caucasian race; provided, how-
ever, that persons not of the
Caucasian race may be employed
on said property by an actual
Caucasian occupant solely in
the capacity of servants of
such occupant. Said property is
intended to be for the exclu-
sive use and occupancy of per-
sons of the Caucasian race.
```

"How could you?" she asked.

"What?"

"You agreed to this when you signed?"

"No! Absolutely not." He slapped the table. "I would never."

Her legs gave way, and she collapsed onto a chair.

"Everything happened so fast," he explained. "Mr. Sweet assured me it was all routine and that no one actually reads everything they sign."

Kay Lynn thought back to being sent for ice cream while Mitch was left with the paperwork. Would she have read the papers if she had been there?

Mitch shook his head. "I distinctly remember him saying these restrictions were to stop businesses from moving into residential areas."

"I feel sick," Kay Lynn said.

"Me too."

Kay Lynn looked around their house. Then she stared at her husband, who looked as sick as she felt.

They'd made it through this terrible war—all of them were scarred inside and out, but they had each made it to the other side of the necessary tragedy. Lenny was home. Kristine was married to David. Her Mitch was alive, mostly recovered, and earning a degree in business. The government acknowledged the great debt the men had paid to this nation and to the world with the GI Bill. It was helping families build new lives after the devastation. After five years of uncertainty, their life was back together on firm ground.

Ken and Kimiko deserved the same, if not more. Surely, they had made an even greater sacrifice. They'd been unjustly imprisoned. He'd fought in Europe and North Africa. *He'd liberated Dachau.*

Rage burned in Kay Lynn. "This cannot be right," she said to Mitch. "How can this be legal?! Doesn't the Constitution guarantee rights to all of us? Ken and Kimiko are United States citizens."

"Mommy!" Lizzie skipped into the room. "I can't believe I forgot to ask about the most exciting thing ever! Did you tell Mrs. Fujioka about next door? What did she say? Are they buying the house?"

Lizzie looked so excited, so hopeful, that Kay Lynn felt her eyes burn. She looked at Mitch. How could they explain what they had agreed to? This horrible situation went against everything they had taught their daughter.

The silence built between them. Kay Lynn searched for the right words, until she finally said, "It's not going to work for them to move here, honey. I'm sorry."

Lizzie's lip quivered. Tears pooled in Kay Lynn's eyes.

"I know, honey," Kay Lynn wiped her own cheek and said to her daughter. "I'm sad too."

Lizzie collapsed onto Kay Lynn's lap. Leaning her face against her mother's shoulder, she cried harder than she had in years, like a toddler who'd skinned a knee. Kay Lynn rubbed Lizzie's back and let her sob. Tears streamed down her own face. She had no soothing words, nothing to ease the pain of this sorrow.

Eventually Lizzie sat up. In a jerky voice she asked, "Donna will still be my friend, right?"

Kay Lynn nodded.

"But it won't be the same." Lizzie's voice quivered.

"Right," Kay Lynn agreed.

"It's already different," Lizzie said. "I just wanted it to go back."

"I know what you mean."

Lizzie took in a deep, jerky breath. She hugged Kay Lynn tight. Kay Lynn hugged back. Lizzie's head went to her ear. When had she gotten so tall? They hadn't embraced like this in months, perhaps more than a year.

Lizzie sighed, pulled back, and got up from Kay Lynn's lap without a word. Kay Lynn watched her daughter walk away.

Mitch spoke into the quiet. "I'm sorry."

"Me too," she snapped.

Her heart raced as she walked away. It wasn't Mitch's fault, as much as she wanted it to be, but she wasn't ready to pretend she wasn't upset.

Kay Lynn sat down at her desk and got out a piece of paper. She began the ritual that had gotten her through the war.

Dear Kimiko,

I'm shaking as I write these words. I just lied to Lizzie. Not lied lied, but I wasn't honest. How can I admit to our daughter what we have done? This goes against everything we've taught her. I feel sick to my stomach. How could I be so stupid and naïve?

Any person whose blood is not entirely that of the
Caucasian race? It makes me sick.

I don't know how I didn't know what we
were choosing when we moved here. I'm so sorry.
Sorry for me, sorry for you, but most of all sorry
for Donna and Lizzie. They shouldn't be separated
by the prejudice of society. They never should have
been separated to begin with. I don't know how to
make this better. I don't know how we will fix this,
but I will never stop trying.

I feel so ill I might vomit.

I wish I'd paid more attention. I admit I saw
the words "restricted deeds," but didn't know
what that meant. Truly I didn't. I NEVER would
have made this choice if we did. If I were a better
person, I might have understood what was behind
those two words, but it didn't mean anything to
me because it didn't apply to me, or affect me. Or I
thought it didn't, but it does.

I want to take it all back. I want my old life.
Our life with my babies and your babies and
our business and walking to stores, Cal, and the
Grands, and no one afraid of the specter of war or
haunted by the horror of what humans can do to
each other. I want to go back in time and remember to appreciate it while I had it because it was
wonderful. Even while it was so hard. Hard in its
hard way. And now, now is hard in its own way.
And wonderful in its own way too. I can't forget to
relish in the joy of now because I don't want to be
writing you a letter in five years bemoaning that
I forgot to appreciate this time with Lizzie and

Timmy and Mitch and, well, all of it. Someday both of my parents will be gone. And Grammy Sadie. It's all so temporary.

I HATE that. But isn't that life? Each day new and different. No two days alike. No two people alike. That knowledge, that absolutely everything is temporary, is so overwhelming that I have to block it out most of the time.

Oh, Kimiko. I guess what I really want to say to you is thank you. For the gift of your friendship and companionship for all those years. It truly was wonderful, and I don't take it for granted now, though I believe I did at the time.

And I'm sad for all the forces that have torn us apart.

I love you. And cherish you. No matter the years and the miles, I will always hold you dear.

Kay Lynn

Kay Lynn reread what she had written, letting her tears flow. It was true. All of it. The sorrow, the confusion, the hope, and most of all her irreplaceable love for Kimiko and gratitude for her companionship for all those years.

Kay Lynn held up the note in her left hand; her right tore it down the middle. She took those two halves and tore them into little pieces. She swept the bits of paper into her trash can and then joined her family playing in their yard.

EPILOGUE

Kay Lynn found their old red wagon in the back of the garage, right next to the Fujiokas' trunk. She'd offered to return it after they bought their bungalow in South Berkeley. The confused expression on her friend's face caused her to take back the suggestion, and she never raised the question of the trunk again. She'd keep it safe for as long as the Fujiokas wished. Kimiko knew where it was.

The filthy wagon was bigger than she remembered. It wouldn't fit in the car with all of them, so Kay Lynn decided against taking it. They would just have to carry the posters in bags slung over their shoulders, like newspaper boys. She went back into the kitchen. Lizzie was finishing up the sandwiches for a picnic lunch at Indian Rock. It had been ages and ages since they'd been there. She put the rest of the food in a basket with plates, cups, and napkins.

A stack of posters sat on the table.

PLEASE!!
VOTE FOR FAIRNESS
NO
ON
PROPOSITION
15

Missy, George, Donna, Timmy, Lizzie, Kay
Lynn & Kimiko

"They look great this size!" Kay Lynn declared. "How many are there?"

"Two hundred fifty, just as you asked," Mitch replied. "Miss Chance made them as large as possible. She says she can't think of a better use of our mimeograph machine and is eager to make as many as you like." He put a finger to his mouth and pursed his lips. "She isn't asking the department chair, and neither am I."

Kay Lynn pantomimed turning a key near her lips to indicate his secret was safe.

She'd already distributed four hundred quarter-sheet versions of this flyer door to door in Lafayette and Orinda. Today she and the kids were going to tack them up on telephone poles in Berkeley with Kimiko and her kids.

Bigoted politicians and greedy businessmen were working hard to prevent some Japanese Americans from returning to their homes and farms even after all they had done for the war. Proposition 15 proposed that the alien land laws be enshrined in the California constitution in order to force the sale of land.

Kay Lynn didn't understand exactly how it was going to work, but she knew its passage would institutionalize ongoing prejudice against Japanese Americans, and be a signal that California was against racial equality.

"Are you sure you don't want me to come with you?" Mitch asked.

Kay Lynn smiled at her husband. She leaned in and kissed him. He smiled back. "Thank you for offering, but no. Without you, we can all pile into one car. Besides, this is ours to do—without our men." Mitch laughed.

"Enjoy a Saturday to yourself," she said to him. "Let's go," she yelled to Timmy and Lizzie.

None of the kids wanted to sit in the front between Kimiko and Kay Lynn. Instead the five of them darted in and out of her sight in the rearview mirror. They were in the midst of some sort of game that involved lying on the floor and on the back seat. It was sweet to see Lizzie actually playing, something she'd mostly outgrown.

"Can we start on Prince Street?" Kay Lynn asked her friend.

Kimiko nodded, the poignancy of going back to their old neighborhood floating between them.

Kay Lynn parked in front of their former home—changed in the year they'd been gone and yet the same. It was painted bright blue, and all her plants had been replaced with easy-to-care-for juniper and boxwood. There wasn't a flower in sight.

"It looks so different," Lizzie said from her side. "Not like our home."

Kay Lynn nodded with a smile. "It's bittersweet to see it."

"Sad and happy at the same time?" Lizzie asked.

"Yes. Always our home because of all the wonderful memories, but not our house anymore," Kay Lynn said.

She looked over at Kimiko, who was having a private reunion with the home they'd been forced to leave.

Kay Lynn gazed at the wisteria across the street. It still had its bright-green leaves, and a few brown pods, but no flowers.

Kimiko came to her side.

Kay Lynn said, "I want to collect a few pods before we leave. Maybe I can get a wisteria to grow in our new yard."

"My mother told me it took three tries," Kimiko replied.

Kay Lynn was confused. "Three tries?"

"To get the wisteria to take in this new land." She continued, "Two seeds sprouted but soon withered and died. The third turned into this vine, blooming decades after it was planted. She doesn't remember what happened to the fourth seed in the pod she brought from Japan."

"Like this?" Timmy shouted from a telephone pole. He was holding up one of the posters as high as he could reach. Georgie and Missy stood close. Donna had the staple gun in her hand, ready to attach it.

"Looks good to me," Kimiko approved.

It took a few tries, but the team of children succeeded in attaching their plea to the curved pole. In the face of all the horrors of the war, it was a very tiny act, but it was something. She was teaching her children to stand against hatred and bigotry—no matter how small their action was.

They continued down the path they used to walk to Lincoln School, tacking up signs as they went along. They crossed Harper Street. Ahead of them, Kay Lynn saw the telephone pole where Donna and Lizzie had attempted to read the evacuation order in April 1942. She flushed with anger at the memory.

"Our turn!" Kay Lynn declared. "Mrs. Fujioka and I are putting up this one."

Kimiko took a paper from Donna and held it against the pole. Kay Lynn leaned into the staple gun, pressing it hard against the wood. Pulling the lever, rage and sorrow shot into the pole with the staple. And then she did it again, three more times.

She smiled at Kimiko, holding contradictory, complicated thoughts and feelings. She missed her old home—and treasured their new one. She longed for the naïve security she used to feel, and was grateful to know her own strength and resilience. Before the war she believed that the march toward kindness and universal human rights was inevitable, but now she understood that it was a battle to be waged home by home and street by street, including her own, not just across the seas.

Regular people had to stand up for regular people, not leave it to the men in charge.

"I'm so glad we're doing this together." Kay Lynn looked into Kimiko's deep-brown eyes.

"Me too," Kimiko replied. "And with our children."

Their small army of seven walked to the next pole and the next and the next and the next: securing their plea for love and justice with four small staples.

CHARACTER LIST

PRIMARY CHARACTERS

Kay Lynn (Wagner) Brooke: Mother of Lizzie and Timmy, wife of Mitch, and friend to Kimiko

Hazel: The Fujiokas' dog

Kimiko (Hori) Fujioka: Kay Lynn's friend, neighbor, and business partner

Kristine Stevens: Kay Lynn's half sister

Lenny (Leonard) Stevens: Kay Lynn's half brother

Leo (Poppa) Stevens: Kay Lynn's stepfather, who raised her

Lizzie Brooke: Kay Lynn and Mitch's daughter

May (Momma; Ma; Nana May) (Wagner) Stevens: Kay Lynn's mother

Mitch Brooke: Kay Lynn's husband

Timmy Brooke: Kay Lynn and Mitch's son

Sadie (Grammy Sadie) (Johnson) Wagner: Kay Lynn's grandmother

Donna Fujioka: Lizzie's best friend, and Kimiko and Ken's daughter

George (Georgie) Fujioka: Timmy's friend, and Kimiko and Ken's son

Grandmother Barrow: Kay Lynn's biological paternal grandmother, and Jonathon Barrow's mother

Jonathon Barrow: Kay Lynn's biological father

Ken (Kenji) Fujioka: Kimiko's husband, and Donna, George, and Missy's father

Maggie (Smith) Hays: Second cousin to May, and daughter of Naomi and Willie Smith

Missy Fujioka: Kimiko and Ken's youngest daughter

Mr. Cuthbert: Moves into the Fujiokas' house next to the Brookes after the Fujiokas are relocated

Mrs. Hori: Kimiko's mother, who came to the US from Japan in 1912 as a picture bride

Naomi (Cousin Naomi) (Wallace) Smith: Willie's wife, and Sadie's first cousin by marriage

Sam (Uncle Sam) Johnson: Kay Lynn's great-uncle, May's uncle, and Grammy Sadie's brother

AUTHOR'S NOTE

This book is one story in a long answer to my question, *How did we get here?* I started this journey with *Yellow Crocus*. I imagine I will end it sometime in the 2000s, but no guarantees. I'm not naturally a writer, but I'm immensely curious about families and social change. Writing about a fictional family through several multigenerational novels has been a powerful and intimate way to explore the caste/ social system baked into the United States.

When I started *Falling Wisteria*, I knew I wanted this story to be set in Berkeley, my home for thirty years, and that Kay Lynn would be the main character. It seemed likely that redlining, the Port Chicago explosion, and Japanese internment would be central to Kay Lynn's experience.

I distinctly remember learning about Japanese internment/relocation when I was in fifth grade in 1975. My teacher Paul Moore casually asked two students in our class if their families had been held in relocation camps. I don't remember why the topic came up, but I absolutely remember the impact on me. I couldn't believe that something so huge had happened in my hometown and that none of us were talking about it, nor was it in our textbooks. I quickly put together that my brother's best friend's family had been in a camp during the war. The nobility of the United States during World War II diminished in my heart and mind.

When I told friends, family, neighbors, and readers that my next novel would include the forced relocation of Japanese Americans, many of them had personal stories about it. A neighbor told me he found pictures from an internment camp in the attic of a home he'd bought. A reader mentioned that he inherited a box of belonging that his grandparents kept for a Japanese American family that had been relocated. A family friend recounted her mother sobbing after going to a closing sale at a nursery owned by a family about to be sent to Tanforan.

Early feedback from beta readers about this novel criticized it for Kay Lynn's arc. She's a fairly passive main character, and throughout the novel she seems confused by all the changes. She just wants life to return to normal. The story ends with Kay Lynn taking an action that is against her values, but was the easiest option to gain security for her family. Much larger forces set the systems in place for her to make that choice for her family without understanding that the benefits she was receiving were part of a system that was unjust and inequitable.

Kay Lynn is also insensitive to the racialized oppression in the United States. Her attitude of "color blindness" is very typical in liberal white communities. My mother very much taught me it is bad to be prejudiced, and made *prejudice* and *racism* parallel terms. Since we aren't prejudiced (her language in the 1970s), we aren't racist. Today we know that racialized bias is socialized into all of us from a very young age.

I didn't teach my children that we aren't racist; instead I strove to teach my children to recognize and overcome the racialized privileges built into our nation. That through an honest understanding of human-made systems of oppression, we've made strides toward human rights for all people—and we have a long way to go before we have a truly just society.

It's also clear to me that I wrote this novel on the other side of COVID. I'm not surprised that my main character feels battered about by forces so much bigger than she. Her focus gets smaller and smaller as the story continues. She feels selfish to focus on her family, but doesn't have the strength to do more. During much of the pandemic, keeping up with the news of the world seemed an exercise in futility.

This story ends with Kay Lynn aware of the injustice of the housing discrimination laws. That's the beginning of her arc to join the social justice movements that led to fair housing laws, women having more control over their bodies, the Americans with Disabilities Act, and marriage equality. For some, these are political movements or abstract ideas, but for me, they are personal. I'm deeply grateful for the people who came before me that fought for the rights my daughters and I have today.

I don't believe it is foolish to believe those same rights and economic opportunities can be extended to all humans all over the world in the next fifty years.

I grew up with two visions of our future: *Star Trek* and *Mad Max*. I'm aiming for the *Star Trek* future. In *Star Trek* life is not zero sum— my thriving doesn't come at the expense of yours. There is great evidence that we all do better when we all do better.

In January of 1941, President Roosevelt articulated a vision in which all humans throughout the world would have freedom of speech, freedom of worship, and freedom from want and fear. A year later he signed Executive Order 9066. The error of the latter does not diminish the beauty of the former.

I still believe in his vision and in the possibility of that future.

ACKNOWLEDGMENTS

I overflow with gratitude for all that has conspired to allow me to bring the stories of my heart and soul into being.

Thank you to the readers who have reviewed, purchased, and spread the word about my novels.

I'm grateful for

—conversations and resources about the Japanese relocation and internment from Kimi Hill, Donna Fujioka, and Kenji Oshima; the Bancroft Library at UC Berkeley; and the Manzanar National Historic Site

—Kimiko Fujioka Guillermo, George Guillermo, Donna Fujioka, Kalin Brooke, and Mitch Brooke for letting me name main characters after them

—Brian Brackney for his steadfast support and interest in my writing

—Jodie Matthies for arranging the visit to the exhibit at the Bancroft Library at UC Berkeley

—Hazel Nut, the best canine companion ever

—the beta readers who gave me kind and honest feedback to make this a better story: Rinda Bartley, Kelly Kist x2, Darlanne Mulmat, Margie Biblin, Kimi Hill, Jamie Ibrahim, Donna Fujioka, Meri Lane, Laura Sueoka, Mona Ibrahim, Lori Ashikawa, Kimiko Fujioka Guillermo, Rachel Ibrahim, and Heather MacCleod

—editors Erin Adair-Hodges and Shaundale Rénā

—Danielle Marshall for her faith in my ability to tell this story

—Lesley Worrell for the beautiful book cover

—technical assistance with children's writing from Eva Ulmer, Ruby Weiss, and Maya Ibrahim-Bartley

—the many wonderful people at Amazon Publishing, Lake Union, and Amazon Crossing that bless me with their hard work and devotion to bringing these stories to readers around the world: Danielle Marshall, Chantelle Aimée Osman, Ronit Wagman, Jodi Warshaw, Gabriella Dumpit, Alex Levenberg, Carissa Bluestone, Angela Elson, Tiffany, Phyllis, and all of you whose names I don't know (extra shout-out to marketing, whose emails bring great joy to my day every single time I get one)

—Terry Goodman—always

—my agent, Annelise Robey of Jane Rotrosen Agency

—my growing family—what a joy!

BIBLIOGRAPHY AND
RESOURCES

American Babylon: Race and the Struggle for Postwar Oakland by Robert O. Self

The Color of Law: A Forgotten History of How Our Government Segregated America by Richard Rothstein

Dear Miss Breed: True Stories of the Japanese American Incarceration during World War II and a Librarian Who Made a Difference by Joanne Oppenheim

Farewell to Manzanar by Jeanne Wakatsuki Houston and James D. Houston

Infamy: The Shocking Story of the Japanese American Internment in World War II by Richard Reeves

No There There: Race, Class, and Political Community in Oakland by Chris Rhomberg

Oakland: The Story of a City by Beth Bagwell

Only What We Could Carry: The Japanese American Internment Experience edited with an introduction by Lawson Fusao Inada

Picture Bride Stories by Barbara F. Kawakami

The Port Chicago 50: Disaster, Mutiny, and the Fight for Civil Rights by Steve Sheinkin

The Port Chicago Mutiny: The Story of the Largest Mass Mutiny Trial in U.S. Naval History by Robert L. Allen

Seen and Unseen: What Dorothea Lange, Toyo Miyatake, and Ansel Adams's Photographs Reveal About the Japanese American Incarceration by Elizabeth Partridge and Lauren Tamaki

The Warmth of Other Suns: The Epic Story of America's Great Migration by Isabel Wilkerson

Manzanar National Historic Site

Newspapers.com

The Oakland Tribune

The Bancroft Library at the University of California, Berkeley

Encyclopedia.densho.org

BOOK CLUB QUESTIONS

1. What was your favorite part of the book?
2. What was your least favorite?
3. Have any scenes stuck with you?
4. Are there any standout sentences, conversations, or imagery?
5. If you have read others in the Yellow Crocus family saga, how does this fit in with the others?
6. Would you want to read another book by this author?
7. What surprised you most about the book?
8. What would you ask the author if you could?
9. In the author's note, Laila Ibrahim says the COVID pandemic shaped her telling of this story. Can you see the pandemic's influence on this novel?
10. How does the book's title work in relation to the book's contents? If you could give the book a new title, what would it be?
11. Do you think you'll remember this novel in a few months or years?
12. Who would you recommend this book to?
13. Are there lingering questions from the book you're still thinking about?

ABOUT THE AUTHOR

Photo © 2022 Mitch Brooke

Laila Ibrahim is the bestselling author of *After the Rain, Scarlet Carnation, Golden Poppies, Paper Wife, Mustard Seed,* and *Yellow Crocus.* Before becoming a novelist, she worked as a preschool director, a birth doula, and a religious educator. Drawing from her experience in these positions, along with her education in developmental psychology and attachment theory, she finds rich inspiration for her novels. She's a devout Unitarian Universalist, determined to do her part to add a little more love and justice to our beautiful and painful world. She lives with her wonderful wife, Rinda, and two other families in a small cohousing community in Berkeley, California. Her children and their families are her pride and joy. When she isn't writing, she likes to cuddle with her dog Hazel, take walks with friends, study the Enneagram, do jigsaw puzzles, play games, work in the garden, travel, cook, and eat all kinds of delicious food. For more information, visit lailaibrahim.com.